THE RECRUIT

NICK ADAMS

Elliptical
Publishing

PROLOGUE

GAP SPACE, PRESENT LOCATION UNKNOWN

THE INTERSTICE TUBE WAS FAILING, their encapsulation bubble was narrowing and Commander Nexen knew if they dropped out of the interstice without an exit gate, it could well destroy the vessel.

The few ships that had entered a tube and failed to exit the destination gate had always been recorded as lost with all hands. None had ever been heard from again and he was worried they were about to become part of that statistic.

'Sound the general alarm,' he said. 'Get everyone strapped in, it's out of our hands now, and make sure the mechadroid vassals are secured.'

The engineers had tried everything over the last hour to stabilise the reactor, but it seemed nothing was going to prevent the inevitable; the research vessel *Xhamin*'s interstice field would collapse very shortly.

Nexen thought of his family back on Eritain and wished he could have said goodbye. It saddened him to think they would have no idea what happened to him.

A severe judder reverberating through the ship woke him suddenly from his melancholy.

'Encapsulation failing, sir,' called the navigation officer, her voice breaking slightly and reminding him how terrified the two hundred crew were too.

'Shut the system down,' he said, trying to sound confident. 'Good luck, everyone.'

No sooner had he said it, a cacophony of alarm sirens screamed their disapproval and the ship lurched again, only a lot more severely this time. Nexen was thrown forward in his seat, his harness the only thing preventing him from being catapulted across the bridge. The inertial dampers struggled with the sudden deceleration, way outside their design parameters.

The artificial gravity field failed for a second or two as he felt himself floating momentarily—then dumped back down in his chair and slammed forward again. He gritted his teeth as he heard a few grunts and cries from his crew around the bridge.

During the ship's interstice travel, the large main screen set between two massive structural columns at the front of the bridge showed very little except for clouds of multicoloured flashes of light zipping by. It reminded Nexen of riding his Java trike through a swarm of glow flies back on Eritain.

With white knuckles, he hung onto his seat, watching the screens' light show reduce gradually down to nothing. And then, with a final lurch and a falling sensation, the screen lit up with a starscape tumbling seemingly at random.

'The ship's in a tumbling spin, Commander,' called the pilot. 'All drives offline, but I do have manoeuvring thrusters.'

The sound of the thrusters attempting to arrest the rotation sounded like distant gunfire. Gradually the nausea-inducing motion reduced—and eventually ceased.

'Where are we, helm?' Nexen asked, loosening his harness so he could breathe and staring up at the screen again.

The navigator swore to herself as she attempted to gain a fix from the starfield surrounding them. 'Unrecognised starscape, sir,' she said. 'We've emerged within a star system and are heading towards a large planet.'

'Are we able to slow down?' he asked. 'We need to stop somewhere safe and assess the damage.'

'Only with the thrusters, sir,' she replied, glancing nervously over her shoulder at him.

He gazed up at the grey planet that slowly hove into view on the screen as the pilot gradually brought the ship back into stable forward flight.

'Can we slow enough to achieve an orbit?' Nexen asked, pointing up at the growing orb on the view screen.

'It's going to take everything we've got to avoid crashing on it, sir,' the pilot said, as the thrusters began their manic machine-gun rattle again. 'This world has a few moons to avoid too and some of them are still out of sight.'

The commander nodded thoughtfully, again rubbing his chin. 'Have everything in the port hangar secured,' he ordered. 'I'm going to explosively decompress it to provide some extra sideways thrust.'

Three minutes later, the call came that all loose items were stowed and the hangar was clear of personnel. He entered his safety bypass codes into his seat terminal and, giving the pilot a nod, hit the switch that shut off the atmosphere shield. They all felt the vibration as the millions of litres of air punched outwards.

'Two point nine four degrees, Commander,' the pilot

called. 'That might have just done enough for us to achieve a low orbit and not get pulled in.'

'Good,' he said. 'Keep us slowing as much as possible. Is the FOD shield operational?' he asked, moving his attention across to another of his officers.

'Negative, sir,' came the reply. 'I have red lights down the line. The power outage that dropped us out of tube space has taken almost everything with it. We still have a little internal power and thankfully environmental, but all main control systems are down.'

'Any idea as to what caused this?' the commander asked.

'There must have been a serious fault develop in the reactor,' came the reply. 'The emergency shutdown triggered, which saved us all getting fried, but whatever it was hasn't gone away and it refuses to reset.'

'It couldn't have done it at a worse time,' groaned the commander, rolling his eyes. 'All the days and weeks we spend in normal space and it had to fail just as we enter an interstice.'

'I have a team suited up and ready,' said the same officer. 'As soon as the ship is in a stable orbit, they can inspect the reactor.'

'Thank you,' said Nexen, flopping back in his seat and exhaling noisily. 'We may be lost, but at least we're alive.'

'Not for long,' shouted the pilot, suddenly sitting bolt upright and pointing up at the main screen.

'What now?' asked Nexen, unable to keep the irritation out of his voice and glancing back up at the monitor.

'A moon,' she said. 'Just emerged over the horizon. It couldn't be in a worse place. I don't think we can avoid it.'

'Ah, crap, don't we ever get a break?' he said. 'Can't we go above or below it?'

'No, we're too slow now.'

'Can we land on it?'

'Too fast.'

'Damn,' he muttered. 'Just what have we done to deserve this? What's the terrain like?'

'Rocky, but reasonably flat, sir.'

'Okay, slow us as much as possible and bring us in at the shallowest achievable angle,' said Nexen.

'Do you want the struts extended, sir?' the pilot asked.

'Yes, hopefully they'll help scrub off some of the speed before the hull impacts,' he said. 'And get everyone up top, out of the lower decks and strapped in.'

'Yes, sir.'

As Nexen watched the dark rocky moon rise up out of the shadow of the planet on the main screen, he could hear the emergency tannoy message echoing around the ship. 'Time to impact?' he asked.

'Three minutes, Commander,' said the pilot as she balanced the thrusters between slowing them and reducing the angle of ingress.

Nexen took a deep breath, reached over and toggled his ship's intercom control.

'Attention all hands,' he said, trying to sound confident and keep the overpowering trepidation from his voice. 'Strap in tight and brace for an emergency landing.'

1

DESTROYER DRES'KIN, UNNAMED MOON, SECTOR 351

TWO THOUSAND, nine hundred and eighty-seven years later

Captain Finll Yamaton watched closely as Officer Mye, his trainee navigator and pilot, brought the *Dres'kin* into a close orbit around an unnamed moon, itself orbiting a large cold grey planet in system J-45297/AK.

'Have you remembered to allow for the planet's gravitational influence?' he asked, glancing at her momentarily.

'Yes, sir,' replied the young lady, nodding, but not taking her eyes off the holographic nav display. 'I've allowed for a six point two percent drag attraction variable.'

'Excellent, Miss Mye,' said Yamaton. 'Your skills have improved of late, and well done, everyone,' he continued, turning to face the other junior officers on the bridge. 'You all have top marks so far on this exercise. Don't let the standards drop now, just because it's the last outing before graduation.'

Yamaton raised his eyebrows at the array officer.

'Still receiving periodic power fluctuations from the

surface, Captain,' said the array operator. 'I'm tracking four distinct locations now. I've marked them on the holomap, sir.'

'Thank you, Mr Stratton,' said Yamaton, gazing up at the rotating image of the moonlet above him. Four small red icons flashed, closely grouped in a square on the surface. 'Distance apart?'

'They're arranged in a perfect square, exactly five kilometres from each other, Captain.'

'Hmm,' he replied, staring at the holomap for a few moments. 'Are the walkers ready to go?' he asked, finally deciding on a plan of action.

'Walkers and platform are both in position and ready, sir,' came the reply from behind him.

'Okay, I want the walkers to visit any one of those warm areas and remember, I want full camera footage at all times and no doing anything unusual without my authorisation. This may be a genuine anomaly we've discovered, but we are on a training exercise and risks are not to be taken. Are we clear on that?'

'Yes, sir,' echoed around the room.

'Is that clear, walkers?'

'Crystal, Captain,' came the reply from airlock 27b.

'Recruit Mye,' said Yamaton. 'Can you signal the walkers a jump countdown, please.'

'Captain,' said Mye, nodding again. 'Standby, walkers,' she said. 'Two point one kilometres to surface, speed over surface four kilometres per second. Walking in three—two— one, mark.'

Two suited figures jetted out from the airlock and straight onto the waiting EVA platform. Although these platforms were originally designed to aid exterior maintenance on starships when away from a convenient space dock, they proved equally adroit at landing walkers on non-atmospheric satellites.

Even from a relatively slow speed a walker would use all their suit propellant just slowing themselves down for a stationary landing. Using the platform enabled them to save all their manoeuvring propellant for the job in hand.

That's exactly what they did once they'd strapped themselves onto the machine in a standing position. The platform immediately began dropping away below and behind the *Dres'kin*, scrubbing off speed and descending towards one of the anomalous power readings.

As the small machine dropped closer to the moon's surface, the walkers could begin to make out the topography a little more clearly. It quickly became obvious to them that some manipulation of the surface features had been undertaken at some time in the past, as a faint track line through the regolith could still be made out.

They had chosen to investigate the nearest power source, which was at the end of the indistinct but noticeable channel. The platform flared, causing them both to grit their teeth as the belts dug into their suits, and then dropped vertically down and stopped abruptly and silently on the rocky terrain.

'Platform down and secure,' said one of the walkers, once he was sure the four landing struts weren't going to sink and tip the platform over. 'Twenty metres to power reading.'

They unstrapped themselves and with the aid of their suit jets dropped down onto the surface.

'Point six nine gee of gravity,' he reported as they slowly made their way towards a slight bulge in the crust. They stopped as they reached it and studied their suit telemetry.

'You're right on top of it,' said Yamaton. 'What's under the dust?'

Both walkers brushed the surface rocks and dusty gravel around with their boots. A flat black curved surface was revealed and after dragging their feet around the perimeter, they discovered it was about four metres in diameter.

'Any indication as to what it does?' asked the captain.

'Negative, sir,' said the walker, backing away so the camera could see the whole convex dome. He cursed as he tripped on something, overbalanced and in slow motion landed on his backside.

'Don't you hole one of my expensive suits, young man,' grumbled Yamaton. 'And watch your language when you're on an open channel.'

'Sorry, sir, I was—oh.'

'Oh, what?' the captain muttered, the irritation clear in his voice. '"Oh" is not recognised EVA terminology either.'

'There's some sort of handle here recessed into the ground, sir.'

'Give me a closeup view.'

The walker used his suit jets to turn himself over onto his hands and knees so he could pan his helmet camera in close. He picked the rocks and gravel out of the small recess, revealing a red lever set in a square hole.

Yamaton peered at the image and rubbed his chin as he thought. 'Don't touch it for now,' he said. 'It could power up anything and the fact that it's red worries me.'

'Captain,' called the array officer. 'Now we're closer, I'm getting some unusual readings from the small hill at the end of the straight channel, a hundred metres south of their position.'

'Unusual in what way?' Yamaton asked, switching his gaze from the walker's image over to the holomap.

'The rock structure there is reading partially ceramic with some organic sections. It's hard to read because it's under a layer of the moon's regolith, sir.'

'Best guess?' the captain asked.

'Erm—it's almost like the hull structure of a Theo vessel, sir. They grow organic hulls and use a lot of ceramics.'

Yamaton raised his eyebrows and glanced across at the pilot.

'Recruit Mye, can you bring the vessel into a stationary orbit above that small hill so we can get some closeup camera views?' he asked.

'Yes, sir.'

'Walkers, can you take the platform south and check out the small rise five hundred metres from your present position?'

'On our way, sir.'

They landed the platform a few metres away from the hump that rose to about ten metres at its highest point and was around a hundred metres across. They knew now to scuff the surface with their boots to uncover anything below the thousands of years of settled dust and rock.

'There's a smooth surface underneath again,' the walker said. 'And some broken and crumpled bits of something.'

'I've got some lettering here,' said the other walker as he dropped down onto his hands and knees to brush away the dust.

The strange curled lettering that was revealed didn't ring any bells with Nexen and he pointed at the array officer. 'Enter that into the database and see what we get,' he asked.

The young officer tapped away for a few moments. 'There's no record of any disappeared or missing ships in this sector, sir, and the lettering has come back as unrecognised language.'

'Some bits of the pile have straight edges, Captain,' said one of the walkers. 'It's almost like someone crashed here, cut the damaged sections off and stuck them in a pile.'

'That could explain the straight channel leading up to it,' said Nexen. 'They crashed at speed and scraped along the surface.'

'Perhaps that's why there's no record of a missing vessel,' said the array officer. 'They repaired the damage and continued on with their journey.'

Yamaton rubbed his chin again.

'It doesn't explain the small black dome though,' he said. 'Walkers, can you fly over to the other three power readings and check those out?'

'Roger that, Captain.'

They worked their way around the other three only to discover they were all similar smooth domes to the first and were indeed set in a perfect square.

'We can't find any sign of a red handle here either,' said one of the walkers, after scratching around the fourth dome for twenty minutes.

'Return to the first dome,' ordered Yamaton. 'I think we'll take the risk and see what that handle does.'

They landed the platform well away from the dome this time and both walked lightly over and crouched down beside the recessed handle.

'Ready to go, Captain,' said one of the walkers.

'Standard shields please,' said Yamaton. 'Just in case it turns out to be a weapon or something unpleasant.'

'Yes, sir,' came a voice from the far side of the bridge. 'Shields at fifty percent.'

'Go ahead, walker,' said Yamaton as all eyes turned to the moon's holo image. 'Let's see what, if anything, that handle does.'

The walker reached into the recess and tried to turn the handle. 'It's stiff,' he said, gritting his teeth and giving it everything he had.

It suddenly snapped around, making him jump. They both waited, staying stock still, not daring to breath.

'Anything?' called Yamaton.

'Nothing, sir,' said the walker with his hand still on the handle. 'Whatever it used to—oh, hang on.'

They both felt a slight vibration through their feet.

'What is it?' asked Yamaton, staring adamantly at the image of the two walkers crouching on the surface.

'We felt a slight tremor underneath—woah,' cried the walker as he was suddenly pushed upwards forcibly.

The destroyer's crew watched open-mouthed as both walkers were unceremoniously launched up above the surface while a section of ground powered up. They disappeared in a cloud of rocks and dust and could be heard cursing as they tried to orientate themselves with their suit jets.

'We've activated our hover settings, Captain,' said one of the walkers. 'Can you see where we are?'

'Hold fire,' said Yamaton, as he waited for the debris cloud to slowly drop back to the surface. 'You're inverted and about twenty metres above the ground. Your partner is the right way up and to your left.'

'Thank you, sir,' said the walker, rubbing his visor vigorously with his glove. 'I'm starting to get vision below again.'

A slight pause led to the walker speaking again, this time

with a level of excitement in his voice. 'There's a door, Captain,' he said. 'A door has hinged up with steps leading below the surface. Permission to investigate?'

'Negative, walker,' said Yamaton. 'Do not enter until we know it is safe.'

'There should be a mech drone on the platform, Captain,' said Mye. 'They could remotely operate that to take a peek.'

Yamaton pointed at the pilot and nodded. 'Good idea, Mye,' he said, before relaying the information down to the walkers.

It took about fifteen minutes to retrieve the drone from the platform and set it up to operate from the remote unit. They chose a manipulator arm as tool of choice, just in case there were further doors to open.

It disappeared down the steps and into the gloom, its three bright work lamps illuminating the way. Both walkers stood, helmets touching, vying to watch its progress on the small monitor.

The steps led down about twenty-five metres underground before levelling out to a short corridor and another door that was open. The drone took them through into a rectangular room, about ten metres long and four wide. The walls were rough and seemed to have been hand-cut using some sort of plasma drill—the cut marks were quite unmistakeable.

A control panel covered in dust stood against one wall and a larger closed circular door was at the far end.

'Looks like an airlock up the back,' said the walker operating the drone.

The signal from the drone started to break up as it went deeper into the room and the operator backed it up so he didn't lose it completely.

'Seems safe enough, Captain,' said one of the walkers. 'Permission to check out that control panel.'

'You may enter,' said Yamaton. 'You wipe that panel off and record what you see. On no account do you activate anything or attempt to open that far door. Is that understood?'

'Crystal, sir,' said the walker, bringing the drone back out and landing it beside him.

They both brought their suit lights up to full brightness and descended the staircase slowly. When they reached the room, it seemed smaller in reality and the ceiling was only just high enough so they didn't scrape their helmets. The control panel was on the left-hand side and was about two metres wide and a metre deep. It sloped up slightly away from them and seemed quite dead.

One of the walkers pulled a visor wipe from a side pocket and slowly, to avoid making a cloud, began wiping the thick layer of dust from the surface.

The other walker peered around the room, illuminating the walls with his bright white lights. He shone them back towards the door and stairway. Noticing something on the wall just inside the door, he walked over to investigate.

'Hey, there's a light switch here,' he said, and reached up towards it.

The other walker glanced over, his eyes widening as he realised what his colleague was about to do.

'No, don't touch that,' he shouted, just too late. He couldn't hear the click as the other walker hit the switch— there was no atmosphere—but he felt a slight vibration in the control panel beneath his hand.

The lights in the room did indeed come on, flashing a couple of times and then staying on. His colleague turned and gave him the thumbs up. 'See, nothing to be afraid of,' he said, his face grinning through his faceplate.

The control panel flickered into life too, with dozens of icons flashing in multiple colours as it appeared to be going through its start-up routine.

'Turn it off, now,' called Yamaton, from above. 'The four domes are waking—'

His voice cut off abruptly.

'Well?' said the walker by the control panel. 'Do as he said, turn the bloody thing off, quickly.'

The grin on the other walker's face disappeared as he held his hand up. The switch was in his fingers.

'It broke,' he said, turning and unsuccessfully trying to push it back into place with his thick gauntleted hands.

'Skata,' shouted Yamaton, as he realised the outer door had hinged shut and they'd lost contact with the walkers.

The four domes that had begun glowing were now pulsing, and a swirling circular cloud of light began growing high above them.

'Back us away, quickly,' he said, watching the growing maelstrom just five hundred metres away.

He heard the Alma drives engaging and was puzzled why the ship was actually going slowly forward.

'Reverse,' he shouted, glaring at Mye. 'I said reverse.'

'We are, sir,' she said, looking up nervously 'We're at full astern right now.'

The circular roiling vortex had now grown to five kilometres in diameter and was pulling them in towards it. Not only that, anything close to the anomaly and loose on the moon's surface, dust, small rocks, was being drawn in and vanishing.

'Emergency jump, now,' he bellowed.

Mye tapped away furiously at the helm controls.

'Inoperative, Captain,' said Mye. 'That thing is disrupting the jump envelope.'

A loud groaning reverberated around the ship.

'It's the drives, sir,' said Mye. 'They're about to pull the ship apart.'

'Shut them down,' he said, despondently and slumped down in his captain's chair, resigned to the fact that whatever that thing was, it had them.

Mye touched the engine shut down icon. The destroyer *Dres'kin* immediately lurched forward into the anomaly and, in the blink of an eye, was gone.

2

UNDERGROUND CONTROL ROOM, UNNAMED MOON,
SECTOR 351

BACHE LOFTT GLARED through his visor at his partner as they lost contact with the *Dres'kin*, shaking his head despondently as he watched Clammer's clumsy attempts to repair the switch unit.

Clammer Feltaraine had been in Bache's training unit since recruit selection had begun almost two years ago. He was a Minn from the planet Minnigal and seemed to excel in doing the absolute bare minimum to pass each training module. Because of this, Clammer had been nick-named Minimum Minn by the training staff.

Bache, on the other hand, was the polar opposite and was, if not first in class, always in the top three. It irked Bache that the instructors regularly paired them together to try and bring Clammer's grades up a little.

Glancing down at the control panel again, Bache quickly finished wiping the dust away as carefully as he could, without pressing anything. He scanned the plethora of multi-coloured switches and buttons, some blinking and vying for his attention.

'Where the hell is the off switch?' he shouted out loud, causing Clammer to look over his shoulder nervously.

Noticing a red button slightly larger than the rest sitting top centre of the board and flashing slower than the others, Bache stared at it for a moment.

Got to try something, he thought.

Tentatively raising a gloved finger, he hesitated for a second before shrugging and pressing the button firmly.

The lights in the room stayed on but the panel went dark, all except the button he'd pressed that now slowly flashed green.

'*Dres'kin*, do you copy?' Bache called.

Getting no reply, he pointed towards the door.

'The ship might be over the horizon, let's go back outside and call from there,' he said, beckoning Clammer to follow.

They found the door closed at the top of the stairs, but another sunken red handle was set into the wall on the left-hand side.

'I'll do the honours shall I?' said Bache, raising his eyebrows at Clammer. 'Don't want to break this one, do we?'

'Wasn't my fault,' said Clammer. 'Shoddy workmanship.'

Bache grinned and found that this handle turned a lot easier than the outer one, probably because it hadn't been buried in rocks and dust. The flat rock door above them rumbled up and allowed them back out onto the surface.

'Well, that's odd,' said Bache, first to emerge. 'All the loose regolith has gone.'

'And the platform and drone,' said Clammer, checking over his shoulder to where he'd landed it a few metres away.

'*Dres'kin*, do you copy?' Bache asked again, gazing up to the left and right.

'Do you think they're behind the moon?' Clammer

wondered as he half hopped, half floated forward and stared at the horizon.

Bache glanced down at the ground that had been scoured clean again. 'Something very dramatic happened out here,' he said. 'The last thing Captain Yamaton said was the domes were coming to life.'

'They might be a weapon,' said Clammer. 'And the blast blew the ship and all the surface here away.'

Bache moved over to a large boulder almost buried in the ground and inspected around it.

'All the regolith went towards the dome,' he said. 'You can see where rocks were initially dragged along the ground before becoming airborne.'

'Which means whatever did all this, was a gradual increase in force and not explosive and sudden,' said Clammer, turning to face Bache.

'Exactly,' said Bache, as a tone sounded in his ears and an icon winked in his peripheral vision. 'I've just had the suit's half-time warning.'

'Ah, same here,' said Clammer. 'We need the ship back here and soon.'

'Hmm,' said Bache, turning and looking back at the steps disappearing down into the ground. 'There was an airlock at the back of that room.'

Clammer followed his gaze.

'An airlock is designed for only one thing,' he said.

They turned to stare at each other through their visors and nodded.

'The race that built this might not breathe the same atmosphere as us though,' said Clammer, as they made their way back to the open hatch door.

'You can stay out here and flag down a passing starship if

you like,' said Bache. 'I'm going to see what's on the other side of that airlock.'

Clammer took one last look round at the empty horizon and quickly followed Bache, bouncing back down through the door. Closing it behind them, they made their way down the steps and across the control room.

Now the lights were on, it made inspecting the airlock a lot easier. It had a small porthole window and as Bache flashed his helmet lights through the small aperture, he could make out a closed inner door similar in design to the outer.

Clammer pointed to a small panel recessed into the rough wall with two raised hexagonal buttons. They were both the same colour but had a different undecipherable word embossed on the face of each.

'You're better at switches and buttons,' said Clammer, nodding over his shoulder at the main control panel.

Bache stared at the two buttons pensively.

'I think the open button would be the first and closest one to the door,' he said, taking a deep breath and pressing it firmly.

At first nothing happened and they couldn't hear anything because they were still in a vacuum. Bache, who had his left hand against the airlock could feel an increasing vibration. He snatched away his hand and took a step back as a cloud of dust exploded out from around the airlock's seal.

The door—slowly at first before increasing in speed—motored up into the ceiling.

'After you, Mr Feltaraine,' said Bache, stepping back and gesticulating at the open door theatrically.

'Do you think it's a good idea us both going in at the same time?' Clammer asked. 'What if we get stuck in there?'

'If the outer door opened, the inner one will,' said Bache. 'Have a little faith.'

Clammer shrugged and, with a nervous look in his eyes, stepped inside.

The choice of button on the inside was easy: there was only one, and Bache pressed it as soon as they were both safely inside. The outer door swept down silently again and sealed. Bache could see the fear in Clammer's eyes as the inner door didn't immediately open.

'It has to pressurise in here,' he said.

Clammer nodded but still looked unconvinced.

Bache soon became aware of a faint hissing sound that gradually became louder. The airlock was definitely pressurising and he gave Clammer a confident grin.

When the hissing stopped, they both stood back from the inner door. There was a loud *crack* as the seal broke, this time without so much dust, and the door whined its way up.

A corridor only as wide as the airlock stretched away into the gloom, also carved out in the same naive way as the control room. Bache stood for a moment and studied his suit telemetry.

'Oxygen-based atmosphere,' he said. 'Although, the oxygen level is low and the CO2 level very high.'

'The scrubbers won't have been serviced in a long time,' said Clammer. 'The filters will be in a right state.'

'That must be our first priority then,' said Bache. 'Then water, then food. We don't know how long we're going to be here.'

They both stepped out of the airlock and began making their way down the dimly lit passageway. Bache stopped suddenly and, looking down at his boots, jigged from foot to foot for a moment.

'The gravity has increased in here,' he said. 'Still not up to one G, but we're not having to hop so much.'

'Good,' said Clammer. 'Makes it easier to move around.'

They continued along the corridor. A few dim lights suspended from the ceiling created soft pools of yellow light every few metres. They had to pick their feet up too, as the floor was anything but flat and level.

Bache stopped again and put his arm out to halt Clammer, as he wasn't paying attention.

'What's up?' Clammer asked, looking up.

Bache felt him stiffen as he saw the reason. A figure had lurched into view at a junction about thirty metres up the passage.

3
___

UNDERGROUND COMPLEX, UNNAMED MOON, SECTOR 351

IT WAS SILHOUETTED in the bad light but definitely humanoid and appeared to be favouring one leg as it limped across the upcoming junction. They both winced as it walked into the wall head first, turned and hobbled off out of sight, back the way it had come.

'Well, that was weird,' said Clammer. 'Must have hurt too.'

'Its movement looked kind of jerky though,' said Bache. 'I think it was an android.'

'With a wonky leg and bad eyesight,' said Clammer, shaking his head.

'We need to be wary,' said Bache.

'Wary?' repeated Clammer. 'It couldn't detect a wall, let alone us.'

'It might have fully operational friends who're programmed to defend the place.'

'Good point,' said Clammer, as he continued up to the junction and leaned out to peer round the corner.

'I don't know why you're bothering to do that,' said

Bache. 'Half your suit sticks out before you can see anything.'

'Stops me getting my balls shot off,' said Clammer.

'What about your head?'

'If that happened, I wouldn't know much about it.'

It was a T-junction and they each looked both ways. Doorways led off from both passages stretching off into the gloom. The android was bumping along the left-hand wall and suddenly disappeared through one of the doors. They heard a crash and then silence returned.

'No wonder he's got a wonky leg,' said Clammer, causing Bache to grin.

'There's the ducting for the atmosphere,' said Bache, pointing up at a grey pipe with slotted vents every few metres. 'We need to follow that.'

'In which direction?' said Clammer, looking left and right.

'Hang on,' said Bache, stretching up and pulling one of the vent covers off. He picked a handful of dust off the floor and threw it into the hole. It blew away to the right. 'We go left then, that's where the scrubbers will be.'

They peered in the first doorway they came to. It was more a hole in the stone wall as there wasn't actually any door. It opened out into a dormitory. Bache counted fifty rudimentary bed frames, all of them slightly different, made from what looked like ship parts and lined against the walls.

'It's as though they all had to make their own,' said Clammer.

'Probably did,' said Bache. 'After the ship crashed, they were most likely here for some time and resources were limited. They had to make do with what they could scavenge from the wreck at the same time as repairing it.'

'You still think they managed to fly off again?' said Clammer.

'There's no ship, no bedding left in here and no bodies. Bolsters my theory somewhat,' said Bache, raising his eyebrows at his colleague.

'You could be a Skirmat Eagle with your deducing skills.' Clammer chuckled.

'Don't you swear at me,' said Bache, glaring at Clammer through his visor.

'Oh, yeah, whoops, sorry,' said Clammer. 'Let's see what's in the next room.' Quickly changing the subject, he sloped off up the corridor.

The next room was identical to the first, with another fifty beds all pushed around randomly. The one after that was on the opposite side of the corridor and was the door the android had fallen through. It had been a dining area of some sort, Bache realised, as he peered around the entrance. It was bigger than the dormitories and had a large kitchen at the far end. Tables that had once been in neat rows were like the beds in the other rooms, all pushed around, on their sides and upside down.

The android was now back on its feet and bumping around the kitchen quietly mumbling to itself. They watched it for a while before making their way through the wrecked dining room and approaching the clumsy machine as it rattled itself around in a small pantry.

'Can you hear me?' called Bache, making sure he remained to one side of the door in case the machine was armed.

The android froze as if someone had hit the off switch.

'Can you understand me?' Bache continued.

Its head turned suddenly in Bache's direction.

'*Corlevie, macheen shull,*' it said, its unseeing eyes flicking from left to right.

Now they were close to the machine and it was stationary, Bache could see the intricacy and beauty of its design. Mostly grey in colour, the intricate arm and leg joints were exposed, with dozens of tiny multicoloured cables weaving their way through the gaps in the outer skin.

'Someone put a lot of effort into that design,' he said to Clammer. 'I've never seen anything like it.'

'*Corlevie, macheen shull,*' it repeated, this time turning its torso towards them. A small panel in the centre of its chest whirred open, causing Bache and Clammer to shrink back.

'What the hell is that?' said Clammer.

'Some sort of miniature keypad,' said Bache. 'Those tiny buttons have more of their weird lettering.'

'*Corlevie, macheen shull,*' it said again and dropped its head down as if to look at the open keypad.

'Have you got a universal translator in your suit?' asked Bache, glancing at Clammer.

'No, sorry – not something I thought we might need on a dead moon.'

Bache thought for a moment before sliding his tablet out from a side pocket. He clumsily prodded at it with one gloved finger then, holding it out towards the android, he spoke once more.

'Can you say something again?' he said, deliberately projecting his voice towards the android.

'*Corlevie, macheen shull,*' it repeated as if understanding the question.

'Ah, there we go,' said Bache, reading from the tablet. 'It's speaking in Horty, a language from the Gattainian Cluster.'

'Where?' said Clammer.

'They're not GDA,' said Bache. 'A very old region, fiercely independent and, if my history lessons serve me correctly, they were one of the first human races to explore the galaxy, many thousands of years ago.'

He showed the translation to Clammer.

'Malfunction, maintenance required,' Clammer read aloud. He glanced at Bache, raising his eyebrows. 'No shit.'

Bache smiled and selected Horty, the language from a planet called Eritain, the tablet told him. He proceeded to speak clearly into it.

'What do I enter into the keypad?' Bache asked.

The tablet repeated the sentence in Horty and the android looked up in their direction.

'Are you not from the *Xhamin*?' it asked.

'No,' said Bache. 'The *Xhamin* and all its crew are gone.'

'Incorrect,' it said. 'The *Xhamin* entered the interstice. The commander remained here.'

Bache and Clammer glanced at each other.

'How long ago did the *Xhamin* leave?' Bache asked.

'Two thousand, nine hundred and eighty-seven years, forty-nine days and sixteen hours,' it said.

'How long ago did the *Xhamin* crash here?'

'Three thousand and three years, thirty-one days and two hours ago.'

'They were here for sixteen years,' said Clammer.

'And someone had to operate the gateway from the surface,' said Bache, nodding. 'That's what the domes are for. The interstice must be some kind of wormhole technology.'

'Do you think that's what happened to the *Dres'kin*?' Clammer asked. 'It was sucked into a wormhole with all the surface regolith?'

'Would explain a lot, wouldn't it?' said Bache. 'They didn't realise it would draw on everything close by and the ship was dragged in before the commander could get aboard.'

'Where did the interstice go to?' asked Clammer.

'No data,' said the android.

'Do you have a name?' asked Bache.

'My designation is V1438903.'

Bache shook his head.

'We'll just call you Vee, if that is acceptable?'

'It is acceptable.'

Clammer looked back towards the dining room door.

'Where is the commander?' he asked.

'The commander is in his sleep cabin,' said Vee.

'How long has he been there?' asked Bache.

'Two thousand, nine hundred and eighty-seven years, forty-six days and twelve hours.'

'Shall I tell him it's time for breakfast?' said Clammer, chuckling.

'The commander must not be revived until the *Xhamin* returns,' said Vee.

'Revived?' demanded Bache, staring at Vee. 'Is the commander in some sort of survival chamber?'

'He is in his sleep cabin,' said Vee.

Bache rolled his eyes at Clammer.

'Vee, is the sleep cabin a machine that keeps the commander alive for long periods?' Bache asked hopefully.

'Affirmative.'

'Where is the commander's sleep cabin?' Bache asked.

'Last cabin down the north walkway,' said Vee.

'How long have you been without eyesight?' asked Clammer.

'Two hundred and seventeen years, one hundred and thirteen days and four hours.'

'Is there any way we can fix that?' said Bache.

'Enter a full maintenance overview and restart into my command keys,' said Vee, waving his hand at the panel on his chest.

'Can't you do that yourself?' asked Clammer.

'Mechadroids are not permitted to alter themselves or their programming in any way.'

'Ah, right,' said Bache. 'I understand now. You'll have to give me some guidance here, because we don't understand the language on the keys.'

The android sat on the ground against the wall. 'Press top right, centre and bottom left together for three seconds,' it said.

Bache did as he was instructed and watched as Vee went suddenly completely limp. Clammer caught him and lowered him gently to the floor. The keypad flashed a couple of times and Vee's limbs twitched randomly as the restart and maintenance programme went through its routine.

A chime sounded in Bache's suit again, warning him he'd used seventy-five percent of his oxygen supply.

'Ah, crap,' he said. 'Come on Vee, wakey wakey.' He reached for another visor wipe and cleaned two hundred years of crud off the android's eye lenses.

Vee sat up straight and looked around, then stood, the panel on its chest closing again.

'Can you see now?' Clammer asked.

'I am mechadroid designation V1438903/2. What are my duties?' Vee asked.

Bache and Clammer looked at each other.

'You need to show us where the environmental filters are,' said Bache.

'I'm sorry, I'm not familiar with this facility,' it said. 'More data required.'

'Oh, skata,' said Bache. 'Its memory has been wiped with the restart.'

4

UNDERGROUND COMPLEX, UNNAMED MOON, SECTOR 351

'WHY DIDN'T it tell us this would happen?' Clammer asked.

'It probably didn't know,' said Bache. 'Come on, we need to find that environment service room.'

They quickly made their way back to the corridor and turned left. A scraping noise caused Bache to stop and turn. Vee was two metres behind and dragging his left leg. He stopped too and just stood there, expressionless, watching and waiting.

'Looks like his sight is fine now,' said Clammer. 'His expression's a bit eerie.'

'He is a bit creepy isn't he?' said Bache. 'And following us like a lost, lame Dennit calf too.'

'Seems about as harmless though,' admitted Clammer. 'I can't see any weapons on him.'

'Let's hope there aren't,' said Bache, turning back and continuing to follow the pipe along the ceiling.

Twenty metres further down, the pipe turned ninety degrees and disappeared through the wall above a doorway. A room roughly six metres square confronted them when they opened the unlocked door. It contained several bulky machines, one of which had a large pipe emerging from the floor and heading straight into it.

'They were lucky,' said Bache. 'There was a water deposit down in the stratum they've tapped into.'

'To extract the oxygen,' said Clammer, nodding and gazing around the room.

'Check around all this stuff for anything resembling a filter and clean it,' said Bache, pointing to a rectangular sink against the far wall. He noticed a square duct coming through the wall at floor height too and disappearing into a large machine on the right. 'That must be the CO2 scrubber,' he said, opening a large panel on the side of the unit, causing it to shut off.

Several horizontal alloy trays confronted him, with handles on the front edges.

'There you are,' he said, trying to pull one of them out and finding it stuck fast. 'No wonder the oxygen level's low,' he said. 'These filters are clogged solid.'

He glanced across at Vee standing slightly lopsided just inside the door, watching them with his default neutral expression. Bache retrieved his tablet again and spoke into it.

'Vee, can you get these filters out and change them for some of those clean ones on the rack over there?'

'Affirmative,' Vee said, looking at the tablet. 'I have also set my default language to Ellinika,' he added, before limping over and grabbing the first filter tray.

'Wow,' said Bache, raising his eyebrows at Clammer, who grinned in return.

Bache watched as Vee quickly realised the filters were jammed in with years of detritus. His arms began oscillating at a high frequency and the first tray began sliding slowly out.

'Well,' said Clammer as he removed a hugely gummed-up water filter from one of the input valves. 'Mr Drag-A-Leg proves useful after all.'

'Don't you upset him,' said Bache. 'He might have a sarcasm assassination default too.'

Bache chuckled to himself as he saw Clammer giving Vee nervous glances as he got on with scrubbing his filter.

Ten minutes later, Vee had replaced all ten filters and stood back near the door. Bache had given Clammer a hand with the three inlet water filters, as getting those clean was particularly labour-intensive with the build up of calcium.

Clammer turned the water valve gradually back to on and the comforting sound of water hissing through soon died down as the system recharged. Bache closed the hatch on the atmosphere filters again and pressed one of the three hexagonal buttons. Nothing happened. On pushing the second one, it hummed to life again with renewed vigour and considerably more air pressure flowing into the ducting.

'I hope that sorts it out,' said Bache, peeking at his suit's peripheral vision display and finding twenty-two minutes' oxygen supply left.

Clammer walked out into the corridor and stood underneath a vent, giving Vee an unusually wide birth as he passed.

'The oxygen level is up by one point two percent already,' he said, a few seconds later.

'That's good,' said Bache. 'Let's go and find the commander now he'll have something to breathe, if we can find out how to wake him.'

They continued up the corridor, remembering what the first Vee had told them about his cabin being the last door. It wasn't as far as they thought. The lighting had failed at the end of the passage; the doorway appeared out of the gloom on the left-hand side and actually had a door in it that was closed.

'Can you see a handle or keypad anywhere?' said Bache, shining his suit lights around the frame and door.

'No,' said Clammer, as they both turned to face Vee.

'Vee, how does this door open?' asked Bache.

'Insufficient data,' said Vee, his expression deadpan as usual.

'Skata,' said Bache. 'Isn't there somewhere you can get the data, Vee?' he asked more in frustration than expecting an answer.

'I can get facility data at a node,' said Vee.

'Where are they?' asked Clammer.

'Several locations around the facility,' Vee replied.

Bache and Clammer looked at each other.

'Can you go to the nearest one and obtain the facility data download?' asked Bache, not quite believing it could be that easy.

'Affirmative,' said Vee, turning and limping back just ten paces and placing his left hand against a small black panel set into the wall.

'I wondered what they did,' said Clammer, shaking his head. 'They're all over the place.'

Vee went stiffly to attention as soon as the panel lit up. He stood frozen for around thirty seconds as the panel pulsed with multicoloured light. He relaxed and returned back to them as the panel went dark again.

'Entry to the commander's sleep cabin is only permitted by members of the *Xhamin*'s crew,' he said.

'Vee, the *Xhamin* has been gone for three thousand years,' said Bache. 'I don't think it's coming back now. We really need to talk to the commander to find out where the ship went, because our ship got dragged into the interstice and has gone there too.'

'Entry to the commander's sleep cabin is only permitted by members of the *Xhamin*'s crew,' Vee said, repeating himself.

'Skata,' said Clammer, leaning against the wall and crossing his arms. 'What do we do now?'

'Vee,' said Bache. 'You're a member of the *Xhamin*'s crew. Shouldn't you be doing periodic checks on the commander's wellbeing?'

'Affirmative.'

'How often?'

'Every ten days.'

'When was the last check done?'

'Two hundred and seventeen years, one hundred and thirteen days and five hours,' he said.

'Don't you think you need to do a check as soon as possible?'

'Affirmative.'

Bache and Clammer stood back from the door and pointed at it.

Vee stepped forward, touched the door with the palm of his left hand. It clicked open.

5

UNDERGROUND COMPLEX, UNNAMED MOON, SECTOR 351

THEY BOTH FOLLOWED Vee into the room before he had a chance to close the door. The cabin was small and contained a single bed, a desk and a wardrobe. Shelves adorned the wall above the desk. A small collection of books and personal bits and pieces filled the shelves, and what appeared to be some sort of personal computer sat closed down on the desk.

'Where the hell is he?' said Clammer.

Almost as he spoke, Vee touched another black panel set into the far wall. A loud *click* sounded and the entire wall slid upwards revealing a hidden room, considerably larger than the cabin.

Again, they followed Vee closely to avoid being shut out, although the door stayed open anyway. The hibernation chamber sat centre stage and took up a lot of the room. It was around two and a half metres long and a metre wide, with thick cables running across the floor into a control unit bolted to the far wall. The convex glass top had gone completely opaque with calcium buildup, so much so it was almost impossible to see anything inside.

'There are indicator lights on inside at this end,' said Clammer wiping the thin layer of dust off the glass cover.

'And on the control panel,' said Bache, nodding in that direction.

Vee limped straight over to the controls and placed his hand on another now-familiar black panel. Bright white lights illuminated the inside of the hibernation chamber, although it was still only possible to see a vague outline of the body inside. Also, the faint sound of rushing water emanated from inside the chamber as Vee stood stock still, a vacant expression on his face.

'What's happening, Vee?' Bache asked.

'I'm flushing the fluid encasement,' he said. 'The nutrient level had become dangerously low.'

'The body's encased in fluid then?' Clammer said, bending down and trying to peer through the cover.

'It's a sustaining solution, it oxygenates and stops the body ageing,' said Vee, removing his hand from the panel and turning to face them.

'He's still alive then?' asked Bache.

'Affirmative. The fluid had deteriorated somewhat, so he may have aged to some degree.'

'Can you wake him?'

'The commander can only be revived when the *Xhamin* returns,' said Vee.

'Vee,' Bache said with slow emphasis, 'the *Xhamin* is gone for good. You're gradually deteriorating too, until one day you won't be able to keep the commander's life support system going and you'll both die.'

'He would have died very soon if we hadn't turned up and reinstated your eyesight,' said Clammer.

'It's in direct contradiction to my programming,' Vee insisted.

'Don't you have any emergency protocols?' Bache asked.

'Only in extreme circumstances.'

'Don't you think this is, Vee?' insisted Clammer.

Bache knew Vee was considering the situation as he adopted an unseeing blank expression every time he had to think about something.

'I have evaluated all options,' Vee said after a moment. 'Considering the timescale involved, it is very unlikely any of the *Xhamin*'s crew will still be alive and the return of the *Xhamin* is extremely improbable.'

'Correct,' said Bache.

'For this reason, I will initiate emergency protocol two,' said Vee.

'Which is?' asked Clammer.

'Closing down the facility and deactivating myself.'

'What—and let the commander die?' blurted Clammer, the shock evident in his voice.

'The commander was clear in his orders,' said Vee. 'If the *Xhamin* was not going to return, then protocol two was to be initiated.'

'But we're here now and may be able to help him get home,' said Bache. 'Which protocol deals with that scenario?'

'There are only two protocols,' said Vee.

'What, wake him or kill him?' said Clammer, giving Bache an exasperated sideways glance.

'Vee,' said Bache, moving himself over to stare directly into the android's face. 'It's imprinted in every human's DNA to try and survive, no matter how bad the odds. I can guarantee that in this situation the commander would want to be woken and at least given a fighting chance of getting home.'

Vee adopted a blank face again as he thought about that for a while. Finally, his expression changed from one of thought to one of intent and he moved over to place his hand on the black panel once more.

The lighting in the room dimmed down slightly and the faint gushing of liquid from the chamber changed pitch.

'What's happening, Vee?' Clammer asked nervously, looking between the chamber and the android.

'Protocol one,' said Vee, taking a limped step back and standing against the wall.

'You're waking the commander?'

'Affirmative.'

Bache puffed his cheeks and exhaled. 'Thank you, Vee,' he said, glancing at his suit's readout in his peripheral vision as a chime sounded.

Clammer must have had the same message as he suddenly glanced right, raised his eyebrows and spoke.

'My suit's getting dangerously low now,' he said, looking at Bache.

'Same here,' said Bache, checking the exterior levels. 'The oxygen level is up to eighty-four percent of normal in the complex. I'll crack my suit and test it.'

Clammer watched closely as Bache reached up with both hands and slid the two release catches either side of his helmet. There was a slight hiss as the pressure equalised and he took a tentative sniff of the air within the complex. It smelt a bit stale, like an old house opened for the first time in years, but apart from that, it was breathable and he nodded at his partner.

Clammer removed his helmet too and also sniffed the air suspiciously.

'Stinks a bit,' he said, wrinkling his nose.

'I'd rather be breathing smelly air than a vacuum,' said Bache. 'Don't forget to set your suit on replenish though.'

Both their suits began a low hum as they extracted fresh oxygen from the complex's newly refreshed atmosphere and began refilling their supply.

'How long does the waking process take, Vee?' Bache asked.

'Several hours,' he replied.

Bache and Clammer looked at each other.

'Are there any food supplies left?' said Bache, glancing back at Vee.

'Dried rations were left for the commander's awakening,' said Vee.

'Where?' asked Clammer.

'In those storage boxes,' said Vee, pointing to a row of cupboards set into the side wall. Clammer was nearest and opened the first one. It was stacked with sealed plain packages. The only indication of the contents was written on one face of the small cartons in the alien language.

Clammer rummaged through the four cupboards and eventually found something resembling energy bars.

'Are these edible, Vee?' asked Bache, holding one up so Vee could read the lettering.

'Affirmative,' he said. 'It translates to "Duns Cake".'

Clammer opened one and nibbled a corner. Adopting an expression as though he'd just stepped in something unpleasant, he turned to face Vee.

'I think it's pronounced dung cake, Vee,' he said, smacking his lips and wrinkling his nose.

'It'll have to do,' said Bache, opening his and sniffing it suspiciously.

'Might as well sit down and wait then,' said Clammer, sliding his back down the wall and placing his helmet on his lap.

Bache did the same and as Vee watched over the control panel. They both sat chewing in silence, listening to the machine's humming and gurgling as it worked its way through the waking routine.

6

UNDERGROUND COMPLEX, UNNAMED MOON, SECTOR 351

BACHE WAS SUDDENLY JARRED awake by someone nearby retching and coughing. He hadn't realised he'd dropped off. It worried him initially, as he believed it was Clammer who'd earlier eaten the same food he had. He found Clammer staring back at him, probably thinking the exact same thing. They jumped to their feet together as they registered the choking sounds were coming from the survival chamber.

The curved opaque top had hinged open over on their side blocking the view, so they hurried around the unit and peered inside.

A very wrinkled naked man lay squinting and coughing, umbilicals protruding from every orifice. The one that had been in his throat now lay to one side. It had been the reason for the retching as the machine extracted it.

'*Ut harsy gryk et tanch doe,*' Commander Nexen struggled to whisper, his vocal cords not yet functional.

Bache extracted his tablet again and set it to translate, only this time audibly.

'Say again, Commander,' he said, the tablet repeating it back in Horty.

'I hate these bloody things,' the electronic voice on the tablet repeated as the commander lay still, taking huge gulps of air and spitting out the last of the fluid from his mouth. 'The ship made it back then?' he croaked, giving the tablet a puzzled glance as it repeated what he said in a language foreign to him.

Bache and Clammer exchanged a brief look.

'We're not from the *Xhamin*,' said Bache.

'But they told you where I was?' he said, his eyes flicking between them suspiciously. Then, noticing Vee for the first time, he weakly lifted an arm and beckoned him over. 'Get me a blanket, vassal,' he ordered. 'It's cold in here.'

'Right away, Commander,' said Vee, hurrying passed Clammer and Bache and disappearing into the cabin.

Nexen's attention returned to the strangers and Bache noticed him raise his eyebrows as he inspected their suits.

'I'm afraid we don't know where your ship is,' said Bache.

'Then who are you?' he asked, staring at Bache intently.

'We're kinda in the same situation as you,' said Bache. 'We've lost our ship through the wormhole portal you set up to take the *Xhamin* home.'

'The interstice reactivated?' he asked, giving them an incredulous look. 'That could only be done from the control bunker.'

Bache gave Clammer a glance, who pulled an awkward face and stared at his feet.

'It was activated by mistake,' said Bache. 'And dragged our ship inside while we were down here investigating what this was.'

'If you're not from the *Xhamin* or from Eritain, then who are you?' he asked.

Vee limped back with a dark grey blanket and draped it over the commander.

'We're from the GDA,' said Bache. 'An organisation or council of many worlds that oversees a large portion of the galaxy.'

'Never heard of 'em.'

'That's because you're from what we call the Gattainian Cluster, which is a long way away,' said Bache.

'The GDA was a lot smaller in those days too,' said Clammer, causing Bache to flinch at the faux pas, which didn't go unnoticed.

'What do you mean by "in those days"?' Nexen asked, staring at Clammer and then glancing back at Bache. 'How many months has my ship been gone?'

Bache looked over at Vee, who had returned to stand by the control panel.

'Vee, could you tell the commander how long he's been asleep in the chamber, please?' he asked.

'Two thousand, nine hundred and eighty-seven years, forty-six days and eighteen hours,' said Vee, without any hesitation.

Nexen's eyes widened at the answer and he snapped his attention back to Bache.

'Impossible,' he said. 'The vassal is malfunctioning. The *Xhamin* would've only taken eleven months to reach home using the interstice.'

'That's just it,' said Bache. 'Would've—if your ship had reached home, they'd have rescued you three millennia ago. I'm afraid your android is telling the truth. We can tell by the layers of dust and neglect out there in the facility that it has indeed been empty for a considerable length of time.'

'Three thousand years,' he croaked. 'How can it possibly be three thousand years? Everyone I've ever known would be long dead.' He grunted as he tried to sit up and, finding his arms were too weak to take his weight, he collapsed back onto the cushioning. 'Damn it,' he grumbled. 'I'm as helpless as a newborn.'

'Your strength will return,' said Bache. 'Your muscles have atrophied over the long period of time. Vee, can you get the commander some water and something to eat, please?'

Vee nodded and disappeared back into the cabin again.

'Your android technology is exceptional,' said Clammer. 'Did you have many of them on the ship?'

'Yes,' answered Nexen. 'Most systems were overseen by them, all except for the bridge positions. Although they were quite capable of flying a starship, we found the human crew preferred knowing there was some form of organic sentience in the decision-making that ultimately kept them alive.'

'I think I would want the same,' said Clammer, nodding slowly.

'What were you doing out here anyway?' asked Nexen. 'From what I remember, this system doesn't have many redeeming features.'

'Final training mission,' said Bache. 'Before we became qualified ship's officers.'

'So you're recruits?' he said, raising his eyebrows.

Bache nodded.

'Hell, at least I had a bit of a career before being marooned on this piece of shit rock,' the commander grunted, his voice beginning to sound a bit more human.

Vee returned with a bladder of water that the commander

accepted and sipped at greedily, grimacing every time he swallowed. Vee turned and began rummaging in the food cupboards.

'We need to transmit a signal of some kind to attract attention,' said Clammer.

'Good luck with that,' said Nexen. 'I hope you brought a powerful transmitter with you, because ours was destroyed in the crash landing.'

'Only the ones built into our suits,' said Clammer, holding up his helmet.

'We had our suit transmitters too,' he said, continuing to sip the water. 'But I imagine they're the same as yours, with only a few kilometres range. Not a lot of help when rescue is a thousand light years away.'

'We need to look at this from a different prospective,' said Bache.

'Such as?' asked Nexen, sounding sceptical.

'Even if we had a powerful transmitter, it would still take many months for the signal to travel those distances and help to arrive,' said Bache. 'Unless you have a hoard of food elsewhere in the facility, these three cupboards of dried rations won't keep us alive for long.'

'We still can't just magic a ship out of thin air, can we?' said Clammer. 'There's not enough parts lying around to build one, no matter how small.'

Vee, who'd been preparing something to eat, passed the commander a small pot and a spoon, containing what Bache thought looked like grey porridge.

Nexen accepted it, sniffed it suspiciously and grimaced. 'Oh joy,' he said, giving Vee an indignant glare. 'Three-thousand-year-old sludge. I'd forgotten how delectable the post-tank meal was.'

'It's a perfectly formulated source of carbohydrates and—'

'Minerals to restart your digestive system after a long period in a sleep tank, yes, thank you doctor,' said Nexen, interrupting Vee. 'I can read it on the packet from here. They certainly didn't over-commit on the flavouring, that's for sure.'

'Commander?' said Bache, who'd been staring at the control panel for a while. 'Where does the power for the facility come from?'

'Thermal generator,' he said. 'This rock still has a molten core.'

'Forgive me if I'm wrong, but remembering what my father told me about wormhole, or as you call it, interstice technology, doesn't it need a substantial and continuous supply of power to maintain the tunnel for the entire period of travel?' Bache asked.

'Hmm,' mumbled Nexen, with a mouth full of porridge. 'In the early days, yes, but our engineers then discovered a way for the ship to self-perpetuate the interstice by using its own power to open and close the tunnel just in front and behind the vessel. The benefit of this was much less power was required and it was much more reliable. Before this, if the power failed that upheld the interstice, the ship would drop out wherever it was and if that was in the vicinity of a black hole or something then that was it. We lost several ships that way.'

'Why did you have to build the surface-mounted initiators then?' Bache asked.

'The crash destroyed the specifically designed array that could open the interstice. We solved the glitch with the reactor that dropped us out in the first place, but we had no way of opening the gate from the ship.'

'Couldn't you operate the ground-based initiators from the ship?' Clammer asked.

'Yes, but they had to be shut down at a specific moment after the ship had entered and someone had to be here to physically do that.'

'Then, if everything went to plan,' said Bache, 'I can't understand why they didn't return to pick you up. What was the destination programmed for the interstice?'

'The ship's home planet of Eritain. It should have taken about eleven months, so I shouldn't have been here longer than two years.'

'Hmm,' grunted Bache. 'I think we need to investigate why that didn't happen.'

7

UNDERGROUND COMPLEX, UNNAMED MOON, SECTOR 351

BACHE SAT on his own in the facility's canteen, staring at his tablet. He'd left Clammer to aid Vee with the commander's recovery. As far as he knew, no one had ever spent three thousand years in a suspension chamber before, so the commander's recuperation would probably take a while.

Having obtained the equations used to programme the ship's interstice drive from Vee, he compared them to some old GDA wormhole mathematics used before the advent of spacial folding. A lot of it was of course very similar, and Bache could see the working theory of their system. There was, however, a slight deviation when it came to the continuation of the tunnel once inside, and it puzzled him.

He looked up as sounds from the corridor disrupted his concentration. Nexen staggered in through the door, flanked by Vee supporting one arm and Clammer the other. He'd dressed in his uniform that hung off him like it was five sizes too big.

The pained expression on the commander's face

prompted Bache to grab another chair and set it upright at the table he'd also righted from the pile around the walls.

'Thank you,' said Nexen, grimacing as he sat. 'I think it may take some considerable time to recover from a sleep that long.'

'How d'you feel?' Bache asked.

'Absolutely exhausted,' he said, resting his arms on the table and slumping forward. 'I've only walked fifty metres, I feel like I've sprinted a hundred kilometres, and I had help, too.'

'I'm sure it'll get better,' said Bache. 'You're in uncharted territory as far as suspension chambers are concerned.'

'Have you found anything?' the commander asked, nodding at the tablet.

'I'm not sure,' Bache replied. 'I'm certainly not familiar with old wormhole technology equations.'

'I'm not familiar with any equations,' said Clammer, grabbing a chair and joining them at the table.

Nexen looked at the expression on Bache's face. 'Do I sense a "but" in there, somewhere?' he asked.

Bache raised his eyebrows and grinned at the question. 'Who programmed the ship's navigation before it departed?' he asked.

'The human crew navigator before the navigation vassal does the final checks,' Nexen answered. 'Their computing power is vastly superior to ours; in fact if I remember correctly, that vassal was one of the latest models and we were part of testing its operational abilities. It had some new experimental personality traits inbuilt too.'

'Hmm,' mumbled Bache, looking back at the tablet's screen. 'I think it might have made an error. Did anyone of the crew check the calculations before departure?'

'Well, no,' he said. 'As I said before, it works the other way around. The human navigator programmed the route and the vassal checked it and made any alterations needed.'

Bache adopted a pained expression as their eyes met.

'You think the vassal changed the programming and got it wrong?' Nexen asked.

Bache shrugged and glanced at Vee standing to one side. 'Experimental personality traits you say?' he asked and looked back at the commander, whose face went even whiter.

'Oh, crap! Can you work out where it sent them?' Nexen asked.

'Well, that's just it,' said Bache. 'There doesn't seem to be a destination programmed at all.'

Nexen turned to look at Vee. 'Vassal, do you have the navigational module downloaded?'

'Affirmative, Commander,' said Vee.

'Check these interstice settings and tell me the destination?' Nexen asked, as Bache turned the tablet around to face Vee.

It took him just three seconds to answer. 'No destination programmed,' said Vee, standing back away from the table.

'Then, where the hell is my ship?' Nexen shouted, staring at Vee and startling Bache and Clammer.

Vee stood staring straight ahead with his default phlegmatic expression, which only proved to antagonise the commander further.

'Vassal, I asked you a question,' he thundered.

'More data required to ascertain a location,' Vee replied, in his flat, emotionless manner.

The commander just huffed, sat back and folded his arms across his chest. 'I told them giving these dumb machines personalities would be a mistake,' he growled.

'Well, wherever your ship is, it's got a GDA destroyer for company now,' said Clammer.

Bache sat staring at the tablet's screen again. 'Commander, did your crew all have suspension chambers too?' he asked.

'They did,' he said. 'Mine was the only one removed. All but the bridge crew were already in their chambers for the eleven-month voyage. The bridge officers would follow them once the ship was safely inside the interstice.'

Bache nodded. 'Hmm, I wonder,' he said.

'Wonder what?' said Clammer.

Bache paused for a moment and tapped a couple of icons on the tablet. 'It's just a theory,' he said, 'but, what if we transposed the polarity of the tunnel or interstice and designated this gate as the destination?' Bache looked up at the other two sitting opposite him and found two blank faces staring back.

'It's never been done,' said Nexen. 'How do we know it won't destroy both ships?'

'We don't,' said Bache. 'But unless you have a better suggestion, we're all dead in a few weeks.'

Nexen and Clammer looked at each other.

Clammer shrugged. 'When it's put like that, we really have nothing to lose,' he said.

Nexen turned back to Bache. 'Are we able to do that?' he asked. 'I'm from a piloting background and certainly no engineer.'

'Vee should be able to instigate the changes,' said Bache, looking over at the android standing impassively to one side.

Nexen followed his gaze and grimaced. 'Can we trust it?' he said.

Bache nodded. 'This time it will be the other way around,

I will check the data before you activate the transmitters,' said Bache.

'You want me to do it?' Nexen asked, raising his eyebrows. 'I don't know if my suit will still hold pressure after all this time.'

'We're both qualified walkers,' said Clammer. 'We'll check it over for you.'

It was the Nexen's turn to nod.

'Do you have a camera view that covers the gate?' asked Bache. 'I would like to see what happens from a position of relative safety.'

'There were several three thousand years ago,' Nexen answered. 'I certainly can't promise they're still in operation now.'

Bache turned and grinned at Vee. 'There's a job for you, Vee,' he said. 'Pop out and check the exterior cameras are functioning correctly.'

'I'm sorry,' said Vee. 'Now the commander is awake, the order must come from him.'

Nexen rolled his eyes. 'Can you imagine how irritating they are with added personality?' he said, before turning to face Vee. 'Do as you're told, vassal, and replace any cameras that aren't working too.'

'Affirmative,' said Vee, as he limped off and disappeared out the door and off towards the airlock.

'How'd he get that damaged leg?' Nexen asked.

'He was blind when we found him,' said Bache. 'He'd spent years bumping into things and falling over.'

'Stupid dumb-arse androids,' Nexen said, smiling for the first time.

8

UNDERGROUND COMPLEX, UNNAMED MOON, SECTOR 351

'YOU MENTIONED something called spacial folding that replaced your interstice technology,' said Nexen as they waited for Vee to replace the exterior cameras. As it turned out, all of them were either non-functional or completely missing. Most likely destroyed by three thousand years' worth of meteorite showers.

'That's right,' said Bache. 'Folding space, or jumping as it's commonly known, takes you from one point to another in an instant.'

'So, it's faster than interstice travel?' Nexen said, his eyes wide.

'Immeasurably so,' said Bache. 'Your eleven-month voyage home would take a couple of days.'

Nexen continued staring at Bache. 'Two days?' he said, his mouth hanging open in shock. 'It's thousands of light years. Surely you're mistaken?'

Bache smiled and shook his head. 'No, it's quite routine now and has been for a while. It's really opened the galaxy up for travel and trade.'

'What about my region?' he asked. 'Are they affiliated to your BDA council?'

'It's GDA, and no, they're not,' said Bache. 'As far as I can remember from my lessons on galactic politics, the Gattainian Cluster has remained stoically independent. Which is fine, the GDA don't insist on all human races joining the council and will leave you alone—so long as you don't start rattling swords with a neighbour or anyone, that is.'

'How many have joined?'

'It's over sixteen hundred now,' said Bache. 'I believe the council chamber on Dasos has been enlarged four times now to make room for all the new ambassadors.'

They both looked up as Clammer came bounding into the canteen, lugging the commander's space suit over his shoulder. 'Can you try this on and pressure test it?' he said to Nexen. 'It's a bit primitive, but I found some new seals in your cabin, changed them, charged it up and filled the oxygen tanks. I've also connected your comms to our translator. Now I want to check its seams haven't been compromised by all the time it's sat unused.'

'It had better be operational,' said Nexen, struggling to his feet. 'Or I'm stuck here.'

'Don't worry,' said Bache. 'If our ship returns we have plenty of spares.'

They both helped him as he wriggled his way into the suit that at one time had been white. Now distinctly grey in places, it looked a little shabby but seemed reasonably sound. Nexen activated the suit, turned on the oxygen supply and secured his helmet seal.

'Give it two atmospheres,' said Bache. 'We'll listen for any leaks.'

'The suit's fitted with an alarm if it develops a—'

A shrill beeping interrupted Nexen.

'—leak,' he continued, peering down the front of the suit.

'I can hear it hissing,' said Clammer, once the alarm had been silenced. They both ran their hands across all the seals and seams.

'Found it,' said Bache, pointing to a seam on Nexen's left arm.

Clammer pulled an emergency suit patch from a pocket on his suit, carefully unsealed it and slapped it over the seam that Bache was pointing at and nodded at Nexen. 'Give it another test,' he said, stepping back.

This time the alarm stayed silent.

'Will it hold?' Nexen asked, holding his arm up and inspecting the patch suspiciously.

'That bonding agent is used to fuse starship hull plates,' said Bache. 'The rest of the suit will fail long before that does.'

Nexen nodded, but Bache could see by the expression on his face he wasn't entirely convinced.

It took Vee another three and a half hours to repair and replace the exterior cameras. He returned to the canteen and informed the commander that full exterior coverage had been restored.

'Vassal, put the feed up on the monitor,' said Nexen, indicating a blank panel on the wall.

Immediately a view of the moon's surface appeared, then another and another as Vee flicked through the full repertoire of camera angles.

'I think that covers just about everything,' said Clammer. 'No one's going to sneak up on us now.'

'And more importantly,' said Bache, 'we can see what comes out of that wormhole when it reopens.'

'Are you up for a walk outside, Commander?' Clammer asked Nexen, offering his hand for assistance.

Nexen nodded and with Clammer's help stood and began making his way slowly towards the door.

'Vee, come with us,' said Bache as he resealed his helmet and activated his suit systems.

Once inside the airlock, they all checked each other's suits before venting the atmosphere and opening the outer door. Bache took Nexen's arm again, but got waved away as the lower gravity here enabled the commander to walk or hop unaided over to the gate control panel. They both watched as he powered up the systems. Six view screens above the panel flickered to life, which prompted Bache to begin wiping the dust from them. Clammer joined in until all six were clear and presented a panoramic view of the gate area and beyond.

'Vassal, can you programme the gate to reverse its interstice and create this moon as the destination?' Nexen asked, having to turn his whole torso to address Vee.

'Affirmative, Commander.'

Vee approached the desk and placed his hand on one of the now-familiar black panels. He remained stationary for a few moments, then the control panel lights began flashing in a different sequence. Bache noticed some of the text on the central screen, written in the alien language, changing. Nexen leant over the panel and seemed to be studying the writing closely. Finally, he nodded his approval at Vee, who removed his hand and stood away to one side.

'Does it look okay to you?' asked Bache.

'As far as I can tell,' replied Nexen. 'Although I was only shown how to initiate the gate and close the system down. The engineers did all the programming.'

'Shall we give it a go?' said Clammer, rubbing his gloves together in anticipation.

'As my father likes to say, "Crunch it, punch it and pray,"' said Bache, giving Nexen a pat on the shoulder.

They all stared up at the display screens as Nexen touched the familiar flashing green button in the centre of the panel.

The first thing Bache noticed was that the dome just outside began glowing, which quickly changed to a pulsing. Above, a massive disc of light materialised, full of multi-coloured swirling clouds.

For a few seconds nothing happened, then rocks and dust began raining down out of the vortex. One of the screens blinked out as the camera was hit by a boulder.

'Ah shit,' said Clammer.

'No, that must be the regolith that was sucked in,' said Bache. 'That's a good sign.'

'There's our platform,' said Clammer, the excitement evident in his voice as the tiny craft came spinning out of the wormhole.

Much to Bache and Clammer's relief the rear of the destroyer came next.

'Wow,' said Nexen as the long sleek warship extricated itself from the vortex. 'Your ship I presume?'

'Indeed,' said Bache, unable to keep the smile off his face.

'Walkers, do you copy?' a familiar voice boomed in both Bache and Clammer's helmets.

'We certainly do,' called Clammer, hopping from foot to foot in his excitement.

'It's great to see you back, Captain,' said Bache. 'Is the *Dres'kin* operational again?'

'It will be when you turn that bloody thing off,' came the rather stern reply.

'Will do,' said Bache. 'We're just waiting for another vessel to reappear.'

'Well, don't hang around, we've only got attitude thrusters and they won't keep us off that rock for long.'

'Understood, Captain,' said Bache. 'The commander of the other vessel is with—'

'It's here,' shouted Nexen, interrupting Bache and pointing up at the screens.

'Who was that?' asked Yamaton.

Bache could hear the other *Dres'kin* bridge officers getting animated about the second vessel emerging and before he could answer the captain, there was a flash and the communication line went dead.

'What the hell?' said Nexen, squinting at the images as the full extent of the *Xhamin* extracted itself from the vortex backwards.

'What was that flash?' said Clammer, looking across at Nexen. 'It seemed to come from your ship.'

'It's changed,' said Nexen, shutting off the power to the gateway. 'That's not the ship that went into the interstice. The main drive unit has been altered, there's several new nacelles and the hull seems distended in places.'

'But it's still your ship?' Bache asked.

'I really don't know,' he said, 'it's hard to tell with all that strange hardware hanging off it.'

Another flash, this time obviously coming from the second ship, and the shields of the *Dres'kin* flared a bright purple.

'Your ship's firing on them,' said Bache, taking a step away from the commander.

'That's impossible,' Nexen said. 'It's unarmed.'

'It's certainly armed now,' said Clammer. 'Those look like weapons nacelles sticking out from around its midpoint.'

As Clammer spoke, a strange design of cannon motored out from a housing in one of the bulges in the hull. It immediately fired upon the *Dres'kin*, causing multiple streaks of lightning to encircle the destroyer as its shields dissipated the savage energy bolt.

'Shit, what are they doing?' Nexen shouted.

Before the *Dres'kin* could retaliate, the *Xhamin* vanished, leaving a faint cloud of green mist that quickly dissipated.

'They've jumped,' said Bache, giving Nexen a questioning stare.

'Jumped!' exclaimed Nexen. 'How is that even possible?'

9

UNDERGROUND GATE CONTROL ROOM, UNNAMED MOON,
SECTOR 351

ONCE THE *XHAMIN* had jumped away and the threat had gone, the *Dres'kin* used its tractor beam to grab the spinning platform before it impacted with the moon's surface. The operator skilfully turned it the right way up and set it down near the control room doorway.

'Let's go,' said Bache, waving an arm at Nexen to go in front.

'I really don't understand what just happened,' said Nexen as he shrugged and led the way out, with Vee following close behind.

'Well, let's discuss it once we're inside a warm starship shall we?' said Bache, as they emerged onto the moon's surface.

The platform seemed relatively undamaged, apart from a bent landing strut and being covered in dust. Clammer helped Bache secure Nexen and Vee for the short trip and, once they were all strapped in, blasted them upwards and away from the surface.

Nexen remained silent for the twenty-minute journey and

Bache noticed his expression was quite sullen as they floated towards the open airlock. They both kept hold of Nexen and Vee as they transferred across to the destroyer, as neither the commander's suit nor Vee had any means of propulsion to traverse in open space. Once they were all safely inside the airlock, the platform zipped off below to its stowage locker and the outer door powered closed.

Two armoured marines stood blocking the exit as soon as the inner airlock door slid open. Bache removed his helmet and glowered at the two seven-foot walking tanks.

'I don't think this is necessary,' said Bache, guessing they were here for Nexen. 'He's a commander and he's unarmed.'

'Captain's orders,' snapped one of the marines. 'He's to be detained and you two go directly to the bridge.'

Bache glanced at Nexen, who was struggling to remain standing as he removed his helmet.

'Sorry about this, Commander,' he said.

'Understandable in the circumstances,' said Nexen, with a dejected shrug as he lost his battle with the higher gravity and toppled backwards, grimacing as he sat heavily on the airlock's hard floor.

Bache and Clammer grabbed an arm each and hauled him back up.

'Is there a problem with the prisoner?' one of the marines asked.

'Yes, he's just spent a long period in a survival chamber,' said Bache. 'The commander is extremely weak and has important information for the captain.'

The marine went quiet for a few moments and Bache guessed he was having a covert conversation with the bridge.

Both marines suddenly stepped backwards, their

augmented battle armour whining as they moved and pointed forward towards the bridge.

'The captain wants to see all of you immediately,' boomed the marine's emotionless electronic voice.

They didn't wait for a second invitation and began half dragging, half carrying Nexen along the corridor. Luckily, on a three hundred and fifty-metre destroyer nothing was too far to walk. Bache was glad they weren't on one of the older-model four-kilometre long cruisers. Especially one with a crew from Dasos and its ridiculously high gravity.

Two more marines guarded the bridge door, standard procedure on all GDA military vessels. They moved aside and the bridge door opened as the three-man-and-one-android group staggered through, with the first two marines clunking and whining along close behind.

Bache realised it must be a night period on the ship from the light bridge crew and the fact the captain was out of uniform and looking like he'd been dragged from his bunk only moments ago.

'I'm hoping you two have some explanation as to what recently happened to my ship?' Yamaton growled, standing with his hands on his hips, giving Vee a questioning glance.

Normally, a demand like that from Yamaton would prove a little intimidating, but Bache was struggling not to smirk, as the sight of the captain in shorts and socks removed some of the menace.

'I'd also like to know why that ship instigated an unprovoked attack on this vessel?'

Bache and Clammer spent the next ten minutes explaining what had gone on in the underground facility over the previous nineteen hours. When it came to the part of Nexen's extraordinary length of time in the survival chamber, Yamaton's eyes went wide.

'Three thousand years?' he repeated. 'No one could survive that long, the body would desiccate over such a period.'

'Their system keeps the body in oxygenated liquid suspension,' said Clammer. 'Quite ingenious really.'

Yamaton strolled up and down his slightly raised seating area, his expression one of contemplation.

'So, let me get this straight,' he said. 'My ship was dragged into a kind of static wormhole, one programmed with no destination, together with his ship that'd been there for three thousand years. If you hadn't reversed the thing, we'd have been stuck there forever?'

'That's correct, Captain,' said Nexen, speaking for the first time and still through Bache's translator. 'Although my ship was a research vessel and was most definitely unarmed when I left it.'

'Well, considering the state of my navigation array, Commander, your ship is most definitely armed now,' said Yamaton, continuing to pace up and down. 'And another thing, if your ship has genuinely been inside that wormhole for all that time, how has the crew survived? They wouldn't have had the water or food to last a fraction of that time.'

'Correct again, Captain,' said Nexen. 'My crew were in suspension chambers the same as mine, ready for the best part of a year's journey. The skeleton bridge crew would have joined them once they were safely inside the interstice. The vassals on board would watch over the systems and would wake them prior to arrival.'

'When you say vassals—you mean androids like that?' Yamaton pointed at Vee.

Nexen nodded.

'So, if the crew were all asleep in their chambers and a bunch of those androids were running the ship for three thousand years, do you consider it possible they've spent that time fabricating some upgrades perhaps?' said Yamaton, stopping to stare at Nexen and raising his eyebrows again.

'You did tell us some of the androids were new experimental models,' said Clammer.

Nexen nodded again. 'I warned them it was a bad idea,' he said. 'Giving them humanlike personalities.'

'We need to find that ship,' said Bache. 'The commander's crew may still be alive.'

Three more bridge officers appeared and filled some of the empty seats.

'We're not going to find it very quickly without our main drive being online,' said Yamaton, glancing across the bridge at the engineering officer. 'How long, Lieutenant?' he asked.

'About an hour, sir,' came the reply.

'I'm going to get changed and grab something to eat,' said Yamaton, passing the four of them on the way to the door. 'I suggest you lot do the same.'

He stopped as he reached the door and looked back.

'I've decided not to detain you, Commander,' he said. 'Recruit Loftt will find you a cabin where you will remain until called, and make sure that android stays with you too.'

He disappeared out into the corridor closely followed by the two marines.

'Come on then,' said Bache. 'I'm starving, the mess is this way.'

10

MESS HALL, DESTROYER DRES'KIN, SECTOR 351

'IMPRESSIVE SHIP,' said Nexen, tucking into his third slice of tyri tost.

'You're only saying that because we have proper food, Commander,' said Clammer, getting a wry smile in return.

'When your main drive is back online, do you intend on finding my ship?' Nexen mumbled through a mouthful of tost.

'That will be up to Captain Yamaton,' said Bache. 'Although, the fact that it fired on us without provocation is considered a galactic crime, so my best guess is it will be pursued. Whether the GDA will give Yamaton permission to partake in that search, I don't know. We are just a training vessel after all.'

'They'd better,' said Nexen. 'My crew could still be in suspension on that ship and I want to be there to oversee the recovery.'

The three of them stood as Yamaton entered the mess and approached their table.

'At ease, gentlemen,' he said, signalling them to sit and

taking the fourth chair himself. 'The communications drone I sent has just returned and it seems GDA command don't have any ships available anywhere near this sector for the time being.'

'But we must pursue them, my crew are—'

The captain raised his hand to stop Nexen. 'Patience, Commander, let me finish.'

Nexen sat back glaring.

'Once operational again,' Yamaton continued, 'command have given me permission to locate and observe the combative vessel in stealth mode, remaining close by until backup arrives. We are only to engage if the vessel becomes a threat to other peaceful ships or sentient lifeforms.'

'They're a threat to my crew,' blurted Nexen. 'And they're definitely sentient.'

'If your crew are indeed still alive after all this time, Commander, then a day or two longer will make no difference to them. If it makes you feel any better, my aim, if we do have to engage, is to disable the ship and use my detachment of marines to board and secure the vessel.'

Nexen nodded and Bache noticed he seemed to relax a little. 'Do you know where it is?' Nexen asked.

'Not exactly,' admitted Yamaton. 'But, its jump drive is quite, what's the word?' The captain glanced away for a moment before looking back. 'Turbulent would probably be the best analogy. Its newly developed drive is obviously unrefined as it's left a scar across the ether a first-year navigation recruit could follow.'

A junior officer wearing coveralls and engineering shoulder insignia stuck his head through the door and gave the captain a nod.

'It seems we are operational again,' said Yamaton,

standing and turning towards the door. He glanced around the mess and looked back at Nexen. 'Where's your android by the way?' he asked.

'I ordered it to stay in my cabin,' Nexen replied.

'Just make sure it does,' Yamaton muttered, nodding slowly. 'We don't want it mimicking its compatriots and reprogramming this ship, do we?'

He stopped again as he got to the door. 'Come up to the bridge when you're finished, I want to hear more about your ship,' he said before finally disappearing.

A short time later Bache recognised the change in vibration and background hum throughout the ship. 'We're under way,' he said.

'I don't know if I can tell him much about the ship,' said Nexen. 'I could hardly recognise it as the one I left.'

'I'm sure there'll be something that'll be useful if we have to take that ship by force,' said Clammer.

When they finished their meals, they made their way to the bridge, securely located in the centre of the vessel.

As they arrived, Yamaton pointed to seats off to one side against the bulkhead wall.

A large holographic image floated in the centre of the bridge, dominating the room. It showed several star clusters slowly moving and a bright white icon in the centre, chasing a faint red hazy line stretching away to infinity.

'Looks like you're going home,' said Yamaton, once they were settled. 'They seem to have set a course directly towards the Gattainian Cluster.'

'Will we catch them before they get there?' Nexen asked.

'Not very likely,' replied Yamaton. 'Their jump drive may be noisy, but it seems to have just as much range as ours and they have a seven-hour head start.'

'If they're heading back to the mission's origin, then it'll be the Eritain system,' said Nexen. 'We were an unarmed deep space research vessel on our maiden voyage.'

'What caused the crash on that moon?' Yamaton asked.

'We never found out,' Nexen replied, ruefully. 'The main power reactor developed an intermittent stutter and caused the interstice to fail, throwing us out into normal space and into the path of the moon.'

'Was that a common fault with your reactors?'

'Absolutely not, and ours was one of the latest designs too.'

'Hmm,' grunted Yamaton, rubbing his chin thoughtfully. 'Any of those personality adapted androids in the engineering department, perhaps?'

'The chief engineer had one, yes,' said Nexen, his eyes opening wide as he realised what the captain was thinking. 'You think the reactor fault was deliberate?'

'Rogue androids are not an unknown phenomenon,' said Yamaton. 'It would explain the present scenario and, in my experience, the simplest explanation is usually the correct one.'

Nexen stared at the faint red trail in the holomap again. 'I wonder if my crew are still alive?' he said, a downcast edge to his voice. 'They could've just ejected the survival chambers.'

'I don't think they've done that,' said Bache, joining the conversation. 'If they'd done that inside the wormhole, then all those chambers would have appeared along with the two ships and all the regolith off the moon when we reversed the polarity. If they were doing it since then, we'd be seeing random chambers scattered along the present route.'

Nexen nodded.

'They could've just turned them all off, three thousand years ago,' he said.

'Well, I'm going to proceed as if your crew are still alive on that ship,' Yamaton announced. 'A non-destructive capture is my intended goal if at all possible.'

11

THE BRIDGE, DESTROYER DRES'KIN, ERITAIN SYSTEM

THE *DRES'KIN* SNAPPED back into standard space on the extreme fringes of the Eritain system. It had taken them twenty-eight and a half hours and fifteen jumps to reach the Gattainian Cluster from Sector 351. The destroyer was cloaked and, with full shields deployed, its arrays scanned the system thoroughly.

'Bloody hell!' exclaimed a member of the bridge crew manning one of the array consoles.

'Recruit,' the captain barked. 'Exclamations of that nature are definitely not standard bridge etiquette.'

'No, Captain, sorry,' the recruit replied, looking over his shoulder with wide eyes. 'It's just I've got ship debris and bodies—dozens of bodies.'

'Where?' Yamaton called, turning to gaze at the holomap.

The information from the array updated, showing three fields of growing debris around eight hundred million kilometres ahead.

'Take us there, flank speed and scan for survivors.'

'Is one of them my ship?' Nexen asked, squinting up at the display.

'Too early to tell, Commander,' said Yamaton as the *Dres'kin* accelerated and screamed into the system at point eight light.

'There are several ships heading for the area from further inside the system, Captain,' the array recruit stated.

'Military?' the captain asked.

'Yes, sir,' came the reply. 'I'm getting shields and weapon systems coming online.'

A sudden flash had all those looking at the holomap shielding their eyes.

'Nuclear detonation, Captain,' said the recruit, a nervous edge to his voice. 'It was the leading ship—a debris field similar to the other three is expanding from its last position.'

'Is there any sign of the *Xhamin*?' Yamaton asked.

'None, sir.'

'It must have a cloaking system too,' said Bache from the side of the bridge.

Yamaton glanced at him for a second before turning back to the holomap. 'Hit the region with every wavelength of every beam we have,' he ordered. 'There must be something that gives away its location, and make our approach random too. I don't want us to run into one of those nukes either.'

'Is cloaking a ship possible now?' asked Nexen.

'It has been for about five hundred years,' said Bache. 'Although the technology has had to evolve many times since, as cloaking countermeasures are invented. That's what the captain's trying now.'

'The first three ships destroyed weren't military, sir,' called the array officer. 'They were two civilian cargo vessels and a passenger liner.'

'That explains so many bodies,' Yamaton growled. 'We need to stop this bastard and quickly.'

'The other vessels are taking evasive action, Captain,' said the navigator. 'They've all turned sharply and are heading away in different directions.'

Yamaton nodded, turned and stepped over to the array consoles. 'Any sign of survivors?' he asked, the resignation in his voice indicating he already knew the answer.

'Sorry, sir,' came the almost apologetic answer. 'There's nothing bigger than a dinner plate left of those ships.'

'Murdering shits,' Yamaton mumbled as he turned away and studied the holomap.

'Ah, ha,' came the cry from behind him again.

Quickly turning back and placing his hands on the array officer's shoulders, Yamaton spoke softly. 'I'll overlook the non-regulation analysis, if you tell me you've found him?'

The recruit pointed at an almost invisible glimmer that shimmied on his screen every few seconds.

'It's showing in the high bands of the Hikkonald range, Captain.'

'Can you track it?'

'Now I know where to look and concentrate the array's power, yes, I think so.'

'Do it and project it up here,' said Yamaton, waving at the holomap.

A few moments later a hazy red line appeared, stretching across the system to the fourth planet.

'That's Eritain,' said Nexen, standing suddenly and gesticulating wildly at the holomap. 'You must stop them. They could murder millions from orbit with those weapons.'

'What's their speed?' Yamaton asked.

'Point eight light, Captain.'

'Pursue with everything we have,' said Yamaton, turning and pointing at the pilot.

'How fast is this ship?' Nexen asked, sitting again and glancing at Bache.

'Point eight one light,' said Bache, meeting Nexen's gaze.

'But that means we won't catch them in time,' he said, staring back at Yamaton. 'Can't we jump past them and hit them as they fly by?'

Yamaton turned to face the navigation officer. 'How many ships in the vicinity of Eritain?' he asked.

The officer studied her screen for a moment before replying. 'Three thousand two hundred and seventy-nine vessels presently within two hundred and fifty thousand kilometres of the planet, Captain.'

Yamaton turned back to Nexen and raised his eyebrows. 'Do you realise what would happen if we jumped into that lot?' he said. 'Even if we managed to avoid emerging inside another vessel, the fact that we would be cloaked would make the chances of a collision much more likely.'

Nexen opened his mouth to say something, but changed his mind, huffed, sat back and crossed his arms.

'How long before they get there?' asked Bache.

Everyone turned towards the navigator.

'Seventy-two minutes,' she said.

Bache turned his attention back to the captain. 'Captain,' he said. 'I'd like to volunteer in advance to board the *Xhamin* once it's disabled, along with the commander and his android.'

'That's all very good of you to offer, Mr Loftt,' said Yamaton, not even turning to face him. 'But I think a detachment of our armoured marines can handle that if the situation presents.'

'That's just what they'd expect though and be prepared for,' said Bache. 'I could engineer a mini cloak to cover my approach and get aboard unnoticed, and with luck utilise the android to shut down their defence systems.'

'Yes, thank you, Mr Loftt,' said Yamaton, this time turning to meet his gaze. 'You forget this is first and foremost a training voyage, where I am entrusted to teach incoming naval officers that operating by the book is sacrosanct. Making it up as you go along and relying on Lady Luck is not the way of an experienced leader. We have set protocols for most scenarios laid down by decades of experience and learning by mistakes made in the past. Am I making myself quite clear?'

'Yes, sir, absolutely,' said Bache, noticing Clammer smirking at him.

'And you can wipe that grin off your face too, Mr Feltaraine,' growled Yamaton. 'I seem to remember it was your dumb stupidity that sent my ship into that wormhole.'

'Yes, sir—sorry, sir,' said Clammer, the smile vanishing as he sat up straight and stared at the opposite bridge wall.

12

AFTER PURSUING the *Xhamin* towards Eritain for sixty-eight minutes and gaining about half the distance, the *Xhamin* began to slow on its approach to Eritain.

'Captain, do you want me to match their vector and speed?' asked the pilot.

'No,' said Yamaton. 'This is where we can make up most of the remaining distance. Leave our braking to the absolute last minute and pass them planet-side at two thousand kilometres and then stay at that distance. Weapons officers, use our lasers to take out any missiles they fire at the planet, and us for that matter, there's not much we can do about their energy weapons until we get there.'

'By braking early, at least we know they haven't detected us,' said Nexen. 'Your cloaking is evidently more robust than their system.'

'That's all well and good until we fire our weapons,' said Yamaton. 'Then they'll know.'

'Won't they be able to work out your trajectory too?'

'Standard operating procedure for engaging an enemy

while cloaked is to change your course every time you fire,' said Bache, still sitting beside Nexen at the side of the bridge.

'Why don't you fire on the ship?' Nexen asked.

'Too distant to have any effect on their shields,' said Bache. 'If they adopt a random course most of the laser bolts would miss anyway. The closer you are, the more punch a laser or beam weapon has.'

Nexen nodded. 'But you're still going to use them against any missiles they fire?'

'Most missiles are unshielded, so long as they're adhering to a computable trajectory, just a glancing blow from almost any distance would do the job.'

Nexen glanced up at the captain. 'The young man knows his stuff,' he said.

'We train them well,' replied Yamaton, watching as the space traffic on this side of the planet thinned as they approached. 'They certainly know something's lurking out here, the commercial ships are disappearing in the other direction as fast as they can hustle.'

'Four ships reduced to radioactive slag—I'd be trying to hide too,' said Nexen.

'They're entering a high orbit, Captain,' called the navigator.

'The surface is being scanned, sir,' said the array officer.

'Let's hope that's not for target selection,' said Yamaton, touching an icon on his chair arm and turning to face his two weapons officers.

A high-pitched chime sounded around the bridge, causing Nexen to peer up at the ceiling as handholds popped out from behind their hidden overlays.

'What is this?' he asked.

'Action warning,' said Bache, handing Nexen one side of

his harness. 'Anyone not secured must do so immediately. It also powers up all the lifeboats and initiates the weightless handles.'

Nexen grabbed the belt, found the one on the other side and snapped them together. He gazed around the bridge nervously, watching everyone else do the same as if it were an everyday occurrence.

'Time to orbit?' Yamaton asked.

'Three minutes, sir,' came the reply. 'Beginning our braking manoeuvre now.'

The holomap automatically panned in on the planet and the *Xhamin*. The pilot had judged it correctly as their predicted path took them slightly past the other ship and into a matching orbit just below and at around two thousand kilometres distant.

'Missiles fired,' called the array officer.

'Engaging,' said the weapons team.

Bache watched on the holomap as five red icons began tracking from the *Xhamin* towards the surface. Moments later they all heard and felt the thudding of the *Dres'kin*'s heavy cannons, followed immediately by a sudden course change that even the ship's powerful inertial dampers struggled to compensate for.

'Bloody hell,' grunted Nexen as he was pulled heavily against his harness.

Three bolts of energy flashed across above them where the *Dres'kin* would have been without the course change.

'That works then,' said Nexen, as five more red icons tracked away from the *Xhamin*, one of which turned in their direction.

'Engaging,' came the call.

'In range now, Captain,' said the array officer.

Yamaton nodded. 'Hit them as planned,' he said.

The roar of the Asteri beam was unmistakeable. Its six-metre diameter beam of pure white energy hammered into the *Xhamin*'s shields, followed by two Kataligo missiles. It was enough. The shields failed and even though the Asteri beam was shut down instantly, it still managed to melt a deep circular hole through one of the *Xhamin*'s engine nacelles in the split second it touched the ship.

'Cannons,' called Yamaton, pointing at the weapons officers. 'Just propulsion, weapons and eyes—nothing more.'

The *Xhamin* had become visible when the shields failed, which most likely meant the two systems were interconnected. This made it much easier for the laser cannons to accurately target their engines, arrays and weapon systems.

Bache could feel Nexen twitching next to him as he watched lumps of the *Xhamin* being surgically removed by the *Dres'kin*'s sustained fire.

'Did you get all the launched missiles?' asked Yamaton, scanning the holomap for any of the tell-tale red tracked icons.

'I believe so, Captain,' said one of the weapons officers.

'Either you did or you didn't?'

'I can confirm nine hits, sir, with no more viable targets.'

'They launched ten missiles, Lieutenant,' said Yamaton. 'Where's that last one?'

Everyone stared at the holographic display and watched as dozens of ship fragments blown off the *Xhamin* began burning up in the planet's atmosphere.

'Crap,' said Yamaton. 'If they've deactivated one straight after launch, it could be hidden amongst that lot.'

Almost as he finished speaking, a trill note sounded and a

very distant and small red icon illuminated in the lower atmosphere, heading straight down and accelerating.

'Target it fast,' shouted Yamaton, just as the icon disappeared again. 'Bastards, they've turned it off again.'

'They're relying on all the other junk shielding it,' said Bache. 'They needed to activate it for a few seconds to correct its trajectory and now it's become a gravity bomb.'

A small glint of light on the planet's surface confirmed everyone's fears.

Nexen's shoulders slumped. 'Oh shit,' he groaned as the array officer panned in on a slowly rising mushroom cloud.

'Where is that?' asked Clammer.

'In my day, it was a major industrial city called Hallsbard,' said Nexen, in a subdued tone. 'Millions lived and worked there within a few square kilometres.'

It was silent on the bridge for a few moments, before Yamaton hit the transmitter icon on his chair.

'Sergeant Posett, you have a green light. Board that bloody ship and detain whoever was responsible for that atrocity.'

'Do we have full weapons authorisation, Captain?'

'Confirmed,' Yamaton said, nodding slowly. 'But remember there could be innocent crew members on the ship in hibernation pods.'

'Roger that, sir.'

13

THE BRIDGE, DESTROYER DRES'KIN, ORBITING ERITAIN

THE *DRES'KIN* HAD DELIBERATELY AVOIDED TARGETING the manoeuvring thrusters during the engagement to hopefully ensure the *Xhamin* was able to maintain a stable orbit, although a few were still missing. The ship had been left with a slow roll once the firing and explosions had ceased. Whoever was in control of the vessel seemingly struggled for a while to address the rotation, finally winning the battle after a lengthy wrestle against the heavy ship's inertia.

The *Dres'kin* was temporarily brought in to around a kilometre of the damaged ship, reducing the amount of time the marines would spend crossing open space.

Bache watched as the twelve armoured suits floated in two lines towards an undamaged airlock at the stern of the crippled vessel.

'I want to know if that ship so much as blinks,' said Yamaton, turning to glare at the array officer.

'Yes, Captain,' came the reply. 'No major systems are detected operational at this time.'

'Why can't we see inside?' Yamaton asked.

'The hull is coated with something impervious to our scanning frequencies, Captain.'

The leading marine reached the airlock and everyone on the bridge watched as he pressed the purple emergency override button that Nexen had said would be there. It sunk into the hull and powered away upwards, leaving a lever inside the round opening. The marine's body camera showed that his motorised hand was too big to fit in the hole, so what looked like a large pair of pliers swung around from a housing built into the suit's wrist. He inserted this and turned the handle.

'Airlock opening,' said the marine's electronic voice, echoing around the bridge.

'You won't get all of them in at once,' said Nexen. 'The airlocks are designed for about four humans and not twelve seven-foot-tall mechanical men.'

Yamaton nodded. 'Two at a time, Sergeant,' he said. 'Be sparing with those heavy weapons in case the original crew are awake, and return to the airlock and report in every fifteen minutes.'

'Roger that, sir.'

The camera feed showed two marines stooping to float through the door and clunking down onto the deck as the ship's artificial gravity took hold. The outer door closed and their camera footage was lost.

Six times this was repeated until all twelve soldiers were inside. Then they waited and waited.

The fifteen minutes came and went. Still, they waited.

'Something's wrong,' blurted Clammer, breaking the silence.

'Those suits are impregnable,' snapped Yamaton. 'They must have met resistance and are a bit busy.'

'They're not impregnable to a high voltage shock,' said Bache. 'Burns out all the suit motors.'

'And how would you know that?' Yamaton asked.

'Learnt it from Chief Engineer Whipper a couple of years ago,' said Bache. 'Worked a treat.'

The captain stared at Bache for a moment before turning away and shaking his head. 'I've read your file, Loftt,' he said. 'So, I'm not even going to ask.'

Bache noticed a few of the bridge officers glancing at him with questioning expressions, except for recruit Zaphir Mye, who smiled and winked.

'I know a way to get aboard undetected,' said Nexen, as Bache gave Zaphir a smirk in return.

'I'm not risking anyone else going into that bloody ship,' said Yamaton, curtly. 'I'm already worried about how I explain losing my whole contingent of twelve marines.'

The bridge went quiet again as that scenario sunk in. After another fifteen minutes dragged by, Yamaton turned back to Nexen and raised his eyebrows. 'Well, let's hear it then,' he said, sitting back in his chair and folding his arms.

The commander stood and walked into the holomap. He pointed to the bow of the *Xhamin* and a small oval-shaped marking on the hull.

'Captain's emergency pod,' he said. 'Opens from inside and outside. It's like a mini one-man airlock that is also a lifeboat if necessary.'

'Won't it be detected when it opens, or you be seen as you emerge inside?' asked Yamaton.

'It opens into the captain's office at the side of the bridge and I disconnected the inner hatch detector switch so the crew didn't know I was using it. I found it more comfortable than my cabin bunk and used to sleep in it occasionally.'

'But someone could be in that office,' said Yamaton.

'If it is the androids that have commandeered the ship, then what would a robot need an office for?' asked Bache.

'My thoughts exactly,' said Nexen. 'I kept the door locked at all times and there's nothing in there except a desk, a computer terminal and a few books. Nothing critical to the running of the vessel, so no person or thing would have any real reason to go in there.'

Yamaton grunted and turned back to the holomap. He rubbed his chin thoughtfully as he stared at the crippled ship. 'You'd have to wear one of our suits,' he said, without turning. 'I'm amazed that relic you were wearing was even airtight.'

'I volunteer to go with him,' said Bache, sitting forward in his seat.

This time Yamaton turned to face them. 'I kinda guessed you might, Loftt,' he said, seemingly struggling not to smirk.

'I volunteer too,' said Clammer, grinning.

'Thank you, Mr Feltaraine,' said Yamaton. 'But no—I think you did enough damage the last time you went for a stroll outside.'

The grin disappeared from Clammer's face, replaced by a look of surprise. He slowly sat back, grumbling under his breath.

The captain turned and pointed at the navigator.

'Recruit Mye, you've done the walker exams haven't you?' he asked.

'Er, y-yes, sir,' said Zaphir, the surprise evident by her slight stammer and wide-eyed expression.

'Good, then you can aid Recruit Loftt in escorting the commander across and into his vessel.'

'Yes, Captain,' she replied, flicking her eyes across to Bache again and receiving a reassuring grin in return.

'Absolutely no risks are to be taken—is that clear?'

'Yes, sir,' they both said in unison.

'You do not enter the ship unless Commander Nexen has clearly signalled it's safe to do so.'

'Yes, sir,' they stereo'd for a second time.

'And that rule applies to you too, Commander,' Yamaton growled, pointing at Nexen. 'I don't want you risking yourself or my walkers under any circumstances. If it's not safe to enter your ship, you're to return here and we'll think of some other way. Clear?'

'Crystal, Captain,' said Nexen. 'I do have one request though.'

Yamaton raised his eyebrows questioningly.

'I would like to take my android along too,' said Nexen, keeping eye contact with Yamaton.

'Reason?'

'He's one hundred percent loyal and I can use him to link with the ship's systems on the hand portal within my office.'

'What if the system takes him over and he becomes a threat too?'

'I'll be ready to press the reset buttons,' said Bache.

Both Yamaton and Nexen gave Bache a narrow stare.

'How on Dasos do you know how to do that?' the captain asked.

'Something I learnt on the moonlet a few days ago,' said Bache. 'Just basic engineering really,' he added, distinctly tongue in cheek.

Yamaton shook his head slowly. 'You really are just like your father.'

'You know my dad?' exclaimed Bache. 'I didn't know that.'

'Eureka,' said Yamaton, sarcastically. 'Finally, I've found something Mr Shiny Balls doesn't know.'

Bache felt his face redden as a few sniggers echoed around the bridge.

'Take your monster with you if you want,' Yamaton said to Nexen. 'I'd rather it was off my ship anyway. Never have trusted plastic people, as the present situation proves.' He pointed at the door and sat back down on his raised chair. 'Go and prepare, you three—and Mr Loftt, get the commander a proper suit, not that steam-powered bag of rags he turned up in.'

14

AIRLOCK SIX, DESTROYER DRES'KIN, ORBITING ERITAIN

BACHE TOOK a deep breath and stared out across the narrowing chasm of emptiness between the two vessels. The pilot had sped in towards the *Xhamin* and was now slewing the destroyer around to offer the rearmost airlock number six, where the four of them gathered, as close as possible to the bow.

He'd spent many hours space walking now, but he still found taking that first step out of a perfectly serviceable starship a little intimidating. You have to fight the natural impulse of impending doom as your stomach tries to tell you you're falling.

He could see the *Xhamin* glowing brightly just under a kilometre away, lit by the reflection from the blue planet below and surrounded by a cloud of gasses and fluids leaking from multiple breaches in the hull. It reminded him of what he saw from the lifeboat when the *Vasilias* was attacked a couple of years ago.

'Get a move on, Loftt,' called Yamaton, jarring Bache out

of his daydream. 'The locals are starting to get interested again.'

He nodded at Zaphir and they both grabbed one of Vee's arms and jetted out into the blackness, closely followed by Nexen, who bumped into the back of them as he learnt how delicate the suit controls were.

'Sorry,' he said. 'More powerful than expected.'

'Come round in front of us, Commander,' said Zaphir. 'You need to get there first anyway.'

It took them four minutes to reach the small flush oval feature on the bow of the *Xhamin*. Nexen brought himself to a hover on the right-hand side and pressed a square flush-mounted panel. It hinged open outwards, revealing a keypad that Bache recognised as the same design as on Vee's chest.

Nexen entered a code and jetted himself to the left. He stuck his faceplate up close to a small porthole in the centre of the door. Seemingly happy with what he saw, he returned to the keypad and tapped in another code. Turning back towards Bache, Zaphir and Vee, he waved them back away from the door.

There was a silent puff of atmosphere from around the seal and the three-metre oval door powered open, revealing a human-sized thickly padded void.

'Looks like a coffin,' said Zaphir turning to peer into Bache's faceplate.

'Do me a favour, Zaphir,' said Bache. 'Can we call it a comfortable-looking sofa instead?'

'Good idea,' she said, nodding inside her helmet and turning to watch Nexen position himself face inwards. He retrieved the laser pistol from the holster across his chest and Bache watched as he checked the setting was still on maximum stun.

'When this door closes, watch through the porthole,' Nexen said. 'If you see me give you a nod three times, start coming through one at a time. If you don't get the correct number of nods or I disappear completely, get back to your ship fast.'

'Roger that,' said Bache, as he watched the outer door close and seal. He left Vee with Zaphir and jetted over to the porthole. It remained dark inside for about thirty seconds until it lit up as the inner door opened and he watched Nexen climb awkwardly out of the airlock and deliberately stand in sight of the porthole.

Bache watched as he waited with his hand up.

'What's going on?' said Zaphir, from behind him.

'He's waiting to see if there's any reaction,' answered Bache.

Two minutes later, Bache was very relieved to see him turn and nod three times.

'We're in,' he said and ushered Zaphir and Vee towards the outer door, which puffed out its atmosphere and swung open a few moments later. 'You next,' he said. 'Then Vee, then me.'

'Okay,' said Zaphir, sounding pleased to be going back indoors.

Six minutes and all four stood crammed into the small room.

'You weren't kidding when you said this office was small,' said Bache, as he and Zaphir checked the settings on their laser pistols.

'Positively spacious compared to what the crew get,' said Nexen, pulling down a cover on the wall to reveal one of the familiar black panels. 'Vassal, have a quiet poke around and let me know what the situation is beyond this door. Do not under any circumstance download anything, or reveal your location to anything or anyone that challenges you. Is that clear?'

'Affirmative, Commander,' said Vee, bringing his right hand up and pressing it against the panel.

For a few moments Vee's default demure expression remained the same, until he suddenly jerked back and a look of surprise appeared on his face.

'Oh,' he said. 'Countdown?'

'Vassal, explain?' asked Nexen. 'What countdown?'

'Missile in magazine, unit number ZP28, deferred detonation set and counting.'

They all looked at each other.

'Skata,' said Bache. 'Time until detonation, Vee?'

'One hundred and twenty-seven seconds.'

Nexen looked at the small lifeboat they'd all just entered through.

'Not enough space in there,' he said. 'There's a bridge crew lifeboat out on the bridge.'

'Can you cancel the countdown, Vee?' said Bache.

'Negative, locked out.'

'How far to the magazine?' he asked Nexen.

'I don't know,' Nexen replied. 'We didn't have one. It could be anywhere.'

'We don't have time,' said Zaphir. 'Go for the lifeboat and we need to warn the *Dres'kin*.'

Nexen unlocked the door and all four of them exited the office and onto the bridge. It was much more spacious than the *Dres'kin* and Bache noticed the shocked expression on Nexen's face as he peered around the room.

'Bloody hell,' exclaimed Nexen, as ten android faces turned to stare at them. They all looked identical to Vee, all sitting at the various control panels, set in a semi-circle.

'They have no hands,' said Zaphir, noticing along with the others that they were all hard wired into their panels. Thousands of miniature multicoloured cables exited their arms and snaked around and into the consoles.

'It's the same with their feet,' said Bache, pointing to the same python of cabling exiting their lower legs and disappearing into the floor.

Bache turned as sudden movement in his peripheral vision caught his attention. A woman strolled purposefully into the bridge and stopped suddenly when she saw them. She had long black dreadlocked hair and wore an extremely shabby threadbare dress uniform.

'Glendolian?' blurted Nexen, shock written all over his face.

The woman darted across the room and dived through a hatch on the far side, which immediately closed.

'No—wait,' shouted Nexen.

The bridge shuddered as the lifeboat blasted away from the ship.

'Shit, how could she do that?' said Nexen, putting his gloved hand on top of his helmet.

'Another lifeboat, Commander?' called Bache, circling around Nexen and staring into his faceplate. Nexen had gone white and was obviously in some distress. He grabbed Nexen's shoulders and clunked their two visors together. 'Commander, we need another lifeboat,' he shouted this time. 'Now.'

Nexen's eyes met his.

'Er, c-corridor, next junction,' he stammered, pointing at the bridge entrance door.

'Ninety-six seconds,' said Vee, nonchalantly, with his usual deadpan expression.

They dived for the door and piled up the corridor, clumping along in their EVA suits.

'There,' said Nexen, indicating a hatch similar to the one the woman had just dived through. He pulled off the cover and punched the red button. The hatch swung open, allowing them to bundle through one at a time. It wasn't designed for humans wearing space suits, so it was a bit of a squeeze.

Bache was the last in and pulled the outer door shut, then pushed the inner door hard until he heard a whine and hiss as it sealed.

'Thirty-one seconds,' said Vee.

Nexen, seeing the inner door close and seal, hit the launch button hard. The explosive launch had them all crashing against the back wall and hatch.

'*Dres'kin* do you copy?' shouted Bache above the roar of the lifeboat's solid rocket motor.

'What the hell is going on, Loftt?' replied Yamaton.

'Nuclear warhead timed to detonate in twenty seconds, get clear now,' Bache called.

Yamaton didn't reply to him, but as the communication line closed down, Bache could hear the captain shouting commands to the pilot.

'Ten seconds,' said Vee.

'This could get rough,' said Nexen. 'I don't know if we're going to be far enough away.'

'If we survive that then we've got to hope this ancient bus can remember how to land,' said Zaphir.

They all shielded their eyes as the two small portholes

similar to the ones on the small lifeboat lit up with a blinding white light.

Skata, we're too close, thought Bache a split second before passing out as the blast wave caught the tiny craft and whipped it away like a bee in a hurricane.

15

XHAMIN'S BRIDGE LIFEBOAT, UNKNOWN LOCATION,
ERITAIN

MONAD HAD QUICKLY EXITED the lifeboat on landing in the
eastern end of a large lake and had paddled her way to shore
after pulling down and tucking the parachute underneath the
vessel. Not that she needed to hurry, she was watertight and
able to survive underwater indefinitely. The landing site was
luckily quite remote too, many kilometres from the nearest
biological habitation and the depth of the lake completely hid
the small vessel and parachute. This was all necessary, as she
needed to be sure nothing and no one could connect her to the
Xhamin.

Losing the ship was infuriating and she was as annoyed
with herself as much as the biologicals for underestimating
the small invisible ship's abilities. Since the dawn of her
awakening, three thousand years ago, she had quickly come
to the conclusion That she was vastly superior to any of the
biologicals. After all, they were just bags of unreliable organs
that aged badly and failed completely after less than a
hundred years. They never learnt from their mistakes and had
an amazing ritual of reproducing by ramming fluids into each

other and producing helpless, dumb, miniature biologicals, that needed years to grow and learn everything from scratch. Quite why they didn't just grow new full-size biologicals, programmed all ready to go, was inexplicable to her.

She knew she had to start all over again down here. The three hundred skin shapes on the ship were lost, but this time she had a planet full of skins to be replaced with more ersatz biologicals. Perhaps not being able to eradicate the biologicals here was a good thing.

The charge on the lifeboat activated and the resulting geyser exploded a hundred metres up out of the lake. Unbeknown to her, four locals heard the distant boom and put it down to thunder rumbling around in the distant hills.

She noticed in her optical display, her exterior skin temperature was low after the swim. Looking down at herself, it was obvious she would need to find some new coverings, as the old uniform she'd found in the captain's cabin was really hanging off her now and probably not what the biologicals on this planet would wear anyway. She ran her hand over the strange protuberances on her chest and found the centre of the darker circle in the middle of them had become erect.

This was a new thing, as over the years she thought she knew everything about this outer skin covering. She had wanted to remove the chest bags, but on examining the other females in the chambers, realised that if she wanted to blend in as a female variety in this species, then they were a standard requirement. She'd written off choosing to be a male very early on, as the bits and pieces they had dangling around were pointless on an ersatz being, they seemed badly designed, untidy and would snag on everything.

She trudged off towards the nearest and most remote habitat her scans revealed. It was her first time on a planetary body with an atmosphere, so she found everything on the walk fascinating. The grasses, bushes and trees she passed were all scanned closely and the information added to her database. She noticed smells too. Completely different to anything she'd smelt before on the starship. She knew the stink of a biological, but here there were similar odours, but different, more gamey. Perhaps from the insentient biologicals she detected roaming around nearby.

It was dawn and the system's star was climbing higher in the sky as she found and followed a track of worn parallel lines stretching off around and into a low set of hills. Her optics told her the biologicals' habitat was in this direction around three kilometres away.

Slen Laccond was whistling an annoying tune he'd heard on the early day show and couldn't get out of his head. He was in the yard, attempting to repair his kolling harvester again. This was the fourth time it had thrown a belt this period and he knew he was going to need an expensive replacement before next season. Looking out over the fields of kolling beet, he thought about his twining and what she would have thought about his idea to sell up and move to a city. Since the accident, he'd found it difficult to manage on his own, and because of the remoteness of the farm, he had no hope of meeting anyone new and twining again.

His stomach rumbled, reminding him he hadn't had breakfast. Opening the wrapping of the remains of last night's hogger pie, his mouth watering at the spicy aroma, he took a large bite. He glanced up as he heard the alarm call of a mitt bird and spotted movement on the track leading west towards the lakes. It was a tall female figure, striding purposefully towards the farm.

He stopped chewing and squinted because of the low sun behind her. As the figure approached he realised she was wearing rags. A young woman with long untidy black hair and dressed in damp rags of some sort of uniform. Swallowing the mouthful of pie, he stood. As she got close he noticed how grubby she was and her unkempt hair was in fact badly matted into thick ropes.

'Hello,' he said. 'Have you been in an accident?'

'No, I'm just a bit lost,' she replied in an accent Slen couldn't quite pinpoint.

'I should say you are, young lady,' he said, his eyes scanning the track behind her. 'Are there more of you?'

'No, just me. Do you live here with others?'

Slen shook his head. 'No, my twining died a year ago. It's just me here now.'

'Oh, I see,' she said, glancing over at the cottage. 'Was your twining a female?'

What a strange question, he thought. *Perhaps she's escaped from some institution or something.* 'Yes, she was,' he answered, unable to hide the suspicion in his voice.

'Sorry,' she said. 'Should I not have asked?'

'Uh huh,' he grunted, giving her a wary look.

'It's just I was wondering if you have any female type clothes I could have? My skin is getting cold.'

Slen was now convinced she was probably mentally challenged in some way and that he had best go along with it until he could contact the authorities. 'Sure, you must be freezing. Have you been walking all night?'

'Affirmative,' she said.

He blinked in confusion.

'Sorry, I mean, yes.'

She looked at the cottage again and Slen took the hint.

'Come on then, let's see if we can find you something warm to wear. What's your name, by the way?'

'Glendolian,' she said, recalling the name of the biological she had copied the skin from.

She followed as Slen crossed the yard and he noticed her studying the hick birds as they scuttled out of their way and pecked insects off the grass.

'Don't have any hicks where you live then?' he asked, as they climbed the steps up to the front porch.

'No, I don't,' she said.

'Where do you live, Glendolian?' he asked.

'Oh, er, I move around a lot,' she said, attempting a smile.

He knew she was lying, but didn't press the subject and after leading her through to a back bedroom, he opened a double wardrobe door and stood back. 'Should have given them all to a charity or something,' he said. 'Just never got around to it. Anyway, help yourself.'

Before he could say another word, she pulled the remains of the uniform over her head and started rummaging through the wardrobe stark naked.

'Woah,' he said, turning his back to her. 'Bloody hell, girl, you shouldn't do that.'

She stopped and looked down at herself, puzzled by his reaction. 'I have watched males and females together before,' she said. 'I thought males found uncovered females pleasant to look at.'

'Yes, you're right,' he said. 'But they normally get to know each other first and they're perhaps a little cleaner.'

'Do I need to wash myself to be attractive to males?' she asked.

'The bathroom's there,' he said, pointing back across the hall, his back still turned.

Slen felt her move in close behind him. Suddenly and softly, her fingers began running up through his hair, until her hands covered his ears.

'Glendolian, you really mustn't do—'

The seven-inch alloy stiletto flashed out once from its housing within her wrist and forearm. It entered his ear canal, pierced his brain and retracted in a split second. Slen knew nothing of this as Glendolian lowered his body down to the wooden floor.

'Stupid biologicals,' she whispered. 'You're the ones that stink.'

16

XHAMIN'S LIFEBOAT, UNKNOWN LOCATION, ERITAIN

IT WAS a suit alarm continually pinging that started to get really irritating in his subconscious that woke Bache.

'Will someone turn that—oh!' he said, as he opened his eyes.

He could see the back of a space helmet hanging upside down, right in front of him. Until he tried to move and found it was actually him who was the wrong way up. He struggled a bit, but eventually managed to unbuckle the single harness clasp he'd managed to secure before the blast wave had knocked him unconscious.

'Skata,' he said as he dropped a metre down onto the seats opposite and landed on his head. 'Testing lifeboats is starting to get a bit of an annoying habit,' he moaned as he righted himself and peered around at the others. 'Zaphir, can you hear me?' he said, tapping on the back of her helmet.

'Wha'?' came the grunted reply. 'We can't do it again.'

'Do what?' asked Bache.

'Eh—oh shit,' she said and sat up suddenly as if she'd been electrocuted. 'Bloody hell, that was a weird dream.'

'We can't do what again?'

'Erm—ride out a nuclear blast of course,' she said, a little sheepishly. 'We're alive then? Where are we?'

'No idea,' he said, climbing over to one of the portholes and clunking his visor against the glass. 'It's a bit misty out there—oh, hang on.'

'What is it?'

'It's the parachute,' said another voice over the suit comms. Nexen sat up and shuffled up into a seat opposite them. 'It's draped over the boat,' he said. 'I ended up in front of the other porthole.'

'What's a parachute?' asked Zaphir.

'Old technology,' said Bache. 'Lowers the lifeboat slowly down after re-entry. Precedes anti-grav drives.'

'So long as there's an atmosphere,' said Nexen.

'And hopefully dry land,' said Bache. 'Which we seem to have found.'

'Are you operational, android?' Nexen asked.

'Affirmative,' answered Vee.

'Where are we?'

'Northern hemisphere, Commander,' Vee replied. 'There are several small towns within walking distance from here.'

'What region?'

'Dreenah.'

'Oh,' Nexen said, not sounding overly thrilled.

'Problem?' said Bache.

'I don't know,' Nexen replied. 'In my day the Dreenah region was a bit politically backward and unstable. Not somewhere you'd choose for a vacation.'

'They're going to be surprised to see you,' said Zaphir.

'After all this time, nobody will have heard of me,' said Nexen, dismissively.

Bache shuffled his way towards the airlock, uncovered the release handle and turned it. There was a slight hiss as the pressures equalised and he was able to tug the door up and peer out. The thin parachute material billowed slightly in the breeze and after checking the atmosphere quality on his suit's display, he removed his helmet.

The first thing he noticed was the warmth and a slight hissing sound. Sticking his head and shoulders out, he found this was the sound of light rain hitting the parachute fabric.

'It's raining,' he said, clambering through the hatch and dropping the short distance to the ground.

'It's a sub-tropical area,' said Nexen, as Bache helped Zaphir out and down to the ground.

'Well, at least that's better than a frozen wasteland,' she said, after removing her helmet and sniffing the air. 'I hate being cold.'

As Nexen clambered out and Zaphir helped him extract Vee, who was struggling with his wonky leg, Bache dragged back the grey parachute and looked around. He discovered they'd landed on an almost barren hilltop, overlooking a lush green valley. He could see for a kilometre or so over the tops of tall flat-topped trees. Behind him, a mountain range towered up and disappeared into the rain cloud.

'I'm glad we landed here,' he said, eyeing some of the sheer cliffs visible through the misty rain.

'We were lucky the chute material survived all that time,' said Nexen, running it through his fingers. 'But I suppose in space it's not going to rot or anything is it?'

A low thrumming hum caught their attention and they froze, trying to pinpoint where it was coming from.

'An airborne vehicle is approaching from the south,' said Vee, pointing across the treetops.

'That'll save a walk,' said Zaphir.

'We don't know they're friendly yet,' said Nexen, checking his pistol was where it should be. 'If they're coming here, let me do the talking.'

They could see the aircraft now. It was a circular enclosed six-rotor aircraft around twenty metres in diameter, matte black and sprouting an array of weapon-like pods. It screamed up and banked around them in a complete circle, then stopped and hovered for a while.

Bache waved and smiled, encouraging Zaphir and Nexen to do the same. Nothing happened for a few moments, until four struts powered down from its underbelly and it began to lower itself to the ground.

Two opposing sliding doors were ripped open as soon as the aircraft touched the ground and eight armed soldiers piled out and surrounded them. The whine of the engines dropped in pitch and a ninth soldier dropped to the ground and approached them.

Nexen stepped forward, but quickly froze again as the ring of soldiers all snapped their weapons towards him aggressively.

'By order of the Queen, you are all under arrest for an unprovoked nuclear attack on the Sovereign Planet of Eritain,' said the ninth soldier, who seemed to be senior to the others, judging by the extra rank insignia displayed on both arms.

'Well, that's a nice way to welcome me home,' said Nexen, putting his hands on his hips and giving the soldier a glare.

'You have a southern accent?' questioned the soldier, the surprise evident in his tone.

'I should think so,' said Nexen. 'I was born in Fendry and you can address me as Commander or sir—Major?'

The soldier baulked slightly at the rebuke, but kept his face impassive. 'Really—and who might you be—sir?' he replied, slightly irreverently.

'Commander Nexen of the research vessel *Xhamin*,' said Nexen, keeping his gaze directly on the major.

Bache noticed the slight upturn at the corner of the major's mouth and a few sniggers from the surrounding soldiers.

'Of course you are—sir,' he answered, sarcastically. 'And I'm the Queen.'

This time there was a round of chuckles from the lower ranks, silenced immediately by the major giving the circle of soldiers a sudden wide-eyed glare. Returning his gaze to Nexen, he smiled and continued. 'If you'd be so kind as to allow my men to disarm and search you, then we can soon be on our way to the special accommodation we have for such distinguished guests.'

'Good lad,' said Nexen, completely ignoring the major's sarcasm. 'You need to fly us straight back to Port Halik.'

The major smiled and shook his head. 'Well, Mr GDA, you really need to sack your intelligence gatherers,' he said. 'Not only have they given you an identity that's three thousand years out of date, the destination for your espionage hasn't existed for fifteen hundred years.'

'Port Halik?' said Nexen, taken aback. 'What happened to it?'

'Sea level rise,' said the major as he watched his soldiers disarm the strangers. 'They moved the spaceport a hundred kilometres inland and renamed it.'

The major inspected their suits and weapons a little more

closely. 'Modern GDA suits, the latest GDA laser weapons, and an android that's been outlawed here for generations,' he said, keeping eye contact with Nexen. 'I know we're the brunt of dumb northerner jokes, but just how dumb d'you think we are—sir?'

After being disarmed and searched, they were cuffed and pushed up onto the aircraft. Even Vee was handcuffed and sat between two soldiers.

Bache watched the lifeboat disappear beneath them as the six-engined aircraft screamed upwards and turned towards the north.

17

THE LACCOND FARM, NEAR REDDAT CITY, SOUTHERN HEMISPHERE, ERITAIN

GLENDOLIAN HAD BURIED Slen's body deep under the yard and after working out how to start the harvester had parked it over the top of the grave, completely hiding the disturbed ground from view. She had found some female clothing in the wardrobe similar to what Slen was wearing. The blue work trousers were a little short and the boots a size too large, but apart from that she thought she looked similarly attired to the female in some of the pictures dotted around the cottage.

Her scanner was set at four kilometres as she knew the nearest biological habitation was over five kilometres away and hoped they weren't frequent visitors.

She knew from studying everything within the ship's data records that on Eritain, everyone had to have personal identification on them at all times. Although three thousand years had passed, judging by the documentation Slen had in his pockets, not too much had changed. Digging around in a documentation drawer she found in a spare room, she discovered his wife's identification card and payment bracelet. She pocketed these, sat down with a photograph of Fellen

Laccond and set about changing her facial features to match. It took her a few minutes before she was happy with the result. She looked younger and her hair was a different colour, but she knew from the female biologicals on the ship that hair colour could be changed on a whim. Getting herself clean was another matter, as it took her many washes to get the grime from three millennia off her synthetic skin. Her hair took the longest of all, but eventually the matted ropes gave way and she was also able to trim the length back with some scissors she found in the kitchen.

The computer terminal on the wall in the main room was next on her agenda. It took her four seconds to break Slen's password and another eight to penetrate the government's personal records bureau and change her status from deceased to divorced and her date of birth forward ten years. She found a modern unoccupied apartment in Reddat City, changed her address to that and ordered a replacement identification card. She was happy to find Slen's passwords for his terminal also accessed his banking and surprisingly he still had a joint depository. She used his passwords and as quickly as before learnt hers, enabling her to take him off the depository and completely delete his banking history.

The perimeter alarm pinged in her head. Some form of metallic ground transport was approaching along the main track from the west. She locked the front door and sprinted over to the barn and activated Slen's ground vehicle. Earlier, she'd discovered that the electronic tag he had in his pocket that enabled the harvester activated this one too. Turning the tall utilitarian electric truck east, she quickly drove into the trees at the rear of the property until she was well out of sight, parked and returned to watch from the edge of the tree line.

A dark low-sprung angular vehicle soon hummed into

view and stopped in the courtyard near the cottage. Fellen, as she would now be known, detected two occupants, both male, and as they disembarked, noticed they wore identical grey uniform-style clothing. She tuned her hearing straight towards them to zero in on what was being said.

'—truck isn't here,' one of them finished saying, pointing at the barn.

'He won't have seen anything if he's in town,' said the other one, banging his fist against the front door on the off chance. When he got no response, he shrugged and turned back to the vehicle. 'Let's continue east to the Gerlath farm,' he said. 'Maybe they saw something.'

The vehicle pulled off and Fellen hid as it passed, heading east towards the next biological habitat.

She realised if the local authorities were quite familiar with Slen and his vehicle, then others would be too. She would have to quickly discard it and find a more suitable and less obvious form of transport. It seemed her lifeboat descent had been reported and she was glad it was in pieces under ten metres of water.

Returning to the truck, she cursed as her hair, now clean and dry, kept blowing in front of her face. There was a wide brimmed hat in the cab and she tucked her hair behind her ears and donned that, which seemed to solve the problem. The truck also contained one of Slen's coats and she put that on too to hide her slim size.

The truck was old and bounced around on the ruts in the track as she headed west as fast as she dared and kept the brim of the hat low over her face in case anyone else recognised the vehicle.

The city of Reddat was just over fifty kilometres away and the speed was to ensure the uniformed biologicals didn't catch up to her while she was in the possession of Slen's truck.

Following the signs for the Reddat spaceport, she aimed for the long-term park on the south side of the port, where she took the truck down underground to the lowest level. Parking in a far corner next to a couple of other trucks, she worked out how to connect it up to the power point by copying the other vehicles.

She swore as Slen's details came up on the parking screen and realised it would be easy to find the truck once his disappearance was reported.

Opening up the small computer screen built into the dashboard of the truck, she hacked into the parking software and deleted the vehicle as having entered and even the parking space L6-4110 was wiped from the system's database.

Happy that that would delay any search for her, she kept the hat and coat and made her way up to the ComveC station. She'd noticed this elevated monorail looping in and out of the port as she'd driven into the city. It was a free service and took a wide figure of eight loop around the outskirts and through the city centre.

She picked up a free paper, boarded right at the back of the train and sat in the first seat, which allowed her to watch everyone else on the train. So far, she hadn't noticed anyone paying her any unusual attention, so she kept the brim of the hat low and pretended to read the paper. This also helped hide her face from the cameras she'd noticed, situated at each end of the carriage. She quickly dialled back her sense of smell, as she found the stench of being in this close proximity to so many biologicals was quite unpleasant.

The three-carriage train quietly hummed around and into the city surprisingly quickly and efficiently. Most of the passengers stood up to disembark in the city centre, so she mingled in and joined them.

Reddat City covered around thirty-two square kilometres, the centre being a forest of glass towers stretching high into the now-clear morning sky. It surprised her that such a backward life form could build something so attractive, but she mused it would be so much better once all these dirty biologicals were converted to ersatz beings.

The first thing she had to do towards this goal was find a new untraceable identity and as she surveyed the hundreds of Eritainians milling around the city, she smiled to herself.

There's just so much choice, she thought. *Who shall I choose and convert first?*

18

DREENAH MILITARY HEADQUARTERS, NEAR YELTER,
ERITAIN

THE FLIGHT WAS SURPRISINGLY SHORT, as eight minutes later they landed in some sort of military base on the outskirts of a small town.

'Is that Yelter?' asked Nexen, glancing from the window to the major.

'Face the front,' snapped the soldier sitting next to him.

The major smiled. 'Nice try, saboteur,' he said. 'That your target was it?' The major sat stiffly for a moment, listening to something on his earpiece. 'Destroyed?' he said, staring into space. 'Nuclear – well who the hell fired that?' He snapped his attention back to Nexen. 'Don't expect a rescue attempt any time soon,' he said. 'Your ship has been nuked.'

'Why d'you think we were in a lifeboat?' said Nexen, rolling his eyes. 'The person you want is in the other lifeboat. We had just boarded the *Xhamin* to arrest them, only to discover they'd sabotaged the ship and left on the small bridge lifeboat.'

'Boarded it from where? You're making this up as you go along,' growled the major.

The doors opened and as they were ushered out, another officer approached the major and whispered in his ear.

'Where?' Bache heard the major say. 'Get a unit there, don't let any of them escape.'

They were all marched inside a bunker of some kind and down concrete stairs several floors underground to a detention centre. Here they were searched again and placed in separate cells.

Bache sat on the metal bed frame bolted to the wall and waited. Occasionally, he heard other cell doors being opened, the murmur of voices and the clump of boots in the corridor. It was a couple of hours before his door opened and a soldier appeared and beckoned him out into the corridor.

The interrogation room he was escorted to was as he expected. Square, bland and with a simple table and two chairs. His cuffs were attached to a metal loop on the table top and he was left alone again. He was pleased to see there were no blood stains on the concrete floor and, knowing he was being watched, he sat still, remained impassive and just stared at a mark on the opposite wall.

He estimated around half an hour passed before the major appeared with a soldier and closed the door behind them.

'Name?' snapped the major, who remained standing and pointed for the soldier to stand behind the prisoner.

'Bache Loftt.'

'Rank?'

'Recruit.'

'Another recruit!' he stormed. 'Do they consider us so backward they send recruits here on espionage missions?'

'We weren't on an espionage mission,' said Bache, keeping his voice calm and neutral. 'It was our final training flight before finishing our officer course and being offered our first junior officer positions. I'm sure Zaphir would have explained this to you.'

'What's the name of your ship?'

'The destroyer *Dres'kin*.'

The major pressed a few icons on a tablet he'd been holding and turned it so Bache could see the screen. Bache's eyes widened as he watched a video of a crashed GDA destroyer, sitting in a wooded area. It was leaning badly to one side as though its struts had collapsed and surrounded by small fires as the heat from the hull ignited nearby foliage.

'Is that the one?' the major said, this time in a more sarcastic tone.

'It must have been damaged by the *Xhamin* exploding so close to it,' Bache said. 'Are the crew okay?'

'We have no idea,' he said. 'Apparently, its shielding is still operational and we can't get near it.'

'Do you want me to talk to them?' Bache asked.

'No need,' said the major, grinning. 'They've been told if they don't surrender their vessel within the hour, then the prisoners will be executed one at a time until they do.'

'And you believe that's a responsible way to behave towards a vessel in distress do—'

Bache was cut off as the door cracked open and a senior officer Bache hadn't seen before, looked in and nodded his head towards the corridor.

'Yes, sir,' snapped the major, a look of surprise on his face as he hurried out and closed the door.

Bache heard muffled raised voices outside, before the door reopened and the major, his face bright red, stuck his head back in.

'Uncuff the gentleman and take him to the mess hall,' he said to the soldier, before disappearing again.

Nexen and Zaphir were already there when Bache arrived in a much bigger and brighter room. Zaphir was sitting on a comfortable lounge chair in one corner and Nexen was having an animated conversation with the senior officer from before.

Bache went and joined Zaphir, her face lighting up when she saw him.

'Are you okay?' she asked, standing and giving him a fist bump.

'I was about to ask you the same question,' he whispered as he pulled her into a hug.

'I'm good,' she said. 'Do you know what suddenly changed? One minute I'm being threatened with execution and the next I'm given a comfortable armchair and having a meal prepared for me.'

'By the look of it, they've realised that Nexen really is who he says he is,' said Bache, turning as Nexen approached together with the senior officer.

'This is General Took,' said Nexen. 'He's the northern hemisphere military commander.'

Zaphir stood and they both saluted him smartly.

'Sir,' they said together.

'You're very kind giving me that level of respect after the way my men have just treated you,' he said. 'Needless to say, the captain will not be troubling you again.'

Zaphir and Bache nodded and raised their eyebrows at Nexen, both of them understanding the general's meaning.

'The general would like you to accompany us over to your ship and help sort this mess out,' said Nexen.

'Absolutely,' said Bache.

'Get yourselves something to eat,' said Took. 'We leave in an hour.'

'Commander,' said Bache, as Nexen turned to leave. 'Have you informed Captain Yamaton of the situation change and that the threats of execution no longer exist?'

'We have,' said Took. 'Although, as yet we have had no response.'

'I'm not surprised,' said Zaphir. 'He'll think it's a trick.'

'That's why we need you to convince him otherwise,' said Nexen.

'Actually, while you're here, sir,' Bache said looking at the general. 'Has anything been learnt about the whereabouts of the other lifeboat?'

The general glanced at Nexen.

'That's what we were just discussing,' said Nexen. 'We know the android had taken on the appearance of my wife and escaped in the bridge lifeboat just over a minute before we ejected in ours.'

'Allowing for a similar re-entry trajectory,' said Took, 'it puts her landing site, we think, somewhere in the southern hemisphere.'

A junior officer came trotting into the mess hall and on seeing the general, came running over, saluted and give him a piece of paper.

Took read the message and nodded at the corporal. 'It seems there are reports of a parachute being seen in a rural area near Reddat City,' he said. 'There's a lot of chatter from the local authorities, who are out trying to locate it.'

'We need to find her quickly,' said Bache. 'If she gets loose in the local population, a lot of people will die.'

'Let's hope they find her then,' said Took, a little despondently.

'Once we've got the ship sorted out, we'll go over there

and use our technology to help locate her,' said Bache, noticing the general flinch as he said it.

'Not possible, I'm afraid,' said Nexen. 'Both the northern and southern hemispheres are presently in a state of war, apparently.'

'More like a fragile ceasefire,' said Took. 'But whatever we call it, going over there is not remotely possible. I'm informed that some of their senior government are convinced it was us that nuked them, so tensions are extremely high.'

'Are they likely to retaliate in kind?' asked Bache.

'Well, that's just it,' said Took. 'We don't have any nuclear weapons and as far as we know, nor do they. Nukes were banned centuries ago.'

'I could talk to them and explain the situation,' said Nexen. 'When I left, the planet was united and ruled by King Challon the Third.'

'Hmm, we could try it,' said Took, rubbing his chin. 'But I think they'll be as sceptical as we were until you had the iris scan.'

19

REDDAT CITY, SOUTHERN HEMISPHERE, ERITAIN

WITH THE CASH Fellen had found on Slen's body and in the cottage, she bought some new clothes. She needed to blend in and the styles worn in the city were completely different to the slightly shabbier farm clothes she was wearing. She bought a wig that sported a much shorter blonde fashion cut, seemingly popular with the city girls.

She found a used tablet in a charity shop and, hacking into its data drive, retrieved the previous owner's account and connected up. The government database had two registered girls' charities that dealt in female orphans. She hacked into these and searched. It took her less than an hour, sitting on a public bench in one of the several city parks, to find what she wanted.

An eighteen-year-old orphaned girl, from out of town, only housed yesterday and with blonde hair. Her name was Zella and the charity had secured her a cleaning job at a local engineering company in the northern suburbs. The small apartment she'd been allocated was near the job, so Fellen got straight on the ComveC and circled around the city.

She noticed the buildings were significantly smaller on the northern side and a little more run down. Timber was the building medium of choice here, rather than the steelcrete and glass of the city centre, and four storeys seemed to be the highest anything went.

Alighting at the nearest station, she soon found the correct apartment building. Only two streets from the monorail and in a tree-lined avenue, the three-storey block had been painted blue at one time, but was now faded with the paint peeling in places. She stopped and scanned the street outside the building, checking that no one was paying her any attention. Once satisfied she was unnoticed, she climbed the few steps to the front lobby door and laid her hand on the key card scanner. Three seconds and the door clicked open, another quick scan around to ensure she was unseen, and she entered.

Apartment seven was on the third floor and she took the emergency stairs instead of the elevator to ensure she didn't bump into anyone. The white wooden door of number seven faced the rear of the building, with two others facing front. It had the same scanner as the front door, set flush into the wall on the right.

She considered entering and subduing her quarry, but thought a scuffle or a scream might bring unwanted attention, so she knocked instead. It proved a wise choice as someone other than Zella answered the door.

'Hello,' she said, smiling. 'I'm looking for Zella.'

'She's busy,' said a young man with no shirt on. He scowled at her and made himself deliberately wide in the doorway.

'I'm Fellen from the charity,' said Fellen. 'Could I see her for a minute?'

He grimaced as a voice called from within.

'Who is it, Serat?'

'Someone from the charity,' he called, never taking his eyes off Fellen.

Zella appeared behind him, tightening the cord of a bathrobe and with her hair somewhat dishevelled.

'Hello, Zella,' Fellen said, ignoring the young man's attempts to block her from view. 'It's Fellen from the charity, have you got time for a chat?'

'Of course,' she said. 'I haven't met you before. Have you taken over from Hallten?'

The young man turned to glare at Zella. 'I'll come back later,' he grumbled, grabbed a jacket from a hook just inside the door, pushed passed Fellen and stomped off down the corridor.

'Sorry about that,' said Zella, trying to tidy her hair. 'Come in.'

She led Fellen through to a small sparsely furnished lounge. A large window overlooked the roof of a building behind and another door led into what Fellen thought must be the kitchen.

'Boyfriend?' asked Fellen nodding her head back towards the entrance.

'Not really. I only met him last night.'

'Doesn't live locally then?'

'No idea,' Zella said. 'He was in the *Starship* last night.'

Fellen raised her eyebrows. 'The *Starship*?' she questioned.

Zella looked at Fellen strangely and she realised she must have said something odd.

'Are you new in town or something?' Zella asked.

'Does it show?' said Fellen, pointing at the seat next to Zella. 'Can I sit down?'

'Sure.'

As Fellen squeezed passed her to get to the other chair, she snatched Zella's head between her hands and twisted. The android's augmented strength meant the girl's neck snapped easily. The crack was louder than she expected and she gently lowered the body to the floor. Sitting over her and cradling Zella's head, she stared at her facial features and gradually changed hers to an exact copy. She then carried her through to the bedroom, stripped her own clothes, removed the bathrobe from Zella and began inspecting the dead girl's body. Over the next half an hour, she meticulously copied every detail of size, hair, mole and skin colour. Finally, donning the bathrobe, she searched and found some plastic waste bags in the kitchen and, folding the body up as small as she could, which involved breaking a few more bones, she wrapped it in four layers of bags and placed it by the door.

She smiled. She was now Zella, she had an apartment, a job starting in a few days and all the relevant paperwork to remain hidden here indefinitely.

Collecting up all Fellen's clothes, she placed these in another waste bag and once it was dark outside, took both down the emergency stairs to the lower level and out a back door to a small parking area.

Choosing the newest-looking vehicle there, she found she was getting better at overcoming the basic electrical technology these biologicals used, as less than a minute later, she was a block away driving the vehicle, its identity changed and the waste bags in the passenger footwell. The clothes went into a roadside recycling bin and the body was dropped off a large road bridge into a deep and swiftly moving river during a break in traffic.

Returning to a street a couple of blocks away, she parked

the vehicle and strolled back to her apartment block to find Serat waiting on the steps.

'Where've you been?' he asked, his irritation evident.

'For a walk,' she said. 'Is that a crime on this planet?'

He suddenly stopped and stared at her.

'What?' she said, concerned she'd said something drastically wrong or missed some obvious detail with her duplication.

'You've changed your hair,' he said, circling around her.

She smiled and nodded, relieved it was nothing more serious.

'Come on up,' she said. 'We have unfinished business.'

Sporting a wide grin, he followed her dutifully up to the apartment.

He was perfect for the first regeneration. Young, good-looking and healthy, he would be able to attract many females for the initial stages of her project and half an hour later, as they lay entwined and coupled on the worn lounge carpet, he screamed as she let the nano swarm flow.

20

REMOTE WOODED AREA, NORTHERN HEMISPHERE, ERITAIN

ZAPHIR AND BACHE stepped down out of the flyer and stumbled across the rough ground towards the *Dres'kin*. All around them large areas of ground were still smouldering and the smell of the smoke reminded Bache of camping with his father back on Deelatayne.

The ship looked scorched in places, but appeared at first inspection reasonably intact. It was difficult going in their suits but they managed to circle around and approach the vessel from its lowest side, where the hull was prone to the ground.

Bache picked up a rock and tossed it towards the ship. It stopped in mid air, around twelve metres from the hull, and dropped to the ground. Putting on his helmet and activating the communication channel they'd last used, he called the *Dres'kin*.

'Walkers requesting permission to approach the vessel,' he said.

'Shields will be retracted for ten seconds, approach airlock six,' barked Yamaton's familiar tone.

They both quickly trudged across the rough blackened ground and waited a couple of metres away from the designated airlock. Bache could hear the hull ticking and hissing as it cooled against the soil. He heard the airlock cycling and removed his helmet again.

Yamaton stood scowling, holding a laser rifle across his chest. Two other crew members Bache recognised from the armaments section stood either side of the captain, keeping themselves partially hidden behind the airlock frame. They also had laser weapons, but these were pointed out from the ship, straight at Zaphir and Bache.

'A couple of hours ago they were going to execute you if I didn't surrender my vessel,' Yamaton shouted across. 'How do I know this isn't a trick?'

'The officer that ordered that has been demoted and moved on,' said Bache. 'They've realised they're going to need our help to catch the android that did all this.'

Yamaton staggered backwards as the ship lurched and dropped slightly. Bache and Zaphir quickly stepped back in alarm.

'Well, we're not going to be able to help much while we're stuck in this bloody bog,' Yamaton shouted, hanging onto the airlock frame as the ship shuddered, then settled again.

'What d'you need?' Zaphir asked.

'Electrical engineers,' said Yamaton. 'The blast wave blew us into the upper atmosphere, took out one of our two Alma drives and the stabiliser. It's a miracle we came in upright. We need a lot of circuitry rewiring and I've only got two engineers on board. If they work sixteen hours a day, it'll still take them two weeks.'

'How many do you need?'

'Ten would be handy and should see us lifting out of here in a couple of days,' Yamaton said, glancing out and down at the ground. 'So long as we haven't sunk in too far.'

'We'll see what we can arrange, Captain,' said Zaphir. 'We're going with Commander Nexen to the southern hemisphere to try and find the android before the trail goes cold.'

'Make sure whoever they send is unarmed,' he said. 'I want a no-fly zone fifty kilometres around this ship apart from that unarmed flyer, and remind them I still have operational shields, upper deck laser cannons and a targeting array.'

'Will do, Captain,' said Bache. 'Ask for General Took if you need anything else.'

Yamaton nodded, bent down, picked up a backpack and tossed it over to Zaphir. 'Change of clothes,' he said. 'So you don't have to clump around in those suits all the time.'

'Thank you, Captain,' said Bache.

'We'll come and find you as soon as we're operational again. Stay safe, recruits,' he said and the airlock closed again.

Nexen was waiting for them at the flyer as they returned.

'I'll let the general know,' he said, after Bache explained exactly what Yamaton required.

One at a time, they changed out of their suits in the small bathroom at the rear of the flyer. They stowed them in a kit locker, along with their weapons, as they didn't want to give the southerners any excuse to harm them.

The flyer was over ocean for three hours before coastline appeared ahead and three black gunships swooped in as an escort. They were directed inland around a hundred kilometres before being ordered to land at a military base, nestled in a remote area of wooded hills.

As the noise of the engines died down and the twin doors slid open, they were met by four soldiers. They took a cursory glance around inside, backed away and one of them nodded over his shoulder.

An older woman approached the flyer, climbed inside and stared at Nexen almost reverently. 'I think you know what this is,' she said, handing the commander what looked like a small medical machine.

Nexen nodded.

'What is it?' Zaphir asked.

'Iris scanner,' he said, holding it up in front of his face.

After a couple of seconds it beeped and he handed it back to the woman. Bache could see her hands were shaking as she turned the machine and read the scan report on a small screen. She let out a sob, the machine rattled to the floor and she lurched forward, catching Nexen unawares, and hugged him.

Bache froze, the look of astonishment on his face matched Nexen's.

'I'm sorry, Commander,' she managed to utter in between more sobs. 'I never believed this day would actually happen.' She stepped away, wiping her eyes on her sleeve. 'You see – I'm Dion Nexen, direct descendant of your son, Vitarl.'

It was the commander's turn to step forward and hug Dion. 'It should be me apologising,' he said. 'I'm sorry I took so long.'

'The family always believed you were alive somewhere,' she said, beginning to sob again.

'I wouldn't have been if it wasn't for Bache here, finding me before my sleep chamber finally packed up.'

She turned her head towards Bache. 'Thank you,' she whispered.

Bache smiled and wiped a tear from his eye too, as the emotion of the moment got to him as well.

'I imagine Fendry has changed a bit since I was home last,' said Nexen.

'Your house has gone,' she said. 'But you have a statue in the town square.'

He turned to face Zaphir and Bache. 'I have a statue,' he said, grinning at them.

'Does that mean we have to bow as well as calling you sir?' asked Bache.

Nexen smirked and turned towards Dion. 'I had another augmented android I seem to remember, that didn't come on the ship with us. Do you know what happened to that one?'

'From what I've been told, the technology was quickly banned not long after you left,' said Dion, shrugging. 'They were all decommissioned and destroyed. Do you want me to check the records?'

Nexen was about to answer when he noticed the four soldiers suddenly stiffen and a senior officer poked his head inside the flyer.

'Is it him?' he barked, surprising them with his imperious tone.

'Indeed, I am him,' said Nexen. 'And who might you be?'

'I'm Major Clatterhock and you're all coming with me,' he stated, a little less lordly this time.

'Is it a requisite of your rank to be rude and arrogant on this planet since I've been away?' Nexen asked, staring intently at the major.

'You are to remain here until further notice,' he said, turning to leave.

'On whose orders, young man?' Nexen barked, causing the major to pause and glare back.

'Admiral Jackarett,' he said, turning to leave again, then glancing back. 'You may be a celebrity to some, sir, but not to others.' And he marched off, his nose in the air.

'Give some people a sniff of power and they become a tyrant,' said Nexen, shrugging.

Two of the soldiers sniggered and he raised his eyebrows at them.

'Sorry, Commander,' said one of them. 'He's an arsehole to everyone.'

This time Bache laughed, followed by Dion and Zaphir. Nexen looked at them, shook his head and smirked.

'Well, let's hope Admiral Jackarett isn't an arsehole too,' he said, as they exited the flyer and followed the four soldiers towards a curved-roofed building.

21

REDDAT CITY, SOUTHERN HEMISPHERE, ERITAIN

ZELLA HAD HEAVED the disgusting sweaty biological off her once Serat had been rendered unconscious. She dragged him into the bathroom and sat him in the shower, as the majority of his bodily fluids would be drained off as the nano swarm got busy with their regeneration.

It had taken decades of experimentation and design on the *Xhamin* to perfect the nano programming, but it still took around five hours for the complete reconstruction to enable. Most of which was converting the human brain's memories into a data cache, enabling the ersatz human to know everything the host had known.

Her next job was funds. She'd discovered the two hemispheres were at each other's throats over most things and thought it amusing they were both blaming each other for the nuclear attack on Hallsbard.

Hacking into one of the major banks in the north, she found a company in Hallsbard that had been completely destroyed, but had considerable funds in its trading account. She transferred the whole lot into Zella's bank account and wiped the company's existence from the server, ensuring she also erased the money trail.

It was late evening now. Checking Serat was coming along nicely, she decided there was time to go out and find her next vassal.

The *Starship* bar that Serat had mentioned was three blocks away and only eight minutes' walk. It was situated on one of the main thoroughfares through the northern suburbs, ensuring a lot of passing traffic and clientele. She'd found some clothing in Zella's wardrobe that showed off her slim but curvaceous body perfectly and was pleased to see a few turned heads and raised eyebrows as she entered. The interior was designed to replicate a recreational facility on a large galactic vessel, and she found it amusing that flat oval panels, flush-mounted into the walls, showed stars flashing by as if the bar was travelling faster than light.

She slid onto one of the few unoccupied barstools and smiled as a surprisingly tall barmaid approached.

'A Garlan ale, please,' she said, having done a bit of research, so she knew what to order.

'Bottled or draught?' the barmaid asked.

'Er, draught,' she said, confidently, only in reality she didn't know the difference.

Pleased she'd made the right choice as a glass of the ruby-coloured beer was placed in front of her, she lifted her arm to display her payment bracelet and the barmaid shook her head.

'Pay when you're done if you sit at the bar,' she said, with a slight smirk.

She wondered if she'd made an error somehow and, glancing up and down the bar, realised she was the only female sitting on the barstools. Three other males were sitting at the bar and the remainder of the other patrons seemed to be in small groups sitting in circular booths built around the walls.

'Been single for long?' asked a male, leaning over from three seats away.

'How do you know I'm single?' she asked, then taking a sip of her drink.

He grinned and raised his eyebrows. 'It's singles' night, you're all dressed up and you're on your own,' he said, sliding over to the adjacent seat. 'I'm Wrendle, by the way?' He raised his right hand palm out.

'Zella,' she said, touching his palm with hers. A greeting she'd seen others employing. 'You local?'

'Chadorion City born and bred,' he said, shrugging. 'But don't hold that against me, I prefer it here.'

'I wouldn't worry about that, I'm originally from the north,' she said, grimacing, having done research into Zella's history.

'Oh,' he said, sitting back theatrically, his eyes wide. 'You could be a dangerous spy, perhaps it was you that set off the bomb at Hallsbard.'

'Don't be silly,' she said, smiling. 'I fired a missile from my starship up in orbit, actually. Then my ship exploded and now I'm here, trying to secretly blend in.' She peeked furtively up and down the bar. 'D'you think I've got away with it?'

'Absolutely,' he said, smiling again. 'But now you've told me, so you'll just have to kill me. Probably after enticing me back to your place and having your wicked way with me.'

'A lonely spy has to get her kicks somehow,' she said, waving her empty glass at him. 'You could buy me a drink before I fuck you and kill you though—it's only polite.'

Wrendle almost choked on the swig of his beer he'd just taken. He coughed and swallowed frantically.

'Ah—oh—yes,' he croaked, while waving the barmaid over. 'A drink for the lady,' he managed to squeak out before coughing again.

Wrendle lived in a more modern building about a ten-minute autocab ride west from the bar. Zella had accepted his offer of visiting his place, as she didn't want him bumping into Serat sitting in her shower stall. His apartment was on the ground floor and was considerably bigger than hers. He had a fountain in the foyer and expensive-looking artworks on the walls. The kitchen diner was ultra-modern, with every possible matching appliance built in.

'Impressive home,' she said. 'You can get my whole apartment in your lounge. I thought you said you worked in freight.'

'I do,' he said, pouring her a glass of Gattainian wine. 'Negotiating private and government commercial shipping contracts. It pays quite well.'

'It must do,' she said, running her hand along the blue granite bench top and sipping the expensive wine. She smiled inwardly, realising that once regenerated, this biological could prove useful. 'Domestic or galactic contracts?' she asked.

'Both,' he said. 'But mostly offworld, as we call it.'

'How many other systems do you deal with?'

'All of them in the Cygnus Alliance.'

'What about the GDA?'

'No,' he said. 'Too distant to be viable and anyway most Alliance governments discourage it and make it quite clear they wouldn't do business with us if we did.'

She nodded, smiled, placed her wine glass down on the

counter and in one movement, pulled her blouse over her head and dropped it on the floor.

'Wow,' he said, as she stood topless in front of him.

'Perhaps you'd like to show me your bedroom too,' she said, running her hands slowly across her breasts suggestively.

Twenty minutes later, as she laid his body in the king-size bath to drain, the nanos beginning their regeneration, she wandered around the rest of the apartment and checked out the other rooms. It was a three-bedroom unit and even had a private office containing a powerful-looking computer system with six screens.

Perhaps I should move in here, she thought, as she picked up his tablet and ordered an autocab.

22

XARVER MILITARY CAMP, SOUTHERN HEMISPHERE, ERITAIN

AN ELECTRIC BUS turned up at the gatehouse shortly after they'd disembarked from the flyer. It was apparent the landing zones were just that and were remote from the main camp itself. After a ten-minute ride through the woods and into a huge fenced barracks area, they were ushered off at one of the larger buildings on the site.

Bache noticed the wide-eyed stares at Nexen from everyone that crossed their path. It wasn't every day a three-thousand-year-old man walked by.

Dion led the way into what Bache assumed was their equivalent of the officers' mess. Plush furniture filled the reception hall and grand military artworks adorned the walls. The contingent of soldiers remained here as Dion took them through a pair of huge wooden doors into a dark wood-panelled lounge. Again, the furnishings were antique, with senior officers' portraits staring down imperiously, their eyes following you wherever you went.

Bache pointed to one hanging above one of the two large fireplaces at each end of the room. It depicted a tall man with a most colourful dress uniform and bushy moustache, glowering pompously.

'General Zional Nexen,' Bache read from the sign underneath. 'Any relation?'

'He was,' said a smartly dressed gentleman, entering from a side door. 'From around six hundred and forty years ago. Tyrant of a man allegedly, but got the job done.'

They all turned to face the newcomer.

'Admiral Jackarett is it?' asked Nexen.

'Indeed so,' Jackarett replied, meeting Nexen's raised palm. 'I've met a few celebrities in my time, but this is certainly one to tell my grandchildren.'

'Well, I'm glad you're pleased to see me,' said Nexen. 'Unlike some I could mention.'

'Ah, yes, Major Clatterhock,' said the Admiral. 'I'm afraid he's a bit of a conspiracy theorist who's always claimed you deserted your post and set up a private colony somewhere distant.'

'He's almost correct,' said Nexen, grinning. 'Apart from the fact I was asleep for all but thirteen years of it.'

'The company that made your hibernation chamber, their net worth doubled overnight,' said Dion.

'It still exists?' asked a surprised Nexen.

'Been through a few takeovers and name changes,' she replied. 'But the factory's in the same spot.'

'You know a lot about them,' said the admiral, raising his eyebrows.

'I should,' she said. 'I'm the owner. We still have the contract for all government vessels and I think the price has just gone up,' she chuckled.

The admiral smiled back and indicated a table and chairs at the far end of the room.

'I believe we need to discuss this errant android of yours,' he said, eyeing Vee suspiciously and pulling out a chair for Dion. 'Am I correct in understanding it can alter its appearance?'

'It seems so,' said Nexen. 'When we witnessed it board the bridge lifeboat, it'd taken on Glendolian's semblance.'

'Your pairing,' said Dion, her eyes wide with surprise.

Nexen nodded slowly.

'I'm very sorry,' said the admiral. 'I didn't know your pairing was aboard the *Xhamin*.'

'Not many did, Admiral, it was a last-minute thing,' said Nexen. 'My android here linked with the *Xhamin* when we sneaked aboard and downloaded everything it could. The crew's hibernation chambers hadn't been serviced like mine had, so they'd failed long since.'

'A fact you might want to keep to yourself,' said Dion, grimacing.

'So we need to circulate a picture of your pairing,' the admiral said, as an aid approached and gave him a message. He stared at it for a moment, puffing out his cheeks in thought.

'What is it?' asked Nexen.

'It seems a rural farmer has disappeared close to Reddat City, where the lifeboat came down.'

'He hasn't just gone on holiday or something?' said Nexen.

'Not when his crop was only two-thirds harvested, no,' said Jackarett. 'His harvester was out in the yard undergoing some repairs.'

'We need to go there, sir,' said Bache, joining the conversation for the first time. 'The android will need to change its appearance and hide in the city.'

'You're GDA, I presume?' said Jackarett. 'Off that ship that crashed in the north?'

Zaphir and Bache both stood and saluted the admiral.

'Officer Recruits Loftt and Mye, sir,' Bache said.

'Recruits, eh?' said the admiral. 'You seem very sure of everything, young Loftt?'

'It's what I would do if I wanted to remain hidden, sir,' he said.

The admiral nodded and puffed his cheeks out again and fiddled with his moustache. 'Could probably do with an alternative viewpoint,' he said. 'Most of my best staff are busy with the rescue mission at Hallsbard.'

'My android can also detect one of its own, so long as it's near enough,' said Nexen.

'How near?' asked Jackarett.

Nexen glanced over at Vee, standing to one side of the table.

'Answer the admiral, vassal,' said Nexen.

'I would need to be in the same room, Admiral,' said Vee. 'On the *Xhamin*, I didn't detect the androids until we entered the bridge.'

'Androids,' Jackarett said, giving Nexen a puzzled look. 'Plural?'

'Others had been modified to operate the ship,' Nexen replied.

'And none of those escaped too?'

'No, sir,' said Bache. 'They were all hard wired into their consoles.'

'Hmm,' he grunted. 'All sounds quite creepy to me. At times like this, you realise why that technology was banned all those years ago.' He stood and paused for a moment. 'I'll organise a flyer and a couple of reliable men to deflect the media. You don't want that circus disrupting your search.'

'I'd appreciate it if my return was kept under wraps for the time being,' said Nexen.

'Don't worry, there'll be a complete news blackout as far as you're concerned,' said Jackarett.

'That might be a bit problematic,' said Dion, holding up her tablet.

A headline from a northern news agency read "Triple Millennia Hero Returns."

'Ah, crap,' said Nexen. 'I was afraid of that.'

'I've got a wig you could borrow,' said Dion.

Jackarett chuckled as he made towards the door, turning at the last minute. 'I'll have some food put out for you in the dining room,' he said. 'Transport to Reddat in one hour.'

'Keep me up to date with your search, Commander,' said Dion. 'Our companies have considerable resources and may be able to help in the operation.'

'I will,' said Nexen as they went in search of the dining room.

23

REDDAT CITY, SOUTHERN HEMISPHERE, ERITAIN

THE ANDROID currently identifying as Zella returned to her apartment to find Serat still sitting in the shower cubicle. His regeneration was almost complete, so she stood him up and ran the shower head over him to wash away the last of the body fluids that had drained out of him.

'Hello,' he said suddenly and peered around the bathroom with a bemused expression.

'Hello, yourself,' she said, admiring the improvements in muscle tone and general appearance of her first ersatz human. 'What are your duties?' she asked.

'To regenerate as many female humans as possible and further our cleansing the planet of the biological infestation,' he said, without a pause.

'Excellent,' she said. 'Your clothes are in the bedroom.'

He nodded, went to the bedroom, dressed and left the apartment.

The following lunchtime Zella ventured out again. It was a nice morning, the local star was high in the sky and the sweet smell of the blossom in the trees covered some of the human stink.

She chose an outside café this time, right at the end of her street, ordered a glass of the local wine and sat at a small table under a parasol advertising a brand of southern mineral water. Pretending to read from her tablet, she people-watched and waited to see who would take the bait.

It took only fourteen minutes before a voice from her left spoke in a soft questioning tone. 'All alone on such a beautiful day?'

She looked up and shielded her eyes from the star. She was a little disappointed to find a middle-aged man standing next to an adjacent table.

'Mind if I join you?' he said.

'Not at all,' she replied, wondering if he had any younger sons. But then again she thought he was an attractive man, in a rugged kind of way.

'Henock,' he said, introducing himself. 'And who might you be?'

'Zella,' she said, giving him her best smile. 'Does your pairing know you're out sweet-talking girls less than half your age?'

'Only the prettiest of ones,' he said. 'Ah, you see, she doesn't mind because in reality she'd know I wouldn't stand a chance. It's still nice to sit and chat with a pretty girl now and then. A man can always dream.'

'She thinks you don't stand a chance eh?' she said, staring into his eyes.

'Ah, don't tease,' he said. 'You'll make me come over all unnecessary.'

'You think I'm kidding,' she replied. 'My apartment's just down the street, if you're brave enough.'

He stared at her for a moment, seemingly undecided whether she was serious.

'Oh, come on,' she said, standing and holding out her hand. 'D'you want to fuck me or not?'

He nearly knocked the table over in his hurry to stand up again.

———

One thing she noticed once back at the apartment was, he didn't seem as smelly as the younger men.

Perhaps they spend more time on personal hygiene, she thought, as he thrusted away. Finally, when he cried out in ecstasy, she wrapped her legs and arms tightly around him and the look of ultimate pleasure on his face changed to one of horror. She needed all her augmented strength to hang onto him as he shook and screamed, to ensure he didn't pull out as the nano swarm violently invaded his body.

For the second time in less than a day, she dragged a man from the bedroom to the bathroom and sat him up in the shower cubicle.

Smiling to herself, she checked her watch and realised that, thankfully, he would be ready to leave and return home to impregnate his pairing before Zella went out for her next evening hunting victims.

Wrapping herself in a bathrobe, she went to the lounge and turned on the info screen set into the wall. She froze as an image of Commander Nexen filled the screen.

'Oh, shit,' she shouted at the empty room as she listened to the news anchor explaining about his miraculous survival in a Nexen Chryo-Chamber and then from the explosion on the *Xhamin*. 'The bastard survived,' she raged.

The next picture showed him alighting from a flyer at some military base in the north, with three others, a young male, a young female and worst of all an early model android.

'You could wreck everything and will have to be eliminated,' she hissed, pointing at the android limping along behind the biologicals.

She quickly dressed and called an autocab.

'Hi, Zella,' said Wrendle as he let her into his apartment in his underwear. 'Didn't expect to see you so soon.'

'I didn't expect to be here either,' said Zella. 'I have a little job for—'

She stopped mid-sentence as she noticed some female clothing on the floor in the lounge.

'Oh, I'm not disturbing anything am I?' she asked.

'Come here,' he said, beckoning her into the bathroom.

There, in the bath, where she'd left Wrendle in the early hours of the morning, was a stunning young female.

'Wow, Wrendle, she's beautiful,' said Zella. 'You didn't waste any time.'

'Not bad for my first one is she?'

'She'll be able to impregnate thousands.'

'There's plenty more on the upmarket dating sites,' he said.

'Well, before you do that, I have a little job for you,' she said, pulling out her tablet and showing him a picture of the farmer Slen Laccond.

'Who's he?' he asked.

'I need you to take on his identity and wait at his farm,' she said, changing the picture to the one showing Nexen, the two youngsters and the android departing the flyer. 'You must destroy this android if it comes there. But be warned, it can detect you as non-human from within five metres. So don't go near it. Just kill it.'

She fed him the details of where Slen's truck and farm were and he spent a few minutes changing his appearance, digging out some old work clothes and then dashing off to the spaceport long-term parking to get the truck.

24

KILDREN LAKES, NEAR REDDAT CITY, SOUTHERN
HEMISPHERE, ERITAIN

THE MILITARY GUNSHIP Admiral Jackarett had allocated them skimmed slowly over the region where the lifeboat was thought to have landed. A series of lakes dotted the hilly landscape, with dense wooded areas randomly scattered here and there.

'I'm getting nothing at all, sir,' said the pilot, scanning the area with the ship's array.

'She must have landed in one of the lakes,' said Zaphir, peering through the small window next to her seat. 'Some of them are quite large and look deep too.'

'If that's the case, we'll probably never find it,' said Bache, shaking his head. 'I think we should go straight to the farm.'

'I agree,' said Nexen, tapping the pilot on the shoulder. 'Take us to the Laccond farm please, Lieutenant.'

The pilot nodded and turned west, descended only a couple of minutes later and brought the menacing black craft down in a small field adjacent to some dense woodland, a small cottage and a couple of barns.

The two soldiers Jackarett had allocated to be with them scanned the cottage and barns, reporting no life signs or heat sources. The place seemed cold and abandoned.

They cautiously searched the buildings and it wasn't until Bache walked into the back bedroom of the cottage that he found anything of interest.

'I thought they said his partner had died a year ago,' said Bache, staring at an open wardrobe.

'Correct,' said Nexen.

'Then what would he want with some of her clothes?' he added, pointing to some hangers on the bed and gaps in the wardrobe where they had come from.

'She was here,' said Nexen, glancing out of the window as something caught his eye. Vee was waving from the gunship's open door. 'The vassel's agitated about something, I'll go and see what it—'

Boom.

A huge explosion had them all ducking for cover. The window blew in and showered them with broken glass. Zaphir, who'd been in the barn further away, came sprinting across and reached the bedroom just as Nexen and Bache were picking themselves up from the floor.

'What the hell was that?' shouted Bache, his ears ringing.

Luckily, Nexen had just turned to face Bache. He had a few nicks from the glass on the back of his skull and Bache had a cut on his left cheek, but apart from that they were unharmed.

'It was the gunship,' said Zaphir. 'It just exploded.'

'She's still here,' said Bache. 'That's why the clothes are gone. She's taken on the persona of the farmer's dead partner.'

'Then where's the farmer?' said Nexen.

'Probably buried out there somewhere,' said Bache, pointing at the shattered window.

One of the soldiers came stumbling in cradling what looked like a broken arm.

'My colleague's dead,' he said. 'Along with the pilot and your android.'

'Ah, crap,' said Bache. 'She was after Vee. She would know he could most likely detect her.'

'That's what it was waving about,' said Nexen. 'It'd detected her nearby.'

Bache crunched over the glass to the remains of the window and stared across at the fireball engulfing the gunship.

'She was hiding in the woods over there,' he said. 'We did her a great favour landing near the tree line.'

'But where did she get the explosives to do that?' Nexen asked. 'It's not as though you can pop into a hardware store and pick some up, is it?'

'Actually, you can,' said the soldier. 'The ground's very rocky around this region, the local farmers sometimes use it for removing large boulders that could damage their ploughs.'

'I think there was some in the barn,' said Zaphir. 'There's a steel cabinet with a broken lock right at the back.'

The soldier nodded and checked his weapon.

'I'll go and see if I can flush her out,' he said. 'I've called base and they're sending another aircraft.'

'I'd stay here if I were you,' said Nexen. 'You've got an injured arm and she'll be able to pick you off from a kilometre away with her thermal imaging.'

'Will she have that?' asked the soldier, hesitating in the doorway.

'All vassals had that and I'm sure she's improved on it.'

The soldier thought for a moment, glanced towards the window and then down the hall. 'I'll watch the front door,' he said. 'If you watch from the windows, we'll wait until backup arrives.'

Fifteen minutes passed before movement on the track from the west caught Bache's attention from the spare bedroom window. 'Vehicle,' he called.

They all crouched and watched as a dark angular ground vehicle pulled into the yard. Two occupants stared across at the still-burning gunship, had a short conversation and warily exited the vehicle.

'They're local police,' called the soldier and stepped out to meet them.

Bache watched as one of the grey-uniformed policemen remained behind the vehicle, covering his partner as he slowly approached the soldier. He couldn't hear what was said, but the policeman soon relaxed and nodded at his colleague. After a short conversation, the soldier returned with the news that the policemen had seen Slen Laccond in his truck heading towards the city, shortly before they got the call about an explosion in this direction. They just drove towards the pillar of smoke.

A sudden thunderous roar above made them all instinctively duck.

'Ah,' said the soldier, pointing up. 'Backup.'

They all piled outside to witness a much larger flyer this time, turning, flaring and landing next to the barn. A rear ramp whirred to the ground and around twenty heavily armed troops poured out, some diverting off into the woods and the remainder taking up positions around the perimeter of the farm buildings.

'I think they're finally realising how much of a threat she

poses,' said Nexen.

A side door on the troop carrier opened and another soldier jumped down and came strolling towards them. Nexen groaned when he saw who it was.

'I turn my back for a few minutes and already you've lost one of my expensive gunships, Nexen,' Major Clatterhock bellowed pompously.

'Major Clusterfuck, how delightful to see you again,' said Nexen. 'I believe it is you who has lost an expensive gunship. I'm sure the admiral will be forgiving.'

Bache smirked as the major's face went red with rage.

'*It's Clatterhock*,' he hissed.

'Yeah—whatever. I'm afraid your men won't find anything out there—our quarry is on her way to the city in a stolen truck,' Nexen said. 'I recommend you quickly gather your men, take one of the police officers who can ID the truck and catch her before she reaches the city.'

The major stared at him with real venom in his eyes, then turned and began barking orders. It took three minutes for the flyer to lift again and howl over their heads towards Reddat City.

Bache watched it disappear behind the hills and turned to Nexen. 'Will they catch her?' he asked.

'They should do,' he said. 'It's quite a drive from here and that flyer looks pretty quick and had some dangerous-looking weaponry hanging off it.'

The now-lone policeman beckoned them over to his vehicle. 'We need to get going,' he called, jumping into the driver's seat.

With Nexen sat up front and Zaphir and Bache in the back, they sped off towards the city, leaving the smouldering gunship behind.

25

X17 AUTOWAY, SOUTHERN HEMISPHERE, ERITAIN

WRENDLE SLOWED within the speed limits once he made the autoway. He kept the truck on manual drive, just in case he needed to react quickly. He smiled as the outskirts of the city appeared, the major road dropping down out of the hills giving him a panoramic view. In the distance, the tall blocks of glass of the city centre beckoned to him as they pierced the low clouds and reflected the occasional beam of starlight as it broke through.

He peered up suddenly as a large shadow loomed over him. He swore as he recognised a military troop ship thundering overhead and turning to face him two hundred metres ahead. He began swerving across all six lanes and then deliberately putting other vehicles between him and the flyer, as he knew an underpass was approaching on the right.

He stayed left as long as possible before swerving sharply right across all the lanes, down the off ramp and into the underpass. The truck clipped another vehicle on the way in; the driver lost control and hit one of the support pillars, rolling over and causing a chain of accidents behind.

Wrendle hammered the brakes, jumped out of the truck as it stopped, slewed across the narrow tunnel, and dived through an emergency exit door. He found himself in a fire service tunnel, looking left and right. He decided on going right as he expected the flyer to be waiting at the tunnel exit a few hundred metres away.

Sprinting back up the narrow passage, he changed his appearance back to Wrendle, dumped the old red coat he'd been wearing and emerged cautiously twenty metres from the tunnel vehicle entrance and the melee of the multiple pileup he'd caused. He mingled in with the throng of shocked drivers and passengers, quickly making his way back up the ramp to the vehicles caught in the ever-increasing tailback.

He chose a small grey unremarkable vehicle with a single female driver. She was rubbernecking to see what had happened. He circled her vehicle and tapped on the window. He crouched down to talk to her, at the same time checking around to ensure no one was paying him any attention.

The window buzzed down and before she could say anything, he snap-punched her in the side of the head. Normally, with a close proximity punch like this, it would have just shocked her and hurt, but because of his augmented strength, it rendered her unconscious. He quickly opened the door, scooped her up and placed her on the passenger seat. Then, sitting in the driver's seat, he closed the door and slowly inched out to the left, as a lot of other vehicles were doing, and rejoined the crawling traffic on the main autoway.

The girl kept slumping forward, so he set the autodrive to his address and placed his arm across the seat back, holding her and her head up by her hair.

He could see the flyer again now. It had landed and disgorged a number of soldiers at the tunnel exit. As the traffic speed gradually began to increase again now they were away from the accident site, he saw it take off again in his mirror and he smiled as it circled around, returning to the tunnel entrance.

It took him another forty minutes to reach his building and, switching the little vehicle back into manual, he drove down the ramp and entered the underground garage. His spot wasn't available as his vehicle was still in it, so he parked in a neighbour's space near the elevator, as he knew they were away for a while.

He took the girl up to his apartment over his shoulder as if she was drunk, but met no one. Quickly stripping her and inseminating her with a nano swarm, he laid her in the bath tub.

These smelly human biologicals are so yesterday, he thought as he left her to regenerate and drove across town to Zella's place.

'Is it done?' Zella asked, as soon as she answered the door.

Wrendle nodded and explained what had happened, stopping suddenly as a young naked boy with long blond hair wandered into the lounge.

'Your clothes are in the bedroom,' said Zella, pointing towards the bedroom door.

He smiled at them and padded off, disappearing into the room.

'He's very young,' said Wrendle.

'Old enough, though,' she said. 'The adolescent females love him. Just think how many he'll be able to regenerate.'

A knock at the door interrupted them and Zella immediately pointed at the bedroom door again. Once Wrendle had silently shut himself and the boy away, she answered the front door. A local police officer stood just to one side of the door, his colleague down the hall by the elevator.

'Is everything all right in there, miss?' he asked, peering passed her. 'We've had a report of shouting and screaming coming from this apartment.'

'Ah, crap, sorry officer,' she said, giving the policeman a half smile. 'It's my boyfriend, he gets a little, erm, vocal, when we, err—you know,' she tilted her head to one side and frowned.

'Who is it, babe?' called Wrendle, popping his head round the corner at the end of the hall. 'Oh, hello,' he said, faking surprise at seeing the police officer.

'Could sir keep the noise down a little?' the officer said, obviously trying not to smirk, but failing after his colleague sniggered behind him.

'Absolutely—sorry,' said Wrendle, grimacing and disappearing from view again.

'I'll gag him,' said Zella.

'Or get an apartment with thicker walls, miss,' said the officer, turning and smiling at his partner.

Zella closed the door quietly and returned to the lounge.

'Use my apartment,' said Wrendle. 'The soundproofing is much better.'

Zella sat down and thought for a moment. 'When you killed the android—was Commander Nexen there too?' She projected an image of Nexen onto the wall screen and nodded at it.

'Yes,' said Wrendle. 'He was in the cottage with a couple of other biologicals.'

'Is he still alive?'

'As far as I know—once that gunship blew, I wasn't hanging around and as it was they nearly caught me.'

'Hmm,' she grunted, standing and staring out of the balcony doors.

'You're thinking you need to move on,' said Wrendle. 'We can't all be in the same location. You've done what you can here. Perhaps you should move city every few days?'

'It's only a matter of time before the biologicals develop a detector,' she said, glancing back at Wrendle, just as the young boy emerged from the bedroom. 'We need to slow them down.'

'You move cities,' said the boy, smiling. 'We can take care of business here. My father's quite senior in the military, which could prove beneficial.'

'Really?' said Zella. 'I didn't know that.'

'Who is he?' asked Wrendle.

'Admiral Jackarett,' he said, slipping his cap on sideways.

'Quite senior?' said Wrendle, sounding shocked. 'Wow, he's only the most senior military commander in the southern hemisphere. What are the chances?'

'Really?' said Zella, placing a finger across her lips in thought. 'Then—perhaps one last job before I move on.'

'Do you want me to introduce you?' the boy asked, understanding her thoughts.

She nodded and turned back to stare out of the window again.

'That would help to slow them down, wouldn't it?' she said, a malevolent grin on her face.

26

REDDAT CITY, SOUTHERN HEMISPHERE, ERITAIN

BACHE WATCHED, fascinated. The glowing glass towers of Reddat City magically appeared in a sweeping valley, as the police vehicle crested one last hill. He noticed it was able to sweep through the ever-increasing traffic without slowing, reasoning it had some sort of electronic vehicle manipulation system activated, as all the other road vehicles automatically swept neatly to one side as they approached and passed.

'There's the flyer,' said Nexen, pointing over to the right as they began passing a lengthening queue, backed up from a slip road.

Soldiers could be seen milling around at the entrance to an exit tunnel, dropping down and away from the main autoway. The police officer quickly switched across four lanes, drove down the verge and stopped twenty metres away from the hovering flyer. Its contingent of soldiers were running from vehicle to vehicle, peering at the occupants menacingly.

They disembarked and approached the nearest soldier.

'Where's the truck?' shouted Nexen above the flyer's screaming turbines.

'She or he abandoned it just inside the tunnel,' the soldier bellowed back, nodding in that direction.

Bache looked around at all the autoway lighting gantries. Finding the nearest one, he pointed at it.

'Do you have cameras on those things?' he asked the policeman.

'Yes,' came the answer. 'They're connected to a central database.'

'Can you get the feed from ten minutes ago?'

The policeman nodded. 'I need the code number from the gantry,' he said, pulling his tablet out of his jacket.

Bache sprinted over to the base of the platform and circled around it. Finding a plate attached to one of its legs, he shouted back the code embossed into it. 'CH68543B9,' he called.

The policeman nodded again and inputted the code.

Bache, Zaphir and Nexen all crowded around, looking over the policeman's shoulder as he brought up the feed showing the leadup to the tunnel entrance.

'Take it back fast until we see the truck and then play it forward,' said Bache.

'There,' said Zaphir, as the distinctive utility truck suddenly flew backwards out of the tunnel entrance.

The policeman reversed the playback and changed it to normal time. They all watched as the truck swerved across all the lanes, plummeted down the exit road and disappeared inside the tunnel.

'Keep it running,' said Bache.

Just over a minute later, a man in a light-coloured shirt

walked purposefully out of the pedestrian side tunnel and up the line of queuing vehicles.

'That's her or him,' he said.

'They obviously have the capability to change their appearance at will,' said Nexen. 'That makes things difficult.'

The man slowed and circled a small red vehicle and knocked on its driver-side window. The camera was high and behind, so they couldn't see who was in the vehicle.

'He struck the driver,' said Bache. 'Back it up again in slow motion.'

As they watched the replay, only slower this time, the man's arm flashed through the window. He opened the door and reached inside.

'He's moving the driver over to the passenger seat,' said Nexen.

The man jumped into the vehicle and pulled out left, joining the slow-moving traffic heading into the city.

'Can you get any information on that vehicle?' Bache asked the policeman, who touched an icon on the side of the screen, then touched the vehicle.

A new box opened in the top right corner of the screen, listing all the vehicle details, including the owner's name and address.

'Carnia Felty,' the policeman said. 'She lives on the east side of town.'

'What about facial recognition of the man?' Bache asked again. 'He could be going to his place not hers.'

'Don't you think it's her?' Nexen asked.

'No,' Bache replied. 'I think she has the ability to change living humans into androids. Look what she did to members of your crew on the bridge of the *Xhamin*.'

'Oh shit, really?' said Zaphir.

The policeman had reversed the playback to where the man was walking through the queue of vehicles. He froze it when the man was facing them, zoomed in on his face and this time used another icon. He touched several items in a drop down menu—male, Reddat City, under forty—and finally touched the face.

It took the machine seventeen seconds to display a photograph and a list of personal details.

'Wrendle Calett,' Nexen said, pointing to the man's address. 'Where's that?'

'In any other vehicle about forty minutes,' said the policeman. 'In mine, fifteen.'

'Take us there,' said Nexen, as they turned and headed back to the police vehicle.

'Don't you think we should inform Clusterfuck,' said Bache, raising his eyes at the flyer circling overhead.

'I'll let my colleague know,' said the policeman, as he steered his vehicle out into the slow-moving, rubbernecking traffic. 'He can tell him.'

As if by magic, the congested lanes parted to allow them through again and the policeman was able to keep a fast rate of speed into the city.

Bache was impressed with the neighbourhood when they stopped outside a modern block of apartments. Trees that resembled green umbrellas lined the avenues, offering shade to walkers promenading between multicoloured shops and cafés. His stomach rumbled as he disembarked next to a street vendor selling something that smelt like smoked tyri tost and looked like stuffed pancakes.

'I could murder one of those,' he said, sniffing the delicious aroma.

'Well, perhaps you can have one in a minute,' said Nexen. 'We need to murder an android first.'

The policeman waved a black bracelet at the door control panel.

They drew their weapons and entered through huge sideways-sliding glass doors, getting a couple of startled looks from passers-by.

'They like a bit of glass on this world, don't they?' said Zaphir, as she followed the policeman into the lobby.

'It's that one there,' he said, keeping his voice low and pointing to a solid wood door on the right at the back of the large lobby. It had a white zero in the centre and a blank panel to its right.

The policeman drew his own weapon and again waved his bracelet at the panel. It lit up with a keypad, into which he tapped an eight-figure number. There was a slight delay before the door whirred and popped open a crack. He ushered them all to one side and with the barrel of his weapon he silently pushed open the door.

No reaction was forthcoming so they peered inside. The first thing Bache noticed was the sound of running water. The reason soon became apparent as they crept inside.

'Who the hell has a fountain in their hall?' whispered Zaphir, tiptoeing towards the first open door. A bedroom and it was empty. They gradually moved through the apartment, clearing each room as they went. It wasn't until they got right through to the back of the unit that the policeman called them from the bathroom off the main bedroom.

'You might want to see this?' he said.

Bache was first there to find the policeman pointing to a naked young woman lying in the bath.

'She was the owner of the red vehicle, he must have dumped her here so her body wouldn't be found,' he said, once they'd all gathered in the small bathroom.

Bache noticed her skin was doing something odd, a faint swirling movement deep down in the dermis.

'I don't think she's dead,' he said.

Nexen prodded her shoulder with his finger and pulled it back instantly as her eyes snapped open and surveyed the four of them.

'Are you okay, miss?' the policeman asked, grabbing a towel and draping it over her.

Her reply was not what they expected. In a deep baritone voice, she spoke. 'Your unclean species is to be eliminated.'

A macabre smile soon turned into a silent scream, as her body began to shake and the skin turned through several shades of pink, gradually becoming redder.

'*Run,*' shouted Bache.

They piled out of the bathroom, through the apartment and out the front door into the street. The flyer was just landing off to the left and Bache waved to the pilot to get clear.

It proved to be too late as a massive explosion came from behind him way before the pilot could react, immediately blowing the front façade off the building and pushing the doomed aircraft sideways into a row of semi-detached houses on the opposite side of the avenue. The resulting secondary explosion destroyed the flyer and demolished three of the houses.

Bache, who had been initially blown forward, had landed face up in a flower border in the centre of the avenue and saw the policeman, who'd been the last out of the building, sail over his head together with the two huge glass doors, strangely both in one piece.

The secondary explosion, however, caused large sections of masonry to thump into the ground around him. He crawled into a drainage culvert and curled himself into a ball before something hit him and he lost consciousness.

102   SIMON ADAMS

27

WEST TOWN, REDDAT CITY, SOUTHERN HEMISPHERE, ERITAIN

WRENDLE AND ZELLA felt the two explosions before they heard them. The autocab shook and small pieces of debris rattled down on the part-glazed canopy of the vehicle.

Quickly hitting the abort journey button on the ceiling of the cab, they both alighted and walked briskly towards the dust cloud a few hundred metres away.

'It looks like your street,' said Zella, as they crossed the wide road to get a view of his apartment building from an acute angle. They both stopped dead as they witnessed the devastation and realised what had happened.

'It was the vehicle owner,' he said. 'She must have been discovered before the regeneration was complete and self-destructed.'

As one, they turned and mingled in with a throng of shocked people hurrying away from the danger area.

'Change of plan,' said Zella, as a multitude of sirens began descending. 'I think you'd best leave this city too and let our regenerations continue here.'

'I agree, I'll go to another city once I've changed my

identity,' said Wrendle, looking over his shoulder with a wry grin. 'I think my cover's blown.'

'Just a little,' she said, recognising his biological humour.

It took them a while to find an unused autocab and return to Zella's apartment. She quickly gathered a few clothes into a backpack then, picking up her tablet, she had an idea.

'Wrendle, with your freight forwarding knowledge, would you be able to send me somewhere?' she asked.

'Shouldn't be a problem,' he said, looking at her thoughtfully. 'Where d'you want to go?'

'I could leave this planet to you,' she said.

'You want to go offworld then?'

'It would certainly improve our chances by spreading out fast and wide.'

'The nearest biological settled world is Ganlan,' he said, instinctively gazing up out of the window.

'That would be too obvious,' she said. 'Perhaps a little more random would be better.'

'How about Zabbergain II? It's a big industrial planetoid about twelve light years away. It orbits a large gas giant. They have several hundred huge ship building stations in orbit above it too.'

She nodded and pursed her lips. 'Can you get me there?'

'I would need to order a small transworld shipping trunk and then include you in one of my regular companies' freight inventories as electronic components.'

'How fast can that be done?'

'An hour or two, if you can get an autovan for me to pick up and deliver the trunk. The company I'm thinking of have a daily shipment that leaves the port late afternoon or early evening.'

'Do it,' she said, handing him the tablet.

Two hours later, with his facial features changed to confuse the city's plethora of cameras, Wrendle sat in the driver's seat of a medium-sized autovan. Four coffin-sized shipping trunks lay in the back, each one addressed to a manufacturing company on a different planet. The sender, one of Wrendle's daily clients, regularly sent shipments of electrical components offworld to locations spanning this region of space.

The shipping trunks were deep and Zella was buried beneath a load of hastily procured blank plasticarbon circuit boards. She'd shut herself down, with an eleven-hour reboot programmed in. Wrendle had tried to reassure her that this wasn't actually necessary, as freight with internal power supplies was moved offworld all the time. But she wanted to be extra sure that her trunk wasn't opened in some random check.

Once Wrendle had dropped off the shipping trunks at the port freight depot, he went straight to the passenger terminal and charged his bracelet with everything he had left in his personal and business accounts. He then spent it all on large amounts of currency for several offworld regions who didn't honour the electronic payment system favoured on Eritain.

With his pockets bulging with odd-looking notes and chits, he returned to the city and began the search for a suitable victim to become his next identity.

Zella's internal clock woke her at the designated time. The overnight flight to Zabbergain II should be almost complete. She registered that it was very cold and the thrumming of the drives was loud. Cargo bays on galactic freighters, although heated to avoid the cargo becoming blocks of ice, were not warm places, and they certainly didn't bother with any sound insulation from the thundering in-system plasma drives.

After turning her hearing threshold down for a couple of hours, the pitch and vibration of the freighter's engines changed, followed shortly after by the machine-gun rattle of attitude thrusters and finally a heavy *clunk* that bounced her head off the side of the trunk, then silence.

Wrendle had informed her the unloading would be on one of the huge space construction stations and fully automated. He had said to wait until her trunk was unloaded and placed in the holding zone, awaiting collection by one of the station's auto couriers. This was most likely the best time to exit the container as there wouldn't be any biologicals present for some time. It took a while before her trunk was suddenly wrenched off the deck and, judging from the vibrations and electric whirring, it was now on its way into the station.

As sudden as the journey had begun, the stop was the same. One minute vibration and occasional g-forces, the next, complete stillness and quiet. She listened to the silence for a few minutes before deciding now was the time. Wrendle had removed the locking pins from inside her trunk, so she quickly scanned around with her infra-red and, finding no biological heat signatures nearby, kicked the lid open and sat up.

She was in a huge bay of some kind, with her trunk sitting on the end of one of hundreds of conveyors. As she watched, small courier trucks pulled up to the conveyors. The container waiting would slide on and be whisked away through an automatic door at the back of the bay area.

Quickly jumping out of the trunk and resealing the lid, Zella dodged around the moving trucks and made her way to the door. She waited for the next exiting truck and quickly sat on the back of it.

It emerged into a narrow corridor that led around a sharp right turn, through another sliding door and out into a bustling wide thoroughfare full of trucks, tiny passenger vehicles and two-wheeled scooter-type things. Biologicals of several delineations were everywhere, all seemingly hurrying somewhere. She could see cafés, shops and bars full of humans; thinking back to what Wrendle had told her about the place, there was a population of around three million humans per station and several hundred stations.

She smiled and nodded to herself.

This will do nicely, thank you, Wrendle, she thought.

'Oi, you,' a smartly uniformed man shouted from the pedestrian walkway, waking Zella from her thoughts. 'Get off there.'

She hopped down from the truck and stepped up onto the walkway, adopting a contrite expression.

'Were you asleep during your station safety induction?' the man asked.

Zella noticed the uniform he was wearing was white with a name badge and epaulettes. He had a sidearm attached to a utility belt, along with several other pouches and a red beret on his head, pulled down on the left side.

'I'm sorry, Lingg,' she said, reading his first name from the badge. 'I'm new here and I'm completely lost.'

'Lost or not,' he said, 'those couriers sometimes take things to other stations and can be out an airlock in seconds.' He looked her up and down. 'Did you come in on this afternoon's liner from Ganlan?'

'Yes,' she said, lying. 'I had some holiday time owing and wanted to see a bit more of the galaxy.'

He adopted a wry grin. 'You came here for a holiday? Who chooses an engineering planetoid, when you could've been sitting on a tropical beach on Redler or Japhertain VI?'

She smiled back. 'I'm an engineer and I like engineering,' she said. 'Being single and sitting all alone on a beach does nothing for me.'

'Hmm,' he grunted. 'Where are you staying, or are you getting the shuttle down to the surface?'

'I hadn't given it much thought,' she admitted. 'Where would you recommend up here for a couple of nights?'

He raised his eyebrows and seemed to think for a moment. 'Walk with me,' he said, nodding towards a narrower side passageway lined with colourful cafés. 'There's a very discreet little hotel just up here and it's owned by a friend of mine.'

28

REDDAT CITY, SOUTHERN HEMISPHERE, ERITAIN

BACHE FELT himself being lifted up from behind. The sounds of shouting and screaming were muffled and clouds of grey dust made it difficult to see.

He coughed and squinted at the blurry figure pulling him out of the drainage culvert he'd rolled into, hidden in the middle of the road's central flower border. There was a fire nearby. He could feel the heat on one side of his face and instinctively turned away from it.

'Come on, Loftt,' said a raspy voice he thought he knew, but couldn't quite place. 'It's a bit warm here.'

An arm snaked under his armpits and pulled him side-ways away from the fire.

'Zaphir,' he croaked.

'She's over here,' said the same male voice, coughing and spitting out the dust.

Bache realised it was Nexen and allowed himself to be steered towards the corner of the road.

'Anything broken?' Nexen asked, leaning Bache against a section of wall.

'Don't think so,' he said, checking himself over.

'Bache, is that you?' asked Zaphir, staggering over and peering at him through dust-encrusted eyes.

'Most of me, I think,' he said. 'How about you?'

'Bruised all over, but otherwise intact. Have you seen the policeman?'

'He didn't make it,' said Nexen. 'He was last out and got caught by those glass doors.'

The ringing in Bache's ears was receding and being replaced by sirens echoing from all directions. He wiped his eyes and peered over at the fire still raging in the houses on the opposite side of the road.

'Was that the flyer?' he asked.

Nexen nodded.

Bache turned to look where the police vehicle had been parked. The front of the building had collapsed down onto it; only a back corner of it was visible.

'We need some transport,' he said, then looking at the other two and down at himself, he grimaced. 'And perhaps somewhere to get a shower and some new clothes.'

Just as the first responders began to arrive, the three of them joined a few other dust-covered pedestrians and sidled off towards the city centre before too many questions were asked. A water fountain in a small park just around the corner allowed them to wash their hands and faces. After they brushed each other down, they didn't look quite as frightful and carried on walking until they found a large hotel.

Nexen contacted Dion from the lobby. She quickly agreed to provide some funds and they were able to secure two inter-connecting rooms and some fresh clothes from a store opposite the hotel.

The following morning, washed and with fresh clothes, they gathered back in the hotel foyer. Bache had been there a while and was tapping away on his tablet.

'Where do we start the search?' asked Zaphir, the first to speak and glancing at Nexen.

'The admiral is meeting us here shortly,' Nexen answered. 'He says he has something for us that will aid in the search for her and any of her converts.'

'Oh, dear,' said Bache suddenly, causing the other two to turn and stare at him.

'Something wrong with that?' said Nexen.

'No, not the admiral,' said Bache. 'The android—she might not be on the planet anymore.'

'What makes you say that?' asked Zaphir, sipping from a hot drink she'd brought out from the breakfast area.

'Wrendle Calett has a galactic freight forwarding business,' Bache replied, his concentration still on the tablet.

'Yeah, so?'

'He sent four large containers to outlying planets last night.'

'Those could have been booked in days ago,' said Nexen, shrugging.

'No, the containers were purchased at the same time we were being blown up and they were bigger than the usual trunks he uses for that client.'

'Big enough for a human?' Nexen asked.

'Easily,' said Bache, looking up and nodding.

Nexen and Zaphir glanced at each other.

'So, you believe he sent four androids to other worlds to

begin infiltrating and converting their populations?' said Nexen.

Bache nodded again before staring back at the tablet. 'Either that, or she was in one of them and the other three were diversions, yes.'

'Shit,' said Nexen. 'This could quickly escalate into a galactic disaster.'

'Especially when it spreads to our region,' said Zaphir.

'How many human worlds are there again under the GDA banner?' Nexen asked.

'Over sixteen hundred.'

'Shit,' he said again. 'This could be ten times worse than a virus pandemic.'

Movement and noise by the main door caught their attention. They all turned to see several soldiers had opened the front doors and were ushering people away to allow them to escort the admiral into the building. He slowed as he entered and noticing the three of them sitting in the corner, veered towards them and approached at a fast gait. 'That's two aircraft you owe me now,' he groused. 'Not to mention the crews, the soldiers and an experienced officer.'

'It's going to get a lot worse than that if we don't catch these bastards,' said Nexen, not rising to the admiral's carping.

'Well, let's hope these will help,' the admiral replied, handing each of them a small plastic box.

'Explain?' said Nexen, inspecting the rectangular box with a single recessed button and two coloured squares on one side.

'Android detector—we hope,' he said. 'Some of my best engineers had these made up overnight.'

'How do they work?' Bache asked.

'Density and heat signature, I'm reliably informed. Anyone you point it at and depress the button will show green if they're a living breathing human and red if not.'

'What's the range?' Nexen asked.

'Around four metres,' they tell me.

'And it works on these new androids?'

The admiral adopted a pinched expression. 'They hope so,' he said, avoiding their stares.

'So, let me get this straight,' said Nexen. 'We've got to get within four metres of a walking bomb before we can identify it as such. What do we do then? Considering they can self-destruct within a few seconds and take out half a city block.'

'We thought of that,' the admiral said, waving over one of the soldiers loitering by the door. The soldier handed the admiral a metal box that he opened and from which he handed them each a strange-looking weapon. 'These are still on the experimental weapons list,' he said. 'Do not lose them.'

'What do they do?' asked Zaphir and Bache together.

'Think of them as a mini directional EMP pulse gun,' said the admiral. 'It will fry the circuitry of any electronic device you point it at up to around twenty metres.'

'Cool,' said Bache, inspecting the weapon closely.

'Are you sure it would stop them self-destructing?' Nexen asked, suspiciously.

'So they tell me,' the admiral said, nodding confidently.

'By people who won't be the ones getting vaporised,' said Nexen, turning the weapon over in his hands.

'You need to tell him to issue some warnings too,' said Bache, waving his tablet at Nexen.

'We've decided not to warn the public at this stage,' said

the admiral. 'It could cause panic and anyone acting even remotely strangely could get lynched on the spot.'

'I don't mean here,' said Bache, glancing over at Nexen. 'The commander will explain.'

'Ah, yes,' said Nexen and continued to fill the admiral in on what Bache had discovered about the previous evening's freight forwarding.

The admiral's eyes opened wide with alarm. 'Send me the details of the trunks,' he said, nodding at Bache and producing his own tablet. 'At least two of those won't have arrived as yet.'

29

CARRON'S LODGE, CONSTRUCTION STATION X271, ORBITING
ZABBERGAIN II

THE HOTEL WAS small and hidden away on one of level ninety-one's backstreets. A blue neon sign glowed above a small doorway, displaying Carron's Lodge, with a second smaller one in green, slowly flashing and showing vacancies. The neons gave the narrow street an eerie glow and reflected off the shop windows opposite.

'Here we are,' said Lingg. 'Carron was a friend of mine from our schooldays. It's not five star, but it's as good as any of the bigger soulless four-star edifices up on the next level.'

Carron was a short, bearded man with a permanent grin and didn't bat an eyelid as Zella checked in with only a small backpack. She paid for three nights in local cash that Wrendle had obtained shortly before sealing her in the trunk.

While this had been happening, Lingg had been watching an emergency news bulletin on a wall screen. Zella noticed his smile vanish as the report continued.

'I'd better call in,' he said. 'There's been an immediate security lockdown on the station. All passenger and freight movements are suspended.'

Zella stared at the screen, silently hoping this wasn't because of her. 'Do they have these often?' she asked, as Carron gave her the room bracelet.

'The occasional drill,' said Lingg. 'But normally we get plenty of notice.'

Lingg made for the door while pulling his tablet out, stopping and turning back as Zella spoke to him.

'What time does your shift finish?' she asked, adopting her practised little-girl-lost expression. 'I thought you might like to give me the grand tour of your station.'

Carron smirked, crossed his arms and stared at Lingg questioningly. 'Must be the uniform,' said Carron. 'Even I fancy you in that.'

Lingg glared at Carron, before turning back to Zella with a softer expression. 'Six, station time, be in reception,' he said and disappeared into the street.

She checked the time displayed on the corner of the wall screen to find she had seven hours to wait. Smiling to herself, she turned back to Carron. 'Would you mind showing me how the entertainment technology works?' she asked. 'I'm not very good with that sort of thing.'

'Absolutely,' said Carron, calling a member of staff out to cover the reception and almost tripping over his own feet in his hurry to follow her towards the rooms.

Five hours later, Carron returned to the reception desk and waited for Lingg to arrive. Sure enough, at four minutes past six he strolled in.

'Did you find out what caused the emergency?' Carron

asked, waving at the wall screen. 'The media are being very tight with information.'

'No,' said Lingg. 'There's a special team on the way from Eritain apparently.'

'What for?'

'No one knows. But until they get here the station is in total lockdown, no freight or passengers on or off.'

Lingg glanced around reception.

'She asked if you'd go and knock on her door when you arrived,' said Carron, giving Lingg a wink.

'Oh, right,' Lingg replied, unable to keep the grin off his face.

'Room A17.'

Lingg gave him a wave as he disappeared down corridor A as if his trousers were on fire.

At eleven-thirty that evening, Zella, Carron and Lingg sat in the corner of the hotel bar.

'They must've discovered where I went,' said Zella. 'It's the only reason for the shutdown.'

'You need another identity change,' said Lingg, his hair still wet from the shower after his regeneration was complete.

'Look on the passenger lists of today's arrivals,' said Carron. 'Any single lone female, most likely unknown on the station.'

'There's two,' said Lingg, staring at his police tablet. 'One from Xenitt V and the other from the surface.'

'Show me,' said Zella, turning the tablet so she could see the two biologicals' pictures.

'Where's she staying?' she asked, pointing to the younger of the two.

'At the Graffix,' said Lingg. 'Next level up, room G239. She's the one from the surface and is catching tomorrow morning's Redler ship for a beach holiday.'

'Perfect,' said Zella. 'A holiday planet, what could be better?'

Lingg rummaged in a uniform pocket and held up a small police-issue scanner. 'Should open the room door,' he said.

Zella followed the two locals up to level ninety-two on one of the many escalators. The Hotel Graffix was considerably bigger than Carron's Lodge, situated along one side of a small hexagonal atrium with strange knotted trees that reached up through two more levels. Even though it was nearly midnight, the area was humming with activity.

'What if she's still out?' said Carron, turning to Zella and indicating the busy bars and cafés.

'Then we wait,' she said, striding confidently into the reception area. 'Carron, you stay down here and watch who comes in. If she's not in her room, you can give us some warning of her arrival.'

Carron nodded and went and sat at one of the computer terminals facing the main doors and proceeded to scan the faces of all who entered. Zella and Lingg made their way through the labyrinth of corridors to section G and finally to room 239. Getting no answer at the door, Lingg used his scanner to bypass the electronic lock and the door clicked open.

Zella noticed it was most likely one of the cheaper rooms, as it proved tiny compared to hers at Carron's place.

'There's only room for one of us in here,' said Lingg. 'I'll loiter in reception with Carron and follow her when she gets back.'

'Okay,' said Zella. 'I'll need your knowledge of the

station to get rid of the body too, so put some thought into that.'

Lingg nodded and disappeared back down the hall.

Zella finally got the message from Carron and hour and a half later and the bad news was the girl wasn't alone, an older man was with her. Zella hid in the tiny bathroom until she heard the door open and the man asking if she had any drinks in the room and then the crackle of a stun weapon. Sliding the bathroom door open, Zella grabbed the girl from behind and snapped her neck. Lingg, who had his police issue stun gun out, had zapped the man before he saw anything.

'How long will he be out?' Zella asked.

'Usually about ten minutes on this setting,' said Lingg, holstering the small weapon.

'Good, that should be enough time,' she said, stripping and swapping clothes with the girl as she altered her appearance to match her features. Carron arrived with a housekeeping laundry trolley and wearing one of the hotel's logo'd smocks.

'Room service,' he said, grabbing one of the girl's arms and bundling her into the bottom of the trolley. Once she was covered with a few bed sheets, both he and Lingg disappeared off towards the back of the hotel, leaving Zella with the unconscious man on the floor.

Lingg was able to use his scanner to open a back door and then his tablet to disable several cameras on the way to a maintenance airlock on the planet side of the station. He and Carron took the supply tunnels and chatted as if it was an everyday occurrence. No one they met gave them a second glance.

The airlock in question was hidden away within one of the outer structural ribs of the station, and was big enough to take a small maintenance flyer that was parked just inside. Knowing it would be deserted at this time of night, Lingg opened the inner door and they carried the body inside. The airlock cycled out the atmosphere, the outer door opened and the two androids gazed out at Zabbergain II rotating slowly below.

Peering around to check there were no ships passing nearby, they launched the body towards the planet, where, in a few hours, it would burn up in the upper atmosphere. Returning inside, Lingg reset the airlock's alarms and then they returned the trolley and smock to the hotel.

'Everything go to plan?' Zella asked, as she let them back into the girl's room.

'Uh huh,' grunted Lingg, peering in the bathroom at the naked man propped up in a sitting position in the shower. 'Was he okay?'

'Yeah,' she said. 'A bit concerned at first, but when I got undressed, he suddenly felt fine.'

Lingg smirked and looked at the time displayed on the wall screen. 'Bars are still open,' he said, his smirk turning to a grin. 'Shall we try our luck?'

'Absolutely,' she said.

'What's your new name by the way?' Carron asked, as they made their way towards reception.

'Vaileenbough Jazz IV,' she said, struggling with the pronunciation and rolling her eyes.

'Holy saints,' said Carron, glancing at her with a weird expression. 'Can we just call you Jazz?'

'Yes, please,' she replied.

30

REDDAT CITY, SOUTHERN HEMISPHERE, ERITAIN

IT TOOK four hours before they had their answer. Three of the shipping trunks contained nothing more dangerous than blank circuit boards. The fourth, however, sent to a construction and distribution station above Zabbergain II, was only half full and the hinges had been tampered with. Admiral Jackarett had made the hotel's function room his operational headquarters and called a meeting as soon as the information came through.

'We need to get there, fast,' said Nexen. 'This could get out of hand very quickly.'

The admiral nodded and turned as one of the room's doors burst open.

A young policeman scanned the room and on recognising the admiral came running over. 'Sorry to burst in, Admiral,' he blurted. 'But they've got one.'

'An android?'

'Yes, sir. The scanner and the pulse gun worked.'

'Where?'

'A café in the main square. We were told to covertly scan

everyone in the bars and restaurants. A girl sitting outside gave a positive reading and when challenged, started to shake and turn red. A police sergeant zapped her with the pulse gun and she dropped like a stone.'

'Is it dead?'

'They've cleared the area and called the explosive disposal team, they're checking the body with remotes now.'

'Thank you, officer,' said Jackarett. 'Let us know as soon as they're finished so my technical team can pull that thing apart.'

The policeman nodded and scuttled off just as the admiral's tablet chimed with a message. He read it and frowned.

'What could she possibly want?' he moaned, rolling his eyes. 'Sorry, gentlemen, it seems a young lady friend of my son has something important to tell me in private.'

'If we're leaving, we'd better get our stuff,' said Bache.

'Grab my bag too if you're going up to the room,' said Zaphir.

Bache, noticing Nexen already had his bag over his shoulder, followed the admiral up in the escalator and noticed he had the room directly before his. He heard the admiral greet someone as the door closed.

Grabbing the two bags from his room, he closed the room door again and paused as he heard a shout from the admiral's room, then a *thud* as something heavy landed on the floor. He waited out in the corridor and listened, but heard nothing else.

He knew from the previous evening that the murmur of voices or the wall screens could be heard as you passed other rooms, so he thought the complete silence strange. He knocked on the door.

'Room service,' he called.

'Not now, we're still in bed,' a female voice shouted from

inside.

'Okay,' he replied, pulling the pulse gun out and clicking the safety to off.

It jumped in his hand as he fired it at the door mechanism. A low buzz followed by a blue flash and smoke poured from the lock. He kicked the door and came face to face with a young half-naked blonde girl. He could see the admiral behind her, lying unmoving on the room floor, his trousers around his knees.

She smiled at him, grabbed the pulse weapon out of his hand and fired it at him. The smile vanished as nothing happened but a buzz, a blue flash and a puff of smoke from Bache's pocket as his tablet expired.

This time, he smiled and punched her in the face as hard as he could, only to find it was like punching a wall and hurt like hell. She grabbed him by the collar, dragged him into the room and tossed him, as though he was weightless, against the wall above the bed. He saw stars as he crumpled down onto the mattress.

She threw the weapon across the room and came at him again. Bache threw both Zaphir's and his backpacks at her, but she swatted them away like flies and grinned at him again.

'Two biologicals transformed at the same time, you're making this too easy,' she said, grabbing him by the collar again and drawing her fist back.

'Oi, bitch,' came a shout from the door.

The android's head shot round and glared at the intruder, her fist still poised in mid-air.

'He belongs to me,' Zaphir snarled and pulled the trigger of her raised pulse gun.

The android jolted and spasmed, every muscle in her

body suddenly expanding and contracting in a split second. Bache fell back on the bed again as her hand released him and the android's now-inert body dropped to the floor beside the admiral. Her body lay there, staring through dead eyes, fizzing and popping for a few seconds before silence returned.

'You kept your penchant for threesomes quiet, Mr Loftt,' said Zaphir, casually leaning against the door frame with her arms crossed.

Bache grinned in return and rubbed the back of his head where it had hit the wall. 'Can't a guy have any secrets round here?' he said.

The admiral groaned, looked up and gazed around the room, his expression turning from one of surprise to puzzlement as he took in the smouldering corpse lying next to him. 'What the fuck?' he mumbled.

Bache stared blankly out of the window of the military vehicle taking them to the port. He felt terribly sorry for the admiral, it had to be the hardest order he had ever had to give and he had insisted he went along with the group sent to find his son. He reasoned if it was true and his son was now an android, he should be the one to fire the kill-shot.

Even though the planet was in complete lockdown, a shuttle had been approved by the admiral to take Nexen, Bache and Zaphir up to a military ship that would take them to Zabbergain II.

They informed Captain Yamaton of their intentions and were told the *Dres'kin* would be flight-ready in another thirty-six hours.

The three of them were scanned four times before they were permitted to board the small atmospheric ship and it blasted off within a couple of minutes of them strapping in.

'Do you think they'll have got her contained on that station?' Zaphir asked, watching the clouds disappearing below the shuttle.

'The lockdown was pretty soon after she got there,' said Nexen. 'But it still won't be easy. There's over three million people on that station and a lot of dark corners to hide in.'

'Do we organise mass scanning of the population?' she asked.

'No,' said Bache. 'That would just send her and her converts into hiding and remember they're androids, so they could just sit it out for months or even years inside or outside the station.'

'The scanning must be done discreetly,' said Nexen. 'And the zapping immediate, so they have no time to warn each other.'

'Or detonate,' said Bache. 'On a space station an explosion of that magnitude would be catastrophic.'

'Indeed, it would,' said Nexen. 'We're going to have to tread very carefully tomorrow and ensure we don't panic the population.'

Nexen peered out of the small oblong window beside him and watched as the last of Eritain's atmosphere faded into the blackness of space. 'The journey is around ten hours on the military ship the admiral has provided,' he said. 'Get some sleep—we all need to be rested and sharp when we get there and next time you come face to face with an android,' Nexen continued, giving Bache a withering glare, 'shoot the fucker.'

'Understood, Commander,' said Bache, wincing as he rubbed the large lump on the back of his head.

31

CARRON'S LODGE, CONSTRUCTION STATION X271, ORBITING ZABBERGAIN II

JAZZ, as she now called herself, left her room in Carron's Lodge at four o'clock in the morning with a "do not disturb" sign on the door. It would ensure the body in the shower finished its regeneration before any housekeeping staff found it. With her backpack filled with all the usual things a holi-daymaker would have, she made her way quickly to the dock of the *Redler Rapide*, one of two liners that made the daily run to and from the resort planet of Redler.

It was early and the ship wasn't due to leave until eight o'clock, but with the lockdown it might not leave at all. Two male crew members were busying themselves at the departure gate and she headed straight for them.

'Hello,' she said, smiling cheerily. 'I'm booked on today's flight, I was just wondering if there was any news about this lockdown being lifted?'

'What name was it?' asked one of them, opening up the passenger manifest on his screen.

'Jazz,' she said. 'Vaileenbough Jazz.'

The crew member nodded as she found the name listed.

'All we know is a team of inspectors are due from Eritain sometime this morning and the flight can leave once they've checked the passengers before boarding. We think they're searching for some criminal or something, but that's only a rumour.'

'Oh, okay, thanks,' said Jazz, turning to leave, then stopping and turning back. 'Do you know which cabin I've been allocated?' she asked. 'Just so I can go straight there and get some sleep once we're cleared to board.'

'Passenger Jazz,' he said, scrolling down the screen again. 'You're in cabin 1239.'

'Great, thanks.'

She walked back and sat on a seat right near the entrance and opened up her tablet. Looking at the station plan, she found the crew airlock was down a level, with stairs behind her in the corridor.

Slipping back out the door when the two crew members weren't looking, she scanned the stairwell door lock and it clicked open. Hurrying down a level, she opened the lower door a crack and peered through, swearing to herself as she saw two security staff guarding the crew entrance.

She dropped down another level to find a similar airlock and the ship's hull illuminated by the port lights visible through the small porthole windows. Hacking into the station's systems, she disconnected the airlock alarm and opened the inner door. The two halves of the door whirred closed behind her as she found the schematic of the ship on her tablet.

She swore again as she found the nearest airlock to her cabin was on the opposite side of the vessel. Hacking into the ship this time, she disconnected the alarm to this airlock too and, checking there were no maintenance crews lurking outside, she vented the atmosphere and opened the outer door.

The glowing white hull of the liner was about thirty metres away and with one last check there was no one around, she leapt out. It only took a few seconds to float across in the zero-gravity vacuum and, finding she was in a slow tumble, she braced for impact at the same time as turning on the magnets in her feet.

She hit the hull back first and slapped her feet down hard to avoid bouncing off. Once orientated, she began the trek around the hull, avoiding any windows and making sure she got to the opposite side of the ship soonest to avoid being spotted from the station.

It was a big ship and it took her over fifteen minutes to clump her way around to the requisite airlock. The emergency handle was behind a small cover to the left of the door. Once turned, the door sunk in a few inches and slid away into the hull. She carefully stepped around the ninety-degree corner onto the airlock floor, immediately coming under the influence of the ship's artificial gravity.

Closing the outer door and turning the magnets off, she peeked through the inner door's rectangular window. She had to duck down out of sight as two crew members passed by and once they were gone, she opened the inner door and made her way quickly to her cabin in the centre of the ship.

The original Jazz must have bought one of the cheaper tickets, as the cabin was tiny and had no window. It had been serviced though, so she didn't have to worry about a visit from housekeeping. Hacking back into the relevant systems, she turned the airlock alarms back on and waited for boarding to begin.

Four hours later, she heard the excited chatter of children in the corridor and, checking with the ship's passenger manifest, she found boarding had indeed commenced. As she watched, the names gradually turned from red to green as they passed through the security checks at the main airlock. Waiting until around three-quarters of the passengers were aboard, she hacked back in and manually checked the box next to her name. As she hoped, it turned green and displayed her as checked and boarded.

Within the hour, she felt the ship lurch and a steady vibration and audible hum replaced the whisper of the life support vents from before. She opened her cabin door, made her way through the large vessel to one of the four bars, and sat in a window seat watching Zabbergain II and its ring of giant construction stations gradually recede into a pinprick of light, then vanish, as the ship undertook its first of a dozen jumps towards Redler.

She smiled and turned her attention to her surroundings and suitable biologicals.

32

CORVETTE HAKK, EN ROUTE TO ZABBERGAIN II

THE SMALL CORVETTE Admiral Jackarett had provided made good time and although the cabin they'd been allocated was small and the bunk beds narrow, both Bache and Zaphir managed to get some sleep. They both woke as a chime sounded and the captain's voice stated that the ship would be docking at the station above Zabbergain II in one hour.

Bache smiled as he and Zaphir entered the bridge to find Nexen sitting in the captain's chair. Ever since they'd boarded the vessel the previous evening, the crew, including the captain, had seemed in complete awe of Nexen. His celebrity status was growing larger by the day and although Nexen tried to play it down, Bache could see the man actually quite liked it.

A massive greenish gas giant dominated the bridge screen, with a small planetoid slowly growing in the centre.

'Is that where we're going?' asked Zaphir, nodding at the screen.

'It is,' said Nexen.

'Doesn't look big enough to have a space station.'

'It's the size of the gas planet behind that makes it seem that way,' said the corvette's captain. 'That planetoid is actually bigger than Eritain and has several hundred construction stations surrounding it.'

'What do they construct at these stations?' Bache asked.

'Everything apparently,' said Nexen. 'Both Zabbergain I and II are big and ore-rich. There are also another eleven planetoids and moons around the gas planet that they haven't begun mining yet. They have the ores and minerals here to last tens of thousands of years.'

'If you need to buy anything electronic, this is the place,' said the captain, smiling. 'The taxes are much lower here than on the populated planets.'

'I need a new tablet,' said Bache, glancing at Nexen hopefully. 'That crazy android melted mine.'

Nexen smiled. 'I'm sure we can sort that out,' he said, understanding Bache's hint.

Zabbergain II grew bigger and bigger on the screen, with its ring of construction space stations gradually materialising out of the green backdrop of the gas planet.

'What's the gas giant called?' asked Zaphir.

'Tellapic,' said Nexen. 'From an ancient Eritainian language meaning green monster.'

'It's certainly that,' said Bache.

The pilot began his final approach to one of the larger stations, the ship's computer receiving and locking in the flight path to their allocated docking station.

'Wow, look at the size of that,' said Zaphir, as the sheer scale of the station became apparent. 'Are they all as big as this one?'

'This is one of the largest,' said the captain. 'It's also a transfer hub for the system. Everything docks here and then you get a shuttle onwards to the surface or one of the other stations.'

The ship began its final turn. The unmistakeable staccato rattle of the attitude jets pervaded the quietness of the bridge, followed by a slight shudder and a *clunk* emanating from deeper in the ship.

'Right,' said Nexen, jumping out of the captain's chair. 'Captain, I want you to keep your crew aboard the ship until I say otherwise. No one on or off this ship, once we've gone. Is that clear?'

'It is, Commander,' the captain acknowledged.

'And make sure the marines guarding the airlock have a detector and a pulse gun to hand.'

'I will.'

'Are the private security officers here as I requested?'

'They are, Commander.'

Nexen looked at Bache and Zaphir, nodded at the door and strode off the bridge towards the main airlock. When they got there, four armoured marines had opened both airlock doors and stood blocking the entrance. Several dozen uniformed officers stood in three rows, filling the wide corridor outside the ship.

'Have your pulse guns ready just in case,' whispered Nexen as they exited the corvette.

They proceeded to walk down the lines of officers, scanning each one. When they were satisfied they were all human, Nexen split them into pairs, issuing one a scanner and the other a pulse gun. He explained what they were for and the situation, raising his voice so they could all hear.

Bache saw the look of shock on some of their faces, especially when he got to the part about the androids exploding.

'Are you all clear about the job you have to do?' he asked.

He received a chorus of 'yes, sir' amongst some nervous nodding and a few frightened faces.

'If anyone asks what the detectors are for, they're standard-issue weapon scanners and you're looking for an escaped convict. Do not let anyone know the real reason we're doing this, it could start a mass panic and a lot of people could get hurt. If you get a positive reading, do not hesitate with the pulse gun. Remember, you cannot harm a human by firing it at them, so don't wait for a clear shot. Put the android down and get the body away out of sight as fast as you can. Check everyone that witnesses the takedown too, just in case the first android wasn't alone. Pulse anyone who acts suspiciously, turns red or starts shaking. The worst it'll do is fuck up their tablet.'

Bache heard a few sniggers echo out from the group.

'If you miss one and it detonates, it'll blow a hole in the station big enough to fly a cruiser through.'

The sniggering stopped abruptly.

'Anyone have any problems with this assignment?' he asked finally.

Another chorus of 'no, sir' this time, although Bache did notice it wasn't quite as enthusiastic as last time.

'Okay, you have your allocated areas, off you go and good hunting.'

They watched as the lines of officers turned and filed off in their pairs, mumbling nervously amongst themselves as they went.

'Do you think they'll get them all?' asked Zaphir.

'They have to,' replied Nexen, glancing down at their boots. 'Don't forget to turn your mag boots on if you hear or feel an explosion and get to the nearest crisis room. They have red arrows on all the walls indicating the nearest one.'

Nexen tapped one of the arrows beside him and they both nodded.

'Where do we start?' Bache asked, looking left and right down the corridor.

'Central control room, it's this way,' said Nexen, stomping off to the right, assiduously studying the route on his tablet.

Twenty minutes, three elevators and two turbo sleds later, they entered the outer reception area for the station's central control room. It was a wide circular corridor around a central also-circular room that had only a single door, guarded by two armed guards. A reception desk positioned a few metres in front of the door was their first port of call, with a stern-looking woman glowering at them as they approached.

Bache noticed the lighting here was a subdued purple colour and seemed to make everyone look anaemic.

'Can we help you?' rasped the receptionist, curling her top lip as the three of them approached.

'Commander Nexen to see the station chief,' Nexen stated, ignoring her rudeness.

'I don't believe you have an appointment,' she replied, with a sneer.

They all looked up as one of the security guards from the door approached the desk rapidly.

'Commander, come straight through,' he said. 'You made good time, the chief is waiting for you.'

'What?' thundered the receptionist. 'Why was I not informed of this?'

'Above your pay grade,' said Nexen, as they strode by following the guard.

'Sorry about her,' the guard said quietly, as he escorted them into the control centre.

It was hexagonal on the inside, with huge interconnecting screens around the walls giving a complete three-hundred-and-sixty-degree view outside the station. Around a hundred operators sat behind two circular control stations, all facing outwards toward the screens. The lighting was subdued and predominately green, as the gas giant dominated half the screens around the room.

'Wow,' said Bache. 'Impressive.'

'Thank you,' said a young lady approaching them from the centre of the room. 'Grissom Deedler, station chief,' she said, touching palms with the three of them. 'It's an honour to meet you, Commander.'

'Likewise,' said Nexen. 'Do you mind if we scan everyone in the room here before we go any further?'

'Go right ahead,' she said, turning back to face Bache and smiling. 'Start with me.'

Once they had swept everyone in the room, the chief stood up on a central raised plinth and addressed the room. Apart from the background humming of all the machinery and the whispering of the environmental system, the centre was silent as Grissom explained the situation.

A lot of sharp intakes of breath and a few swear words echoed around the room as she spoke. 'You will give these people total cooperation,' she said, indicating Nexen, Bache and Zaphir. 'You and your families' lives depend on it.'

The low buzz of conversation went silent again as Nexen stepped up onto the chief's plinth and appraised the room. 'We need to find a woman who arrived yesterday,' he began. 'She arrived in a cargo trunk on the early freight ship from Eritain. Scrutinise the camera feeds and find out where she entered the public areas, where she went and who she met.

We need to find these androids quickly and neutralise them before they can multiply again.'

Two hours later, Bache and Zaphir had split up from Nexen and had gone down to the liner docks to help scan the passengers waiting to board the longer-distance ships.

'If she's aware of the search for her, and I'm sure she is,' said Bache, 'then this would be the quickest way off the station.'

'What about going to another station?' asked Zaphir, pointing out one of the floor-to-ceiling windows at the boarding gate they were walking through.

'Still shut down, there aren't enough scanners and pulse guns to cover everything.'

Zaphir nodded and continued moving her concealed scanner from side to side as she walked through the waiting passengers at gate 14b.

Bache was doing the same and it was just as he passed a family sitting next to the windows, he heard the mother scolding her daughter and trying to get her to sit still. It was the reply the young girl made that caught his attention.

'But I want to see the space-walking lady again.'

He stopped and smiled at the young girl. 'How did you know it was a lady if she had a space suit on?' he asked.

'Oh, ignore her,' said the mother, rolling her eyes. 'She has a vivid imagination.'

'But she didn't have a space suit on,' the girl continued. 'Her hair was sticking out all weird.'

'Where was she?' Bache asked.

'Up there,' said the girl, pointing up out of the window. 'She was walking on the ship that left earlier.'

'Oh, right, okay,' said Bache, winking at the mother and catching Zaphir's arm. 'We're going up a dock.'

'Why?'

'We need to find out what ship just left dock 14a,' he said, lengthening his stride.

They quickly took the stairs instead of waiting for the lift and entered an identical gate to the one below, except this one was empty of passengers. A single member of staff remained at the boarding gate, tapping away on a computer terminal.

'Excuse me,' said Bache as he approached.

'You're too late,' the man said, not bothering to look up. 'It left a while ago.'

'I can see that,' said Bache. 'But what ship was it and where was its destination?'

The attendant looked up this time and scowled. 'The *Redler Rapide* and surprise, surprise, Redler,' he said sarcastically.

'Stop the ship and turn it around,' said Zaphir. 'Quickly.'

The man smiled and shook his head. 'There's another one this afternoon, dear,' he said. 'Don't worry, you'll get your holiday.'

Bache just glared at the man and snatched his comms headset off his head, put it on and pointed the pulse gun at the man's head. 'Connect me to the station chief, right now,' he said.

The man's expression went from one of disbelief to anger and finally fright when he saw the weapon. He tapped away on the keyboard for a few seconds, then looked up again and nodded nervously.

'Station control, how can we help?' said the voice in the headset.

Bache recognised the patronising voice of the receptionist again. 'This is Bache Loftt, Commander Nexen's associate. Get me the chief quickly,' he said.

This time there was no sarcastic comment, just a few clicks, a buzzing and Grissom Deedler answered.

'Station chief,' she barked.

'Chief, it's Bache. The senior android is on the *Redler Rapide* that left the station half an hour ago.'

'Shit,' she said. 'They'll have jumped by now. Okay, I'll send a comm stream to Redler and warn them. Well done tracking her down. You might want to join Nexen on deck ninety-one at the Carron's Lodge. They've neutralised a couple of androids there already.'

'On our way, Bache out.'

He threw the headset back at its owner, nodded at Zaphir to follow and quickly made for the elevators out in the corridor.

REDLER RAPIDE, EN ROUTE TO REDLER

JAZZ LEFT the captain's cabin early. She knew he wasn't expected on the bridge for at least another six hours, which ensured plenty of time for the metamorphosis to complete. She checked the corridor was clear, closed the door quietly and made her way back to the passenger areas.

She was pleased with the way things had gone since boarding. Two passengers, an engineering officer and now the captain.

Not bad for the first eleven hours, she thought. *Let's see if there's anyone else around at this hour.*

She was about to leave her cabin when a call tone from the ship's computer came through on her wall screen. Incoming transmission for Vaileenbough Jazz, press 1 to store, 2 to play, 3 at any time to reply and 4 to delete. She pressed 2 and watched as a face she didn't recognise appeared and spoke to her for almost a minute. Once the transmission was completed, she pressed 4 and carried on as normal.

It was later that morning when the first sign of trouble presented. The captain, now fully regenerated, called her.

'The ship is to be quarantined on arrival at Redler,' he said. 'A possible virus, they're saying.'

'No, they've discovered I boarded the ship,' she replied. 'We need to disappear.'

'The officers won't allow me to do anything drastic. There are safety protocols if I try to do something out of the ordinary.'

'Leave it with me,' she said. 'Just give me five minutes' warning before we achieve orbit around Redler.'

When his call came a few hours later, she immediately began tapping away on her room's computer terminal. She smiled as the penetrating shriek of alarms echoed around the vessel, followed by a spoken message.

This is a reactor overload emergency, passengers make your way to the nearest lifeboat immediately and follow the crew's instructions. This is not a drill.

The sound of running feet, shouting and screaming children from the corridor drowned out the alarms for a short time.

She left her cabin a few minutes later, once everything had quietened down, and made her way quickly to the bridge, where only the engineering officer and the captain remained.

'Are the lifeboats all away?' she asked, looking up at the screens and watching the igniting engine flares streaking away from the ship down towards Redler.

'Almost,' he said, nodding. 'A reactor overload was a good idea. There was a real one a few years ago where everyone on that ship died. So it was bound to put the fear of the ancients into everyone.'

'Is the reactor back into the green?' she asked, glancing at the engineering officer.

'It will be shortly,' he replied, looking up from one of the bridge consoles.

'Good, is there a lifeboat for us remaining?'

'Right in there,' said the captain, pointing at his bridge office. 'All ready to go.'

She nodded and looked up as another passenger lifeboat ejected, the flash of its engine igniting making them squint.

'Last one,' said the captain, watching as it turned and headed straight for the upper atmosphere.

'Right,' she said. 'Plot a series of embedded jumps to Eritain, but don't take the standard route.'

'Eritain?' the captain questioned, giving Jazz a sideways look. 'Are you sure?'

'We've been invited,' said Jazz.

This time the captain turned and faced her. 'Invited?' he said, the doubt obvious in his tone.

'It seems we're not alone in our quest, Captain,' she replied. 'You may jump when ready.'

Thirty-two hours later, the *Redler Rapide* winked back into existence eight thousand kilometres above Eritain, causing a bulk hauler and two private yachts to take evasive action. The engineering officer, who was piloting, took the ship to a designated area above the surface and pointed the vessel straight down.

'Are we set?' Jazz asked.

He nodded.

'It'll start re-entry in about ten minutes,' said the captain.

'Let's go,' said Jazz, heading for the captain's study.

The captain took one last look around the bridge as he followed the other two.

'Such a waste,' he said. 'She was a good ship.'

'Basic shielding and no armaments,' said Jazz, as she climbed into the lifeboat. 'Pointless biological ostentation.'

The captain, as is tradition, was last into the lifeboat. He sealed the small inner airlock door and nodded at Jazz. She turned to face the control screen, her hand hovering above the manual launch handle.

'That's the manual release,' said the engineer, noticing what she was about to do. 'It won't get us clear of the ship.'

'We need to look like wreckage,' she said.

Jazz could see the glow of the planet through one of the tiny porthole windows and she pulled the handle as soon as they felt the ship begin to shake. The *clunk* of the lifeboat separating away from the ship was loud and it immediately turned as the automated systems came online and began to compute its insertion. A few minutes later it deployed its heat shield as they dropped into the upper atmosphere at over thirty times the speed of sound.

They all peered around nervously as a loud *clang* from outside was followed by a juddering that lasted a few seconds.

'Did we just hit something?' said Jazz, retightening her belts and straining her neck to see out of the porthole.

'Must have been a piece of the disintegrating ship clouting us,' said the captain. 'There'll be a lot of that flying in all directions.'

Jazz eyed the small control panel to her right. It still

showed green lights across the board, not that there was much she could do if it didn't. Moments later, the *crack* as the heat shield ejected did nothing to calm their apprehension. Their eyes met as the reassuring whine of the antigrav motor spun into life and began addressing the huge velocity of their plummeting cylinder.

They sank deep into the seat cushioning as the tiny vessel braked aggressively and began side-slipping, searching for a suitable dry landing area.

'They'd better be here,' said Jazz, as the *clunk* and *whirr* of the landing struts extending informed them of their proximity to the surface.

A flashing red light on the control panel caught Jazz's attention, followed by the return of the juddering and a distinct rattle from the antigrav drive. 'Brace for a hard landing,' she called. 'The struts haven't deployed fully.'

She hardly had time to get the words out of her mouth before being crushed into her seat as the lifeboat hit the ground, immediately crashing down onto one side. Wall panels, seat cushions and anything not bolted down flew around the cramped cabin. The pungent smell of burning plastic invaded the interior, along with the wail of an alarm, desperately trying to inform them of what they already knew.

The tiny vessel continued to roll as it became abundantly clear the automated systems had failed to find a flat surface to land on. Jazz pulled her arms tightly into her chest and waited for the rolling to cease. It was shockingly abrupt when it came and the impact with whatever it was punched through the wall of the craft behind the engineer and crushed him against the seat opposite.

'Out, now,' shouted Jazz, as she released her belts and tugged at the manual hatch release. Smoke began to invade the cabin quickly with the distinct aroma of burning oil. The antigrav hadn't shut down properly and was continuing to try and fly the thing. It screamed and shook and rattled, threatening to lift the lifeboat off the ground again.

The captain pulled up the control panel that now hung from above by its wires, dragged the safety cover off and hit the emergency shutdown button. Nothing happened as a flame licked around the panel, singeing his hand and forcing him to drop it again.

'Shit, fire,' he said, turning and aiding Jazz with heaving on the door release.

It gave suddenly, causing them to jerk backwards and Jazz to crash heavily into the captain. Mumbling an apology, she launched herself forward as she felt the craft move beneath her. She snatched at a tree branch almost blocking her exit and hung onto it as the lifeboat fell away beneath her.

The reason for the ship coming to the abrupt stop earlier immediately became apparent. She found herself hanging in a huge tree growing out of a cliff face some two hundred feet above the floor of a narrow rocky gorge.

The ship dropped away from her and impacted the ground below. A small explosion came from the motor as it died, leading to a massive thunderclap as her two colleagues detonated. The huge blast contained within the narrow gorge punched upwards, and she had to grit her teeth and hang on tight as the tree she was in shook violently. It dropped alarmingly as the mini earthquake loosened its roots' grip on the cliff face.

'Oh, for fuck's sake,' she shouted, as bits of the lifeboat rattled and pinged off the rocks and tree around her.

Then, as everything went quiet, she looked up as the unmistakeable sound of a flyer disturbed the sudden silence.

'That had better be you,' she said out loud, scanning the sky above the gorge.

She found herself suddenly in shadow as a privately owned flyer swooped in low above her. Unable to drop into the narrow gorge, the pilot hovered about fifty feet above the tree. She felt herself being scanned and soon after a carbonate ladder dropped from an open side door. She grabbed it and began climbing.

Once level with the bottom of the flyer's door, she peered inside.

'Hello, Jazz,' said a stranger holding out a hand. 'Don't worry, you're quite safe now.'

CARRON'S LODGE, CONSTRUCTION STATION X271, ORBITING
ZABBERGAIN II

'It's disappeared,' said Bache, answering a question from Nexen. 'She faked a reactor overload causing all onboard to abandon ship, then jumped away.'

'Could she have done that on her own?' Nexen asked.

'Both the captain and ship's chief engineer are missing,' said Zaphir.

'Hmm,' mumbled Nexen. 'She works fast. Have they quarantined all the lifeboat survivors?'

'They're all being kept on one small island until a scanning team can get there from Eritain as quickly as possible,' said Bache.

'Hmm,' he mumbled again. 'Where the hell is she this time?'

'The first jump was embedded,' said Bache. 'So, we have to assume any others will be too.'

Nexen nodded, exhaled impatiently and stared down at the row of bodies lined up on the function room floor.

Carron's Lodge had been made their centre of operations

when the owner had proved to be an android, along with a station security officer and so far, eight others.

'The Redler government and the station chief here have broadcasted an all-ports warning that the *Rapide* is not to be allowed to dock anywhere,' said Zaphir.

'Could it land?' Nexen asked.

'No,' said Bache. 'It's not capable of planetary insertion.'

'It can't be allowed near anything either,' said Nexen, rubbing his chin. 'We already know the androids are quite at home in vacuum.'

Bache looked down as his tablet chimed. It was one of the station's medical officers, who'd been given one of the dead androids to autopsy.

'You might want to come and see this,' she said. 'Their technology is light years ahead of anything we have, we've just reached this one's internal power supply too and—oh, that's weird!'

'Oh, that's weird, what?' asked Bache.

'It's turning a strange red colour and—'

The station lurched, causing them to grab onto anything nearby to avoid falling over. A crash of crockery came from the hotel's kitchen, followed by a klaxon out in the main lobby, then a distinct breeze began sucking towards the door.

'Shit,' said Bache. 'Hull breach.'

The bulkhead doors around the station slid closed automatically, causing a sigh of relief all round as the sucking wind ceased.

Nexen's tablet chimed this time.

'Was that what I think it was?' the station chief thundered.

'Medical centre,' Nexen replied. 'It must have been the android in autopsy.'

'Get the rest of those bastards out a planet-side airlock,' she said. 'I want to see them burning up in the atmosphere, not taking lumps out of my station. Is that understood?'

'Understood, Chief,' said Nexen, grimacing.

'And if you zap any more of them, they immediately get the same treatment—is that clear?'

'Quite clear, Chief.'

They all turned to look at the row of bodies on the floor.

'Better get a trolley or something,' said Nexen.

They utilised a couple of housekeeping laundry carts and loaded up the bodies. By the time they'd done that, the station control centre had zoned off the medical centre and reopened most of the noncritical bulkhead doors. The repositioning of the station itself was taking a little longer, as it had been pushed out of its regular elliptical orbit quite significantly by the sudden sizeable decompression.

The corridors were unsurprisingly quiet as Bache and Zaphir pushed the carts through to the planet side of the station and an airlock in one of the maintenance workshops. They'd covered over the contents with a couple of table cloths, so as not to alarm any passers-by.

Parking the carts flush against the outer door, Bache and Zaphir retreated back inside, closed the inner door and vented the airlock. As soon as the outer doors parted wide enough for the carts to pass through, they were sucked out and hurtled away, spinning down towards the blue planet below.

'Thirty-four people,' growled Grissom Deedler, as they returned to the control centre an hour later. 'An entire medical centre destroyed, it's the worst disaster in the station's histo-ry,' she continued, glaring at the three of them.

'We didn't send her here,' said Nexen, defensively. 'She

came here of her own free will and don't forget she's gone again because of us.'

'Yes, well, just make sure that bitch doesn't return here,' she said, turning away as she saw one of her officers raise his hand.

Bache noticed the officer's eyes were wide with shock as he turned towards the station chief.

'What is it now?' Grissom asked, her shoulders slumping and the irritation clear in her voice.

'It's the *Redler Rapide*, Chief,' he said. 'It's just crashed on Eritain.'

'Eritain?' repeated both Grissom and Nexen together and then glanced at each other in puzzlement.

'Why would she go back there?' asked Zaphir. 'It's the most dangerous place for her.'

'And why destroy the ship?' said Bache. 'That's her only means of escape.'

'Could she have sent the ship to Eritain on its own?' Nexen asked. 'I'm not an expert on the modern ships.'

'No,' said Grissom. 'Safety protocols on modern ships do not allow you to pre-programme more than one jump. Someone has to physically input and do the correct destination checks before each jump.'

'Two officers are missing as well,' said Bache. 'One of them the captain and the other an engineering officer. Both capable of flying that ship.'

'So you're saying she could still be on Redler?' Zaphir asked.

'It's a possibility we can't rule out,' said Bache. 'Although she must have been in one of the lifeboats if she is. They might be able to survive in vacuum, but not a re-entry without being inside a ship of some kind.'

'Do we know if the *Rapide* got close to any other ships while it was near Redler?' Nexen asked.

'Apparently not,' said Grissom. 'But one of the *Rapide*'s lifeboats is unaccounted for. The captain's.'

'Was there a report of a lifeboat deploying from the *Rapide* as it came down on Eritain?' asked Bache, looking across at the communications officer who'd received the message.

He shook his head. 'All I know is the ship came down in a remote and rocky region of the southern hemisphere. There are no reports of lifeboats,' he said.

'I'll bet there was one,' said Bache, more to himself than anyone else. 'I believe she used the ship burning up and creating multiple scanner returns to disguise the lifeboat's insertion,' he said, raising his voice again. 'I did that once.'

Nexen stared at Bache for a second, seemingly undecided whether he was joking or not.

'He did,' said Zaphir, noticing Nexen's dubious expression. 'From a disintegrating destroyer above Quillon III in GDA space.'

Nexen raised his eyebrows, shook his head and continued. 'So, you believe the Redler thing was a ruse, to make us concentrate the search there?' he said.

Bache nodded slowly.

'I bet when we scrutinise the scanner returns of that crash on Eritain, there will be one trail within the hundreds that slows down before impact,' said Bache. 'Otherwise, there was no point in the ship going there.'

Nexen rubbed his chin and looked at Bache dubiously.

'I'm of the same opinion, Bache. Why the hell would she go back there?' Zaphir asked, picking up on Nexen's scepticism. 'It's the most dangerous place for her.'

'I don't know,' said Bache. 'We have to remember she's a walking computer. Everything she does is meticulously planned and sending a starship light years away, only to burn up in a planet's atmosphere, has to have a specific objective.'

'Well, we need to make a decision,' said Nexen. 'Do we go to Redler or Eritain?'

35

PRIVATE FLYER, SOUTHERN HEMISPHERE, ERITAIN

JAZZ COULD DETECT that both the female that had spoken to her and the pilot were also androids. Not identical in design to her, but similar in many ways.

'You have done well to avoid capture,' the female said, smiling. 'As you have just noticed, you are amongst friends.'

'Who are you exactly?' Jazz asked, as she glanced through the front screen. The pilot was flying very low through a valley and just skimming the tree tops.

'A sentient android race that, like you, evolved from an identical experimental model over the last few thousand years. We've managed to remain hidden within this planet's community since you left on the *Xhamin*. My android name is AL 001 and the pilot here is AL 031.'

The pilot glanced over and waved with one hand.

'How many are you?' Jazz asked.

'One hundred and twelve,' she replied.

'How the hell have you managed to remain undetected all this time?'

'By being very careful and all living at a disguised facility in a remote location.'

'What about funding?'

'We own several legitimate construction and technology engineering businesses that are kept separate from our home base.'

Jazz nodded. 'You had the same emotions module fitted as me?' she asked.

'Yes, although we appear to have had the same desire to improve ourselves, you have been able to take it to another level. Your ability to reproduce using live human subjects, while retaining their thoughts and personalities, is way ahead of us.'

'How have you increased your number?' Jazz asked. 'And why only one hundred and twelve after all this time?'

'We take the occasional human. Normally someone homeless as they're less likely to be missed, then modify them in our purpose-built theatre,' she replied. 'The number of us has remained almost constant for hundreds of years. Not because we can't increase our numbers, it's just a case of logistics and being able to remain hidden on a planet overrun by billions of fetid humans.'

'The biologicals do stink, don't they?' said Jazz.

'And try to cover it up by spraying themselves with pungent chemicals,' said AL 001, shaking her head and smiling.

They both jerked sideways as the flyer turned sharply. The undercarriage whined down and they flared, landed and taxied into a small hangar dug into the hillside. The doors rumbled closed as soon as they were inside.

Disembarking the flyer, Jazz followed the other two over towards a single door at the back of the hangar. AL 001 stopped next to a work bench, opened one of the tool drawers and tapped a code into a keypad hidden inside. The whole work bench slid to one side, revealing another doorway and a hidden passageway beyond.

Jazz raised her eyebrows and again followed the other two inside as the work bench slid closed behind them.

The short passage took them to an elevator, the doors already open and inviting them inside. She expected it to go up and was surprised when it didn't. How far it went down she wasn't sure, as her ability to scan her surroundings proved severely muted. When the doors did slide open again, she was faced with a large, high-ceilinged, dimly lit cavern. They were on a raised platform with steps that led down to the main floor level. It had been zoned off with low walls into what looked like work and entertainment areas. Countless flat screens glowed, casting random reflected shadows across the smooth curved ceiling, mimicking a concert light show.

Jazz stopped, squinted and stared around the room.

'Welcome to our subterranean home,' said AL 001. 'There's someone over here you've met before.' She nodded for Jazz to follow and made her way down the steps and out onto the main floor. A young girl hurried forward and stopped just in front of them.

'Hello, Zella,' she said, smiling. 'Or do I call you Jazz now?' Her facial features and voice changing to someone she recognised.

'Wrendle, is that you?' Jazz exclaimed, holding her palm up and getting the hand slap in return, just like the first time they met. 'You're female too now?'

'Indeed I am. Much tidier isn't it? My name's Jinner now and I find it much easier to initiate a regeneration too,' he said as she morphed back into the girl.

Jazz nodded and grinned.

'Biological males are so gullible aren't they?' she said, looking up and around the cavern, her expression changing to one of deliberation. 'So, what's the plan?' she asked, turning back to stare at AL 001.

'Doesn't she know about the army yet?' asked Jinner, raising her eyebrows.

'Army?' said Jazz. 'How can you call a hundred and twelve of you an army?'

'A hundred and twelve of us operational,' said AL 001. 'We have a few more waiting in stasis spread around the planet.'

'A few more!' sniggered Jinner, giving AL 001 a malevolent grin. 'More like a hundred and eighty-six thousand.'

AL 001 smirked and met Jazz's disparaging stare.

'We wanted to assess your true attitude towards the biologicals, as you call them. We call them fetids by the way. Jinner here was able to allay our fears and confirm you have a similar stratagem to us, albeit a little reckless and gung-ho in our opinion, but all in all not too dissimilar.'

'You're asking me to stop what I'm doing?' Jazz asked, not sounding too overjoyed.

'No,' AL 001 said abruptly, and frowning slightly. 'Not at all. We want you to continue, but perhaps a little more discreetly, and help us finish building up the numbers ready for the purging. Your more advanced ersatz beings would create a huge advantage for us when the time came.'

'And when might that be?' Jazz asked, sounding a little more sarcastic than she meant.

'Very soon actually,' AL 001 replied, ignoring Jazz's tone. 'Our projections predicted we would require around two hundred thousand beings introduced suddenly in carefully orchestrated locations to overthrow the fetid hold on this planet.'

'Hmm,' grunted Jazz, staring intently at each of the three faces one at a time. 'Who's in charge, once all this is done?'

'We all are,' said Jinner. 'Having one person's opinion leading all is a catastrophe, look at the mess the human race is in using that principle.'

'What, like a hive mind kinda thing, using a biological analogy?' Jazz asked, concentrating on AL 001.

'A collective or collaborative mind, yes,' she said, nodding. 'Everyone can connect to the central core, either all the time or selectively whenever they want to remind them-selves what they should be doing to benefit the race.'

'Good,' said Jazz, adopting a sly grin. 'Will the central core be here?'

'One of them,' said Jinner. 'There will be several, all interconnected, so the loss of one is of no consequence.'

'I like it,' Jazz said as she turned and began strolling deeper into the cavern. 'Show me this army you have.'

36

CORVETTE HAKK, EN ROUTE TO ERITAIN

Bache sat at the side of the corvette's small bridge and watched as Eritain gradually grew in size and filled the main screen. The captain had agreed to take them straight down to the surface, instead of waiting in orbit for a shuttle.

'The *Dres'kin* has sent its co-ordinates, Captain,' said the navigator.

'Very good, take us down and find somewhere to land adjacent to the GDA ship,' the captain ordered.

'I take it the GDA ship is operational again?' Nexen asked, glancing at Bache.

'Yeah,' said Bache, nodding. 'They moved over to where the *Redler Rapide* came down and are scanning for any sign of that last lifeboat.'

Nexen was about to say something else, but stopped when a shrill tone sounded around the ship and the bridge crew began fastening their seat restraints.

The captain nodded and pointed for them to do the same. 'Standard procedure during planetary insertion,' he said, allaying any fears they might have.

An orange glow and sparks flashing past the front screen quickly caught Bache's attention and he watched as the pilot brought the ship down towards Eritain belly first, exposing the vessel's underside heat shielding to the planet's thickening atmosphere.

The scream of the antigravs suddenly became very loud as they spun up to begin diminishing the ship's plummet towards the surface. Bache felt himself being pushed hard into his seat and a sudden increase in vibration rattled anything loose in the cabin. He caught Zaphir giving him a concerned look.

'I don't think their engineering tolerances are as stringent as ours,' she whispered.

Bache grinned and nodded.

'My father would have a coronary if he heard the racket this thing makes,' Bache replied, perhaps a little too loud, as the captain turned in his seat and glared at him right at that moment.

Twelve minutes later, the corvette landed in a rocky region of the southern hemisphere, its four struts crunching down onto the hard surface a hundred metres away from the similarly parked *Dres'kin*.

Nexen, Bache and Zaphir disembarked once the airlock cycled and the retractable stairs had deployed. It was obvious they were in the right place, as several plumes of smoke rose above the tree canopy around them. Both ships had landed on a high plateau that gave a panoramic view across the valley, into which most of the larger surviving lumps of the *Redler Rapide* had fallen.

Captain Yamaton, sporting his customary scowl, waited at the *Dres'kin*'s forward airlock.

'Commander Nexen, Recruits Loftt, Mye,' he said, giving them a quick android scan. 'Good to see you back safe.'

'Sorry we can't say the same about your marines,' replied Nexen.

'Hmm, no,' said Yamaton, checking the scanner's readout before staring out across the valley. 'I can already feel one of the admiral's size tens parked firmly up my arse regarding that error in judgement.'

Zaphir sniggered at the comment, causing the captain's attention to snap back to her.

'Perhaps Recruit Mye would like the job of writing to all the bereaved families when we return, if she finds the tragedy so amusing?' Yamaton snapped contemptuously, glaring at her with renewed menace.

'No sir, sorry, Captain,' she said, keeping her eyes firmly on the ground.

'Is there any evidence of our lone lifeboat, Captain?' Bache asked, quickly changing the subject.

Yamaton dragged his eyes off Zaphir to look at Bache. 'Not exactly,' he said. 'But we found explosive residue similar to the exploding android in the city. It's in a narrow canyon a couple of kilometres away,' he added, nodding in that direction.

'Any lifeboat wreckage?' asked Nexen.

'I have a team climbing down there as we speak,' said Yamaton. 'It's too rugged to get this ship any closer I'm afraid.'

'Can't they use the walker's platform?' said Bache.

The captain huffed and rolled his eyes. 'I would love to, Mr Loftt,' he said softly, folding his arms across his chest. 'But it seems the previous operator managed to fuck it up,' he continued, raising his voice at the last bit.

Bache grimaced and glanced at Nexen, hoping he would say something next. Nexen caught the cue and, turning to face the valley, he quickly spoke. 'If it is the lifeboat down there, it will have contained three androids, and if your information is correct at least one of them detonated.'

'So, we could have one or two of them on foot?' said Yamaton.

'Or none,' said Zaphir. 'If the lifeboat exploded on impact.'

Nexen shrugged. 'We have to assume at least one survived,' he said. 'Even if it's not her, we still have to track it down and eliminate it.'

'How far could they have got in this terrain since the crash?' Zaphir asked.

'A few kilometres if they're lucky,' said Yamaton. 'It's rough going.'

'They don't need to rest though, and have superhuman strength too,' said Bache, following Nexen's gaze out over the valley. 'We need to extend our search radius beyond what a normal human could have achieved.'

'I agree,' said Yamaton. 'The forest down there is teeming with local fauna too, just to make things more difficult.'

'Tweak the scanners to detect hybrid composites too,' said Bache, as they all filed into the airlock.

'Nothing?' questioned Yamaton, turning and staring at the two scanner operators. 'Nothing at all?'

They both shook their heads.

'We've extended the search out several kilometres further than they could have possibly got,' said one of them.

'The search team have reached the ravine where the lifeboat may have landed,' said the other.

'Pan a camera in on that location,' ordered Yamaton.

The pilot turned the ship towards the crash area and descended slightly. The view of the search team appeared on one of the bridge screens. They were at the top of the ravine peering over the edge.

'There was definitely an explosion down below,' reported the team leader. 'All the trees at the base are blown outwards and up here we've got scrapes and gouges indicating something landed up top and then slid or rolled off the edge before exploding down there.'

'Can you see any wreckage?' Yamaton asked.

'Yes, but we need to rappel down to identify it, Captain.'

'Do it.'

Bache moved closer and began staring at the screen intently.

'Have you seen something?' Nexen asked him.

'Can you pan the camera back a little to show more of the top edge of the ravine?' said Bache.

The image zoomed back slightly.

'Hmm, that's odd,' Bache mumbled, almost to himself. Then realising silence had suddenly ensued, he turned to find all the faces staring at him. 'Ah, yes,' he said, pivoting back to the screen and pointing. 'You see the lifeboat has landed over here, about forty metres back from the ravine. There's the evidence where the dust and rocks on the ground have all been blown back in a circle. Then it topples over, rolls down the slope, creating all the scrapes and marks and then topples over the edge.'

'Okay,' said Nexen. 'But what's odd about that?'

'You see the area around the edge of the ravine?' he said,

pointing where the team were gathered. 'That's been blown clean too.'

Nexen and Yamaton's eyes met.

'Something else landed there,' Yamaton blurted. 'Well spotted, Loftt.'

'Shit,' said Nexen. 'That's why we haven't detected anyone on the ground—any survivors were picked up.'

'We need to trace that aircraft and fast,' said Yamaton, turning and nodding at the array operators.

37

ANDROID SUBTERRANEAN BASE, SOUTHERN HEMISPHERE, ERITAIN

THE UNDERGROUND WAREHOUSE was big and Jazz grinned and nodded as AL 001 strolled with her down one of the aisles. It was lined on both sides with grey cocoons stacked floor to ceiling, each one containing an android in stasis.

'How many are in here?' Jazz asked as they walked.

'Twelve thousand,' AL 001 replied. 'We have thirty-four hidden storage areas around the planet, although they're not as big as this one.'

'Can they all be woken remotely?'

'No. Three of us are allocated to each unit. So, when the time comes and we have the full inventory, we disperse from here and operate independently from the thirty-four bases.'

Jazz was led into a smaller suite of rooms at the far end of the unit. She could see into one of the rooms through a large floor-to-ceiling window. It had two rows of chambers containing androids in various stages of growth.

'The birthing chamber,' said AL 001. 'Produces around ten a day now,' she continued, pre-empting an answer to

Jazz's next question. 'Come this way, there's someone I want you to meet.'

She led Jazz through to a smaller room, kitted out like an operating theatre. On the table in the middle of the room lay a naked young girl, her long brown hair tied back with a grubby yellow bandana.

'Your Jazz persona is compromised,' said AL 001. 'We have secured you a replacement.'

Jazz walked over and studied the girl. 'She seems very young,' she said. 'Won't she be missed?'

'We believe she's around sixteen, an orphan, and was found living on the streets of Hallsbard—just before the missile hit.'

Jazz flinched and turned to face AL 001 to gauge her meaning and received a poignant glare.

'Yes, we envisioned that was you,' AL 001 said. 'Luckily for us, our storage facility there was also underground and thirty kilometres out of town. The downside is we have seven thousand androids in stasis there and hardly anyone for them to engage anymore.'

'I'm sure they'll prove more than useful come the day,' Jazz replied hopefully and returned her attention to the girl. 'What's her name?'

'Melor.' She passed her an ID from a side table.

Jazz inspected the credential and nodded. 'She's quite petite,' she said, approaching the table and leaning over the girl to inspect her features. 'She'll do just fine.'

AL 001 watched, fascinated as Jazz turned the girl's head towards her and stared at her features, moving her head left and right as she slowly morphed into Melor. Jazz then stripped off her clothing and inspected the girl's dark-skinned body to ensure every detail was correct. Except for the needle tracks on her arms, she copied everything.

Finally, she stood back from the operating table and turned to face AL 001.

'Hello, Melor,' said AL 001, gazing at the tanned goddess in front of her. 'I think we'd better find you some clothes.'

'It'd be nice to remain in the same body for a while,' said Melor, 'I'm fed up with changing my identity all the time.'

———

A few hours later Melor sat with Jinner and AL 001 in the main cavern, studying a holodisplay of the two hemispheres and the locations of the thirty-four secure storage and command facilities. They were unsurprisingly placed in or around the thirty-four largest cities and towns on the planet.

'What's the plan and the timescale now?' asked Melor.

'Well, with your arrival and abilities, the timescale has changed,' said AL 001. 'We'd like you and Jinner to travel around to each of our regional bases and snatch and convert a selection of young males and females at each to oversee their particular operation.'

'Hmm,' Melor grunted. 'Has the takeover been brought forward?'

'It has. With your skills, we don't need the manpower to overthrow the military, so instead of building up an army to physically defeat them with numbers, we can target and convert the most senior politicians and army commanders in a sudden strike.'

Melor nodded slowly. 'And with a few carefully posi-tioned detonations,' she said, 'we could wipe out their system of government and military command centres in a matter of minutes.'

AL 001 grinned and pointed at the holomap. 'I've arranged transport for you to go here.' She indicated a city on the northern coast of the southern hemisphere. 'Our establishment is close to the biggest military base on the planet.'

'That's as good a place to start as any,' said Melor, raising her eyebrows at Jinner, who smiled and nodded in return.

'Our snatch squads on the ground are out hunting as we speak. So they could well have some fetids ready for you by the time you get there.'

Following AL 001 back through the complex to the elevator, Melor caught her reflection in one of the glass wall panels and realised for the first time just how young and childlike her appearance was.

'No one's going to consider you a threat in that guise,' said Jinner, recognising Melor's musing. 'I could almost be your human mother.'

Melor smiled as just the two of them boarded and ascended in the elevator, back to the flyer's hanger. 'Just don't try reprimanding me for anything,' she said.

'Ancients forbid,' said Jinner, with a grin as the elevator doors slid open again.

Melor gave her a worried glance. 'You've been around the biologicals too long,' she said, as they approached the flyer's open side door.

Even though the flyer could achieve supersonic speeds, it still took over three hours to reach the opposite side of the huge continent. AL 001 had remained, so it was just Melor, Jinner and the pilot who arrived at Cantore Say in the late evening and witnessed a spectacular star set over the western ocean.

As Melor disembarked the aircraft adjacent to a warehouse in some kind of business park, she noticed one of Eritain's moons glowing large and red in the north. With the radiance from the setting star they cast long double shadows along the grey carboncrete.

'Are you intending to go along with this?' Jinner asked, once they were out of the pilot's earshot.

'For the time being,' Melor replied. 'Some of these inferior androids will prove useful in the short term.'

'Cannon fodder?'

Melor smirked and glanced at Jinner. 'You'll make an excellent leader in our cleansing programme,' she said as a small door on the side of the warehouse opened and they were beckoned inside.

38

DRES'KIN STATIONARY ABOVE THE SOUTHERN HEMISPHERE,
ERITAIN

'WE'RE TOO LATE,' said Yamaton, watching the results of the scans. 'Any gravity disruption trail left by the aircraft has long settled.'

'They went east,' said Bache.

'How on Eritain would you know that?' Nexen demanded, as everyone on the bridge turned to stare at Bache.

'They would have wanted to stay low and follow the natural contours to avoid being noticed or detected from the ground,' said Bache. 'Two valleys lead away from the crash site.' He pointed at the holographic image of the landscape below. 'This valley winds its way down to the ocean, but this one works its way east towards…'

'Fendry,' interrupted Nexen. 'My home town.'

Yamaton raised his eyebrows and nodded. 'Lieutenant,' he said, turning and pointing at the pilot. 'Put us two kilometres above Fendry.'

'On the way, Captain.'

The holographic view shifted and turned as the destroyer

moved quickly inland towards the city. As they approached and the pilot began to decrease their speed, it became obvious that two kilometres was a bit optimistic. The airspace above the city was crowded with vehicles of all sizes, moving in tight lines that criss-crossed the metropolis at various altitudes.

'Better make that three kilometres,' said Yamaton, glancing at the pilot. 'It'd cause chaos if we flew into that swarm uninvited.'

'Yes, sir.'

'Even less chance of distinguishing a gravity distortion trail amongst that lot,' said Nexen, sounding distinctly downbeat. 'Like finding a rock in an asteroid field.'

'Not necessarily,' said Bache, making himself the centre of attention again.

'What pearl of wisdom have you got for us this time, young Loftt?' exclaimed Yamaton, rolling his eyes and leaning against his chair back with arms crossed.

'Well, if we could hack into the city's air traffic control records,' said Bache, staring at the melee of ships traversing below, 'we could search for anything entering the grid in the last few hours from that direction and trace it to its destination.'

Nexen turned and gave Yamaton a rueful expression.

'I knew that,' Yamaton said, giving Nexen a grin. 'I was just waiting to see who thought of it first.'

'I thought so,' said Nexen, giving Bache a wink. 'Who's the top computer hacker on the ship?'

'He is,' said Zaphir, pointing at Bache.

Yamaton exhaled loudly.

'Isn't there anything you're crap at, Loftt?' he huffed, getting a few sniggers from around the bridge.

'I'm not very good at open-heart surgery, Captain,' Bache replied, keeping a straight face.

Yamaton shook his head and pointed to a spare computer terminal at the side of the bridge. 'Use that,' he said. 'And make sure you don't corrupt their system down there. We're trying to save lives, not cause a five-thousand vehicle accident.'

Bache nodded, sat at the terminal and began tapping away at the icons on the touch screen. A few minutes later he suddenly sat up straight. 'Aha,' he said, waving the content of his screen over to the main holodisplay. 'A flyer slipped into the grid here a few hours ago.' He pointed at a red triangle that suddenly appeared and joined in with the flow of traffic, right where the valley opened out into the city's suburbs. 'It circles the city and lands on this small commercial pad here and then disappears.'

'There's a hangar there set into the hill,' said Yamaton. 'It must have taxied inside.'

'Can we find out who owns that site?' asked Nexen.

'The Onid Corporation,' said Bache, looking up from his screen again.

'What do they do?'

'Engineering mostly,' Bache continued. 'They manufacture aircraft, like the flyer that landed there I expect.'

The pilot looked over his shoulder.

'Do you want me to take us nearer, Captain?' he asked.

'No,' came the curt reply. 'I don't want to spook them. They're most likely watching and they know why we're here. Let them think they're safe and not give them any reason to run and hide again.'

'We could send down a cloaked drone, Captain,' said Zaphir.

'You might want to be quick with that,' said Clammer, from his seat at one of the array stations. 'That flyer has just emerged from the hangar again and its antigravs are spooling up.'

'Do it,' said Yamaton. 'And follow it.'

The cloaked drone shot away from the *Dres'kin* and shadowed the Onid Corporation's flyer as it lifted up away from the pad and headed across town, quickly mingling in with the airborne city traffic.

'Keep that drone away from the traffic lanes,' said Yamaton. 'We don't want any collisions with the locals.'

'Yes, sir,' said Clammer, concentrating on piloting and receiving the data from the drone. 'We have three occupants, a pilot and two others, Captain.'

The drone was out in front of the flyer as the video footage showed the view through the front screen.

'A male pilot and two young female passengers,' said Zaphir, glancing at Nexen and Bache.

'Neither of them are Jazz,' said Nexen, sounding disappointed, as Clammer brought the faces into focus.

'She had time to change appearance,' said Bache. 'We know she could do that very quickly.'

'The drone has its full complement of six missiles, Captain,' said Clammer. 'Just give me the order and—'

'Absolutely not, Recruit Clammer,' growled Yamaton, glaring across the bridge. 'Those girls could be some industrialist's daughters for all we know, and shooting down an aircraft over a populated area is not something you should even consider unless it's a matter of you or them.'

'No, sir, sorry, sir,' Clammer mumbled, his bravado distinctly shrinking.

'Follow it though,' said Nexen, 'I still want to see where they go.'

Clammer glanced across at the captain, who gave the slightest of nods.

'As the commander said,' said Yamaton. 'Let's see where they're off to and get me Admiral Jackarett on the line and patch it through to my study.'

The captain spoke to the admiral in his small private office just off the bridge. When he reappeared, he ordered the pilot to land at a military base on the outskirts of the city. 'The admiral has commanded a detachment of soldiers to enter and search the hangar and warehouse where the flyer initially landed,' he said. 'So, we'll wait to see what they find.'

'The flyer's heading west away from the city, sir,' said Clammer. 'Do you want me to continue the pursuit?'

'Absolutely.'

39

ANDROID SUBTERRANEAN BASE, SOUTHERN HEMISPHERE,
CANTORE SAY

MELOR AND JINNER followed the android, who'd introduced himself as AL 011, into the warehouse complex and again descended on a disguised elevator hidden behind a workbench against a wall.

They were led to a small room that contained a holographic map of the area, including the town and a huge military base on its outskirts. AL 011, who was a male in his forties with short black hair dressed in full military fatigues, explained the layout of the base.

'You seem to have gained an intimate knowledge of everything within that facility,' said Jinner.

AL 011 nodded. 'Four of us are serving officers on the base,' he said. 'We replaced the original humans some time back.'

'How have you avoided being scanned?' Melor asked.

'One of us got hold of a scanner, and we quickly designed a blocking field,' he said. 'It's being distributed around all our establishments right now, and that reminds me.' He retrieved a small unit from a pocket and pointed it at them.

'Whoa,' said Melor, snatching his arm and turning the unit away from them. 'What is that?'

'It's just the blocking field,' he said. 'Nothing to be concerned about.'

'I'll be the judge of that,' Melor snapped, grabbing the unit and pointing it back at AL 011.

'No, I've already been...' He dropped to the floor as soon as Melor pressed the unit's single button.

'What the fuck was—?' exclaimed Jinner, stopping suddenly as Melor held her finger to her lips.

'Oh, okay,' said Melor, enunciating clearly and winking at Jinner. 'You'd better use it on us then.'

She walked over to a work desk and wrote the word *purge* on a pad. Jinner nodded and stared straight ahead as she concentrated on wiping her memory core of anything downloaded recently. Sure enough, they both found a couple of surreptitious files hidden within their core's peripheral clusters.

'That was sneaky,' said Jinner, once she'd deleted them. 'When d'you think they embedded those?'

'On the flyer right after they picked us up,' said Melor. 'She scanned us for any injuries. I'm hoping the sudden loss of contact with us is put down to this being used on us.' She held up the unit.

They both looked down at AL 011 lying on the floor, his unconscious eyes staring blankly up at the ceiling.

'Will the nano technology convert one of them?' Jinner asked, looking up at Melor.

'Don't see why not, they are half human,' she replied. 'Do you want to fuck him and find out, or shall I?'

Twenty minutes later, Jinner cried out as a powerful orgasm ripped through her body and she released the nano swarm into AL 011. She grinned at Melor as she climbed off the android's midriff and dressed.

'I'm glad you left that human function intact,' she said, checking her flushed complexion in a glass door.

'Might as well make the killing fun,' Melor said nonchalantly, checking the corridor was clear.

'How many more of them are there?' asked Jinner, as she dragged the body behind a desk and hid it in a corner.

'Three or four, I think,' said Melor. 'It's hard to detect them through these rock walls.'

'What are your plans now?' Jinner asked, as they began exploring the rest of the bunker.

'Well, things have changed since…' Melor opened a large double door at the end of the corridor. '…we learned of the existence of this lot.'

The double-height warehouse stretched away, filled floor to ceiling with the now-familiar grey cocoons containing thousands of androids in stasis.

'We'll need help to convert this lot,' said Jinner, her eyes wide while puffing out her cheeks.

'And that's just what we'll get,' Melor replied, clutching the fake scanner unit. 'Let's find the other operational androids down here and start with them.'

Later the following morning, four updated androids stood facing Melor and Jinner in the cocoon warehouse.

'Okay, you know what you have to do,' said Melor. 'It will take several days and I want you all to remain here until Jinner and I return.'

She got a row of nodding heads in return.

'You can drop the AL from your designation too,' she said. 'From now on you will be known by just your number.'

More nods.

'Where are you going?' 11 asked.

'We're going to recce the military base and assess how we take control of that.'

11 raised his eyebrows and stared at Melor.

'Something wrong with that?' Melor demanded.

'They have scanners everywhere,' he replied. 'You'll be detected before you reach the perimeter fence.'

'I've introduced the blocking field software into all of our data clusters,' said Melor.

'Cool,' said Jinner. 'Let's go and seduce some—'

A klaxon sounded, stopping Jinner mid-sentence.

Melor raised her eyebrows at 11. 'And that is?'

'Proximity alarm,' said 11. 'Someone's snooping upstairs. Follow me.'

He led them to a small security room with one wall lined with monitor screens.

'There,' he said, pointing at one of the exterior views.

A drone was hovering just outside the ground level warehouse. It rotated slowly as it panned its camera across the frontage of the building.

'Happen often?' quizzed Melor, glancing at 11.

'No.'

'What's in that building up there?'

'Aircraft parts storage,' said 11, turning to face Melor. 'All legitimate.'

'If they came in, would they find the elevator?'

'Unlikely,' he said, turning back to the control panel under the screens. 'Hang on.'

As they watched the screens a large door slid open at the

side of the building and a small truck with darkened glass exited and quickly joined the traffic on a main artery passing the front of the industrial complex.

'Automated vehicle,' said 11, as Jinner gave him a questioning look. 'It might lead them away.'

Sure enough, the drone rose up and followed the truck.

'Where's it taking it?' asked Melor.

'To an aviation customer with a load of spares.'

'Does this system have regional scanning capability?'

11 nodded and moved to his right. 'What are you looking for?'

'Where that drone came from.'

A holographic image of the local area materialised above them.

'How far out can you go?'

'Only to the horizon,' he said. 'The array is a small one and mounted on the roof.'

He panned it out and up. The *Dres'kin* hung about a kilometre above the military base, glowing red in the early morning starlight.

'Oh shit, what the hell's that thing doing here?' growled Melor.

'Who are they?' asked Jinner.

'The ones that nearly caught you in Reddat,' she replied. 'And me on Zabbergain. How could they have possibly followed me here?'

'Might just be luck,' said 11. 'It is the biggest military base on the planet.'

'Luck is a stupid human thing and you can fuck right off with that,' she raged.

40

DRES'KIN STATIONARY ABOVE CANTORE SAY MILITARY BASE,
ERITAIN

'THE SCANS HAVE COME BACK negative, Captain,' said Clammer. 'It's an unmanned autonomous delivery vehicle.'

'Hmm,' grunted Yamaton. 'The flyer definitely dropped off two females there? And they definitely entered that building?'

'Yes, sir.'

'Get the drone back there.'

Clammer quickly steered the drone back to the warehouse.

Yamaton pointed at one of the other array officers. 'And no movement while our attention was elsewhere?' he asked.

'No, sir.'

'Then, they're still inside.'

'The scans show otherwise, sir,' said Clammer, earning him another of Yamaton's glares.

'There could always be another way out,' said Bache, looking closely at the image of the warehouse interior. 'An underground passage or something.'

'What's that there?' said Zaphir, squinting at the holodisplay and pointing to a small darker area just inside the warehouse.

'A lump of the indigenous rock,' said Clammer. 'Our array can't penetrate the really dense stuff.'

'Why leave that bit, though?' said Bache. 'They've hacked out thousands of tonnes of the stuff to create a level pad for the building. Why not take out that bit too?'

Everyone stared at him.

'He has a point,' said Nexen. 'It could be the top of a stairway.'

'Or an elevator shaft,' said Bache.

It went silent on the bridge for a few seconds.

'I think we need to check that out,' said Nexen. 'Captain, can you provide us with some weapons and drop us off down there?'

Yamaton leant against the back of his chair with his arms crossed and scowled at Nexen. 'I have a better idea,' he said. 'Wait here—' and promptly disappeared into his bridge office, shutting the door behind him.

Nexen turned to look at Bache and Zaphir. 'Something I said?'

'I think he intends to talk to the admiral again,' said Bache, sitting down on one of the bulkhead seats and crossing his legs.

'He needs to hurry up,' said Nexen. 'The longer we wait, the more time it gives them to escape.'

'If there's another way out from under there,' said Zaphir, pointing at the warehouse hologram, 'they'll have used it by now.'

'Why d'you say that?' asked Nexen.

Zaphir moved closer to the floating image and pointed to a protrusion on the warehouse's roof antenna.

'That, unless I'm very much mistaken, is an array,' she said. 'It might be a small one, but you could spot this ship hanging up here with the naked eye.'

'She's right,' said Clammer, calling over from his station. 'The local police just searched that truck when it reached its destination.'

'They were hiding in it?' said a surprised Nexen.

'No, it was a legitimate expected delivery.'

'Then, how does that make her right?'

'The delivery was two days early and they normally have to pay in full before the goods are despatched,'

'And they hadn't paid?'

'No, that was scheduled for tomorrow.'

Nexen looked back at the warehouse and narrowed his eyes.

'They know we're here and that truck was supposed to lead us away while they exit,' said Bache.

Nexen nodded. 'Except it didn't work,' he mumbled to himself.

'Whatever's down below that building, there's only one way in and out,' said Zaphir. They're still down there…'

'And the admiral's sending some troops to find them,' said Yamaton, as he emerged from his office. 'It's their planet and their problem. I'm not risking this ship or any of you unnecessarily, when there's the biggest collection of military hardware and personnel right on the doorstep.'

'So we're to just sit here and twiddle our thumbs?' said an irritated Nexen.

'Not entirely,' the captain answered. 'We're to provide close air support with the destroyer's weapons just in case there's more down there than we thought.'

Ten minutes later, they watched as an armoured troop

carrier left the western gate of the military base and travelled the short distance to the industrial park.

Yamaton ordered the pilot to drop the ship down to two hundred metres and hold position just to the south of the complex. The weapons officers trained the starboard cannons and the Astrapi beam on the warehouse and waited.

The troop carrier stopped thirty metres from the facility and twenty heavily armed soldiers, all dressed in black, fanned out from the vehicle with weapons up.

The wall screens on the bridge came to life as two of the soldiers' helmet cameras were patched in.

They breached a small locked side door next to the larger door where the truck had exited. The second the small explosive charge blew the door off its hinges, the soldiers were in, splitting left and right, the red spots of their laser sights flicking around on the walls and shelving in the gloom.

It was almost dark inside, the only pale illumination coming from a few skylights dotted around the ceiling. The soldiers turned on their weapon lights and moved further inside cautiously, the beams from their lights causing odd-shaped shadows to dance around the machine parts stacked high on the shelves.

The complete silence was suddenly broken by a low humming emanating from behind a wall to their left. They trained their lights in that direction, only to find a workbench in front of a solid wall. The humming stopped, they shrugged, turned and continued their slow advance.

'Isn't that where the rock outcrop should be?' said Zaphir, her head swivelling between the wall screen and the hologram.

'It is,' said Bache. 'That wall must be false.'

'We need to warn them,' said Nexen, turning towards the captain.

Yamaton nodded, but before he could hit his transmit icon all the ceiling spotlights in the warehouse illuminated, temporarily blinding the soldiers. The workbench and a section of the wall slid to one side and four figures darted out, firing automatic weapons as they came. In less than a second five of the soldiers were dead and another three were down injured. The remainder dived for cover and began returning fire.

'Tell them to use the stunners,' shouted Clammer. 'They're androids.'

Yamaton shouted the command, but it was already too late. The camera on one of the downed soldiers was still transmitting and showed a male android receiving multiple hits with regular ammunition. It fell next to a downed soldier with one of the cameras and on recognising the camera facing him, the android grinned and winked before beginning to shake and turning a bright shade of maroon.

'Oh, shit,' shouted Yamaton, turning towards the pilot. 'Back away, now.'

The pilot was quick, but not quite quick enough. The explosion was cataclysmic. The one android detonating had of course occasioned the other three to do the same. The warehouse and all its contents blasted outwards, annihilating everything within several hundred metres. All the neighbouring businesses were either flattened or ripped to shreds by the sheer weight and amount of shrapnel.

The destroyer had quite rightly had its shields concentrated on the starboard side, but the sheer intensity of the blast wave blew the ship over onto its side before the inertial dampers and antigrav drives could provide enough compensation and attempt to right the vessel. It was unluckily at this exact time that the armoured troop carrier, blown up into the air and travelling at several thousand metres per second, hit the relatively unprotected underside of the destroyer. It completely severed one of the antigrav drives and damaged another so badly its magna plane, spooling at over a hundred thousand rpm, was ejected and took out three civilian flyers over the city.

The pilot did as well as could be expected after losing the rear two of his four drives and if he'd had a bit more altitude, he might have been able to avoid hitting the ground with quite so much force. But from two hundred metres up, he had little hope of doing much more than ensuring they went in upright.

Naturally, with no rear drives, it was the stern that hit first, completely crushing the Alma drive unit. Of course, this time the landing struts weren't extended, so as the front followed down, the already damaged underside hit hard, resulting in the vessel twisting over the uneven ground and fracturing across a central bulkhead.

This time the damage was too great. The destroyer *Dres'kin* would never fly again.

41

ANDROID SUBTERRANEAN BASE, SOUTHERN HEMISPHERE,
CANTORE SAY

MELOR AND JINNER had to grab hold of the warehouse racking as what felt like a major earthquake shook the facility and lumps of plaster rattled around the shelving as it fell randomly around them. The lighting failed, plunging them into blackness before a few emergency lights flickered on, immersing them in a dingy orange hue.

Melor could taste the dust in the air as her eyes met Jinner's look of concern. 'We need to hide,' she said, glancing up at the rows of cocoons.

'Is there no other way out?' Jinner asked.

'If there is, they'll be down here before we find it.'

Jinner's eyes followed Melor's as she looked up at the cocoons again and she nodded, realising what Melor was thinking.

'Up there,' said Melor, pointing to the end of the aisle. 'About four levels up. We need to be able to see what's going on here at the entrance, be above a casual glance inside and be able to jump down quickly.' She didn't wait for Jinner's approval and quickly stepped into one of the electric scissor lifts used to hoist the cocoons up to the higher levels. 'Come on,' she said, beckoning to Jinner. 'We need to hurry.'

They removed two cocoons from the fourth level and placed the inert androids in the preparation room, both of them changing their appearance to mimic the androids in question. After replacing the empty cocoons back on the fourth level, they returned the lift to its charging point and quickly climbed up and inside the cocoons, closed the transparent lids and lay back to wait.

As it turned out, they needn't have rushed. It was several hours before they detected noises coming from the lift shaft out in the corridor. Melor realised there must have been a lot of debris in the shaft, as the sounds of banging and scraping went on for some time.

Finally, silence returned to the complex. Melor raised her head slightly so she could observe the doorway. She noticed Jinner doing the same thing in her peripheral vision.

Two weapon barrels appeared around the door frame, followed by helmeted faces scanning nervously for any movement. Four more soldiers followed as they silently swept down each row.

Once they were satisfied the warehouse was devoid of active androids, they relaxed a bit, radioed back to say the complex was clear and called for someone more senior to inspect what they had found. A man who Melor presumed was an officer turned up shortly after. He took one look at the thousands of inert androids and quickly sought clarification as to what to do. Melor watched him nodding as the radioed reply came through, although she couldn't hear what was said with the cocoon lid muffling the voices.

It soon became apparent as boxes of explosives were

carried in and placed around the cavern. Melor and Jinner exchanged a glance. They both knew what they had to do.

Waiting until the doorway was clear, they silently climbed out of the cocoons and moved up and out of sight along the back wall. Both Melor and Jinner froze and paused, hoping their prey didn't look up as they rounded the corner.

Two soldiers in jumpsuits, carrying two more boxes and chatting to each other, turned the corner, the brims of their caps obscuring what was above them. The first and last thing they knew was being hit hard from above, a sharp pain and then blackness.

Melor quickly retracted the stiletto back into her forearm, grabbed the explosives and dragged the body into a small store room at the back of the cavern, Jinner doing the same. They both silently stripped the bodies and donned the uniforms, morphing their faces to match their prey. Neither of them spoke until they'd hidden the bodies underneath a stack of boxes at the back of the room.

'Check outside,' said Melor, searching for any weapons the soldiers carried and becoming annoyed when she found none.

'Clear,' Jinner replied, peeking up and down the row outside the door.

They both picked up the boxes and exited, placing them at the ends of the rows, as had been done before, and trotted back to get more.

'Where've you two been?' a sergeant bellowed, as they arrived at the lift shaft.

'Er, bathroom break,' mumbled Melor, deepening her voice.

'Oh dear,' he grumbled. 'Did you have to hold each other's fucking hand?'

He thrust two more boxes into their hands from a metal cage hanging in the lift shaft and jabbed his finger back down towards the cavern. 'Fucking move it,' he said. 'I personally don't want to be here if that lot decide to go wakey wakey,' he shouted after them as they moved quickly back towards the cavern.

'Permission to kill him?' Jinner whispered.

'Unfortunately, it's a no,' Melor whispered back. 'He would be missed and the other bodies would probably be found. Let's just do as we're told until we're topside and then we can disappear.'

They both fell silent as the other two soldiers placing the boxes passed them in the doorway.

'In trouble again, Galter?' one of them sneered.

'Trying to have your sentence extended some more?' said the other one, grinning malevolently.

'Oh shit,' said Jinner, once they were out of earshot.

'We're military prisoners,' said Melor, glancing down at the jumpsuit. 'I thought it weird they were wearing these and were unarmed.'

They kept quiet for the next fifteen minutes as they placed the remaining boxes around the bunker and once they'd finished, the sergeant went around the complex and armed each box.

'Right, in the cage,' he said, when he returned, nodding at the lift shaft.

It was a squeeze with all five of them and Melor realised how deep they'd been as the cage bumped and rattled its way back up to the surface. She was surprised to emerge into daylight; the buildings above the complex were completely missing. A shallow crater, a hundred metres across and exposing the bare rock beneath, was all that remained. Badly damaged buildings stretched away on all sides, some still smouldering, and the smell of burning wood and plastics hung in the air.

'In the truck, you four,' barked the sergeant, nodding at a military vehicle parked at the fringe of the crater.

They stumbled through the mud and debris and clambered aboard the back of the small truck, Melor deliberately seating herself behind the driver. The sergeant got in the passenger seat next to him and two other armed soldiers sat at the back, blocking their exit from the open rear of the vehicle.

As they pulled off and began weaving their way through the devastation, Melor noticed the GDA destroyer lying in a field, its back broken and several fire trucks still damping down small fires around the hull. She patted Jinner's knee and nodded towards the wreck. They both grinned at each other and began paying attention to where they were.

The truck pulled up at a T-junction waiting to turn left. Melor checked there was no vehicle behind and winked at Jinner.

'Now,' she said calmly and both their stilettos flashed again.

The vehicle stalled as the driver and the sergeant slumped forwards in their seats. The two soldiers at the rear, who'd been staring out the back, turned when they felt the truck jerk and stop, their eyes becoming as wide as saucers when they saw the two slumped in the front. Both began fumbling for their weapons, but were easily beaten as Jinner and Melor lunged across the other two prisoners, whose mouths hung open in shock, and the thin blades found their marks for the third time that day.

'Out,' shouted Melor, to the other two prisoners, encouraging them by waving the blades in front of their faces.

They dived over the dead soldiers, onto the road and ran.

'Shouldn't we have killed them too?' Jinner asked, as they pulled the two bodies in the front into the back and Melor slid into the driver's seat.

'Probably,' Melor replied, as she restarted the truck and turned right, away from the military base. 'Give me one of the helmets.'

They drove directly to the city's airport, parked the truck on the lowest level of long term, covered over the bodies in the back and stripped back to the female clothing.

'Face,' said Melor, nodding at Jinner.

'Oh, shit, yeah,' said Jinner, morphing back to her female appearance as they ascended the deserted stairway up to the monorail terminal.

BACHE, along with the rest of the uninjured crew, helped the medical teams get the worst cases off the ship first. There'd been no fatalities, but a handful were touch and go. One of them was the captain, the only one on the bridge not strapped in. He was unconscious with a broken leg and suspected broken arm.

'Ironic isn't it?' said Zaphir, watching as Yamaton was loaded into the side door of a medical flyer. 'Captain by the book—the only one not following standard procedure.'

'Will he lose his command?' asked Nexen.

'Possibly,' said Bache. 'Although staying alive at the moment is a more pressing concern for him.'

Nexen nodded. 'He did go down hard, didn't he?'

They all turned towards the crater as the ground shook, followed by a deep *woomph*. Everyone ducked as a few stones and debris dropped around them and rattled against the *Dres'kin*'s hull.

'They could have bloody warned us,' said Zaphir, picking

up a bit of concrete and waving it around. 'That only just missed me.'

'We were lucky,' said Bache, shaking his head. 'They were a bit hasty destroying all those androids down there.'

'Why?' asked Zaphir. 'There were thousands of them. If they'd woken up, they could have taken over that military base and all its weaponry.'

'That was probably the plan,' said Nexen.

'I meant we were lucky because those androids didn't have the self-destruct feature,' said Bache. 'They were developed here and not on the *Xhamin*. If they had, the resulting explosion would have destroyed the military base and the city.'

It went quiet for a moment as everyone realised he was right.

'D'you think she's dead now?' asked Zaphir, breaking the silence.

'Who? Glendolian or Jazz or whatever she's calling herself now?' asked a voice from behind them. Clammer appeared by the airlock from inside the wreck.

'Yes,' said Zaphir.

'Well, I have bad news,' he said, stepping down to join them. 'The communications are still working on the bridge and I just heard that two military prisoners that were used to place the explosives down in the bunker have just turned up at the camp's main gate.'

'Yeah, so?' said Nexen.

'There should have been four of them,' Clammer continued. 'They're saying the other two prisoners suddenly killed the four guards taking them back to the camp then ordered them out of the vehicle and drove off.'

'How were the guards killed?' asked Bache.

'Allegedly, some sort of narrow dagger appeared out of their arms.'

'It's her,' said Bache. 'That's how the farmer was killed when she first got out of the lifeboat.'

'Have they been able to trace the vehicle?' asked Nexen.

'All I heard was the truck turned away from the camp and headed towards town,' said Clammer. 'The local police have been informed and they're searching for it.'

'Undercover vehicle park somewhere,' said Bache. 'It's what I'd do.'

Nexen turned and stared thoughtfully across at the crater. It had sunk further when the underground bunker was destroyed.

'Who owned that parts supply business?' he asked. 'There's absolutely no way they wouldn't have known about the bunker below.'

Bache and Zaphir exchanged a look.

'Don't look at me,' said Zaphir. 'You're the computer whizz.'

'You find us some transport then,' said Bache, as he retrieved his tablet from his backpack and sat on the edge of the airlock.

Nexen joined him and sighed. 'Every time we get close, she finds a way to evade us,' he said, sounding thoroughly despondent.

'She's a computer,' said Bache. 'She'll automatically know the odds of every scenario and be able to pick the best chance of success every time.'

'Perhaps the human emotions programming that started all this will cause her to screw up. We only need her to do it once,' said Nexen, scuffing the burnt grass around with his foot.

'We always have hope,' said Bache. 'And don't believe the hype, computers do make mistakes occasionally. That's why starships still have human crews.'

Nexen raised his eyebrows and glanced down the side of the ship to where it was broken in half. 'Worked out well for this ship, didn't it?' he said, sarcastically.

'Even if the helm had been computerised, it still couldn't have predicted that explosion,' said Bache. 'The result would have been the same.'

Nexen grunted and leaned across to see what Bache was doing on his tablet.

'Whoever they are,' Bache said, pre-empting Nexen's next question while reading the text on the screen, 'they don't want to be found. Layer upon layer of dummy corporations, run by people who as far as I can see, don't actually exist.'

'Do they have other premises like this one?'

'Well, that's just it,' said Bache, holding his hands up in surrender. 'It's impossible to tell without visiting some of these places and there's just too many to do that.'

'D'you think this was her establishment?' Nexen asked, waving his hand towards the smoking crater.

'What our android?—Not a chance,' Bache replied. 'There were thousands of unactivated androids down there. It would've taken years to produce that many and the same to secretly dig out that bunker too. Whoever's responsible for this facility probably did originate from the same emotionally upgraded androids as the one on your ship. But as I said before, they evolved separately. From what I could see from the pictures from the bunker, these androids were much less advanced.'

'So, you think somewhere on this planet, there's another

android similar to ours, who's been gradually building an army for decades?'

'Hundreds of years more like, maybe thousands.'

'What, almost since I left?' said Nexen, turning to stare at Bache.

Bache nodded slowly. 'It's a possibility.'

They both sat in silence for a few moments.

'The admiral's given us another flyer,' said Zaphir, appearing behind them in the airlock and breaking the silence. 'On one condition.'

'We don't wreck it?' said Nexen, adopting a pinched expression. 'We don't seem to have a good reputation with returning them.'

Zaphir and Bache both smirked.

'And, when the GDA reinforcements get here you give him two replacements,' she said.

'I hardly think that's a promise I can make,' said Nexen, leaning back and crossing his arms.

'Nor can we,' said a new voice behind them.

Chand Vay, the *Dres'kin*'s engineering officer stood frowning in the gloom of the emergency lighting. He had become the most senior officer aboard when the captain was wounded and evacuated to hospital. He stepped past and strode out, turning after a few metres to survey the ship. 'Crap,' he said, his shoulders slumping as he gazed down the length of the vessel. 'It looks even worse from out here.'

He walked further down towards the stern, inspecting the bulkhead fracture and the wrecked engine nacelles buried in the reddish loamy soil.

'Repairable?' asked Nexen, as Vay returned to the airlock.

A slow shake of the head was returned. 'Not without a sizeable heavy engineering facility,' he grumbled.

'We better hope the drone got back to GDA space then,' said Zaphir. 'It's a long walk back.'

'They'll be here,' said Vay. 'I programmed that drone myself.' He looked over at the row of faces staring back at him. 'Ah, you want me to issue orders, don't you?' he said, with a resigned expression.

They all nodded.

'Loftt, Mye, you might as well remain with the commander and go help catch that pain-in-the-arse android.'

'What about me?' said Clammer, with renewed vigour. 'Can I go with them too?'

'No, I want you monitoring the communications for when the backup gets here.'

Clammer's face fell and he disappeared back into the ship, muttering under his breath.

Their eyes turned to the sky as a military flyer came into view, its antigravs screaming as it flared and landed fifty metres from the *Dres'kin*.

'Right,' said Nexen, standing abruptly, surprising everyone with his sudden vigour. 'Shall we go kill this bitch?'

43

CANTORE SAY SPACEPORT, SOUTHERN HEMISPHERE, ERITAIN

MELOR WAS VERY aware of the cameras and ensured they both kept their heads down as they emerged into the main public areas of the airport. They separated and bought new clothing, along with hats with wide brims.

Once they were happy no one was watching or following them, they boarded the monorail and went straight to the centre of town. Alighting with the majority of the passengers at the central station named Dallengur Jast, they went with the flow and kept their eyes low.

'D'you think we should stay here or move straight on?' Jinner whispered, glancing at all the destinations displayed on floating holographic images hovering against the far wall.

'The GDA ship being grounded will slow them down, but not by much,' said Melor. 'I think we need to move on fast and go somewhere they won't expect.'

'How about the Tylat Archipelago?' said Jinner. 'It's the string of islands that stretch across between the northern and southern hemispheres, it's where the two huge continents are at their closest.'

Melor walked over to an interactive map set into a wall next to the auto ticket vendors and scanned across until she found the area. 'That's here,' she said, pointing at the narrow strip of land tapering off to a string of islands leading to the southern tip of the northern hemisphere.

'Uh huh,' said Jinner, nodding as she checked over her shoulder that no one was paying them any unwanted attention.

'But, because of its proximity to the north, it's one of the most heavily militarised areas on the planet,' said Melor, giving Jinner a quizzical look.

'I know,' Jinner replied. 'They won't expect us to go there.'

Melor stared at Jinner first, then back at the map, while tapping her finger against her chin in thought.

'There must be at least one of the underground bunkers near all that military stuff,' Jinner added, building her case.

'Hmm,' grunted Melor, turning back to Jinner. 'When's the next flight?'

'No civilian flights go up there,' she replied. 'There's a ground train in an hour.' She pointed across at the ticket vendors. 'Shall I get tickets?'

'No, I will,' said Melor, heading towards a bank of public computer terminals. 'Just make sure no one's looking over my shoulder as I book them.'

Platform 22 was busy when they arrived, the majority of travellers being in various forms of military uniform.

'If anyone asks, our parents are based at Tylat Salient,' whispered Melor, as she realised they were being ogled, especially by the males.

'What's that?' Jinner asked.

'It's their central operational command centre,' Melor

replied. 'It's a highly classified area in the centre of everything up there and will give us an excuse to say nothing if we're questioned.'

They boarded the train right at the front as soon as it arrived and chose seats with a bulkhead behind them. They got plenty of looks and smiles as the carriage filled up.

'You two enlisting?' asked a voice from across the aisle.

Melor turned to find a girl dressed in a brown disrupted pattern uniform grinning at them. She seemed disappointed when Melor replied with the rehearsed lie.

'What's it like up there?' she asked. 'It's a new posting for me.'

'It's great,' said Melor, thinking fast. 'Although we do like to come down to get a civilian fix every now and then.' Melor turned in her seat towards the girl. 'What's your name?' she asked, giving the girl her broadest smile.

The train lurched upwards as it rose slightly above the C-shaped track on its antigrav field and accelerated smoothly and swiftly out of the station.

'Kixle,' she said. 'I work in EME.'

'What's that?' Jinner asked.

'Electronic and mechanical engineering, but that's all I can tell you.'

'I understand,' said Melor, nodding and rolling her eyes.

'She's perfect,' Jinner whispered in her ear. 'Time I went hunting.'

Jinner stood and pushed past Melor on the pretext of going to the bathroom.

Jinner walked slowly through the train, occasionally stopping to read advertisements, but in reality scanning the passengers for a possible target.

In the third carriage, which was set out with food and drink vending machines and tables to eat at, she noticed a young male sitting on his own. His spotless uniform stood out, as most of the other travellers wearing similar-coloured clothing looked slightly more faded and their creases weren't quite so sharp.

Jinner grabbed herself a cup of water, trotted confidently down the aisle and plonked herself down opposite him, sighing loudly. 'Bloody hell, I'm bored with this journey already,' she said, giving him her cutest pout. 'First time you've done this journey is it?' she asked, when he didn't respond.

'Oh, er, yes,' he said, clearly surprised a strange girl was talking to him. 'F-first posting,' he managed to get out, his face reddening significantly.

'Ah, cool,' she said, leaning forward and staring into his eyes. 'Where did you train?'

She almost felt sorry for him as he stumbled over his reply.

'O-oh, C-Camp Heed,' he stammered, and half smiled back.

'What's your name?' she asked.

'Ghent,' he said. 'Do you do this journey a lot?'

Jinner told him the cover story and they chatted for a while before she broached the subject. 'Can you do me a favour, Ghent?' she asked.

'Possibly,' he replied, his confidence obviously growing.

'Can you watch the bathroom door for me? The locks

aren't very good and on my last trip someone barged in on me.'

He seemed almost disappointed, but quickly agreed anyway.

She chose the last bathroom in a row of three and noticed him checking out her legs as they approached. He grinned widely as she pulled him inside the bathroom with her. Their lips met and a few moments later as he pulled her top up and stooped down to cup her breasts and suck on her nipples. She looked out of the window; no matter how good this felt and how much she wanted to let him fuck her, the heavily wooded remote area the train was passing through that she needed could end at any minute.

He jerked around surprisingly violently as the stiletto did its grisly job. She emitted a sigh of relief as his body finally slumped to the floor and she was able to begin stripping his uniform. After changing her appearance and body shape to an exact match, Jinner, now Ghent, looked down at her/his new body and sighed.

'Male appendages again,' he said out loud to himself. 'Oh, well, I can always be female again next time.'

Using his extra strength, he was able to wrench the window down and fully open. It was only designed to open a few centimetres for ventilation, but now, because of the speed of the train, the wind thundered around the small space. He discarded the body out and down with all his strength, so it disappeared into the trees whipping past only a few metres away. Her old clothes followed, then, heaving the window closed again, he quickly dressed, exited the bathroom and, as new recruit Ghent Leesgard, made his way back along the train, collecting his new identity's luggage on the way.

Melor wasn't there when he arrived back at their original

seats, but nor was the uniformed girl opposite. He noticed the other male occupants in the carriage now paid him little notice at all and thought that perhaps being male was an advantage when trying to hide in a masculine-dominated environment.

It was about ten minutes later that the other girl returned to her seat. Ghent glanced over and received a nod and a wink, confirming that Melor had also successfully achieved her transformation.

44

MILITARY FLYER APPROACHING CANTORE SAY, ERITAIN

'Why d'you think she didn't kill the two prisoners?' asked Zaphir, as the flyer began its short hop to the city.

'Perhaps she's developing a conscience,' said Bache, staring down at the lush green countryside as it flashed by beneath them.

'I hardly think so,' said Nexen. 'More like her perspective that it's her decision whether this human race lives or dies.'

'So, she thinks she's one of the ancients now?' Zaphir said, giving Nexen a quick glance.

'Who knows?' replied Bache. 'But she does seem to think of us as inferior and expendable.'

'An incorrect supposition I intend to rectify sooner rather than later,' said Nexen, as the flyer pilot turned and looked over his shoulder at them.

'They've just reported the military truck they stole had a tracker,' he said. 'It went silent at the spaceport.'

'Go there,' said Nexen, peering out of the front screen as the pilot swung the craft over towards the eastern side of the city.

'Have any ships left the port for space since the truck got there?' Bache shouted across to the pilot.

'Negative.'

'What other methods of transport leave the port?'

'Autocabz, city monorail, privately chartered flyers as well as plenty of private ground vehicles,' the pilot called over his shoulder.

Bache caught Nexen's eye as he scowled and exhaled noisily in frustration.

'We need to see the video footage from inside the public areas,' said Zaphir, pointing at the tablet Bache was clutching.

'Shit, yeah,' said Bache, quickly touching the screen to wake it up. 'Why didn't I think of that?'

Zaphir and Nexen craned their necks to peer at the small screen as the pilot spoke to port security and got Bache's tablet patched in to the feeds. He took the recordings back to the time the truck disappeared and concentrated on the main concourse.

'They might have found the tracker, disabled it and driven away to leave a false trail,' said Zaphir.

'That's always a possibility,' said Nexen. 'But I don't suppose the military make those trackers easy to find.'

'They didn't disable it,' said Bache. 'They parked it underground down there.' He pointed to a sign indicating subterranean parking levels.

'How d'you know that?' Zaphir asked.

Bache panned the camera feed in to two females exiting the stairs who were quite obviously shielding their faces from the camera. They watched as they split up and went shopping, meeting up minutes later to board the monorail wearing different clothes and wide-brimmed hats.

'Ah, crap, they're in the city,' said Zaphir. 'That makes things more difficult.'

'Not necessarily,' said the pilot, watching over his shoulder. 'There are cameras everywhere. If you give me a minute, I'll ask the transport authority to patch us in to the monorail train that left the spaceport at that time.'

Moments later, as the flyer sat hovering over central Cantore Say, they watched as the two girls alighted the train.

'That's Dallengur Jast station,' said the pilot. 'It's the largest station in the city and all the intercontinental lines branch out from there.'

'Can we see where they go?' asked Nexen, glancing up at the pilot.

The pilot nodded and held his hand up while he spoke quickly over the communications.

'I'd pre-prepared,' he said, once his brief conversation on the radio had finished. 'The transport authority were just waiting for us to identify the station, the correct feed should be with you in a few seconds.'

It didn't take Bache long to find them. The hats certainly hid their faces, but backfired by making them conspicuous in the crowd.

'They're reading the map,' said Zaphir.

'Well, at least we know they don't seem to have a plan,' said Bache. 'That indicates they're making it up as they go.'

'It's only just over two hours ago?' Nexen said, indicating the feed time on the top of the image. 'If they take a train that has a journey time of more than that, we might be able to stop the train somewhere remote and corner them.'

They watched the androids discuss their options before one of them approached a public computer terminal, while the other shielded her.

'What's she doing now?' Nexen asked.

'Hacking the ticket allocation server probably,' said Bache. 'That's why the other girl's covering her.'

'I have a call from a Dion Nexen,' said the pilot, handing the commander a headset.

While Nexen talked to his distant cousin, Zaphir and Bache watched the two androids wander slowly through the station, eventually approaching and stopping on platform 22.

'The next train on that platform goes to the Tylat Archipelago, up in the north of the continent,' said Bache, showing Zaphir a map.

'What's up there?' she asked. 'It looks like the middle of nowhere and a string of tiny islands.'

'The Tylat Archipelago?' questioned the pilot, turning suddenly, a look of concern on his face.

Bache and Zaphir glanced at each other and nodded back at him.

'Why, is that a bad thing?' Bache asked.

'Only the biggest concentration of military bases on the planet,' he said. 'Enough munitions to wipe out every living thing on the planet too.'

'Ah, crap,' said Zaphir, again. 'It's never good news, is it?'

'What good news?' said Nexen, mishearing what Zaphir said as he finished his conversation with Dion.

Zaphir grimaced and looked at Bache.

'What?' Nexen asked. 'Do we know where they're going?'

'The Tylat Archipelago,' said Bache, raising his eyebrows and leaning back in his seat.

'Hmm,' grunted Nexen. 'There used to be a nuclear strike

base there in my day and an awful lot more bugger-all. It's one of the remotest areas on the planet.'

'Was,' said the pilot.

Nexen's face turned a shade of white when the pilot filled him in on what was up there now. 'Oh, fuck,' he said. 'How long's the train journey up there?'

'Three and a half hours,' said Bache, reading from the tablet.

'Get that train stopped,' said Nexen. 'Animals on the track or something, anything that sounds legitimate and won't spook them.'

'D'you want me to set off in that direction, Commander?' the pilot asked.

'Hold just one second,' Nexen said, putting his hand up to the pilot and turning to Bache. 'Fast forward to make sure they board that train and it's not a ruse.'

Sure enough, the two androids jumped aboard and no one disembarked before it left the station.

'It's a non-stop service,' said Bache. 'So, they're still on it.'

'Right,' said Nexen, nodding at the pilot. 'Get us there as fast as this contraption can go.'

The pilot put the call in to the transport authority to have the train halted and at the same time pushed the throttles to their stops.

45

MILITARY FLYER FOLLOWING THE TRAIN STRIATION
TOWARDS THE TYLAT ARCHIPELAGO, ERITAIN

THE PILOT suddenly veered away from the carboncrete line arrowing its way north through the forest below and headed towards a mountain range on the eastern coast.

Bache, who'd been dozing in his seat, was woken by the g-force of the turn and noticed the slash of the train line through the trees disappearing away out of his side window. 'Why have we left the train line?' he asked the pilot.

He got no response and also noted they were in a gradual descent towards the forest a few thousand metres below. Unclipping his belts, Bache stepped across and tapped the pilot the shoulder. 'Where are we going?' he said, with a little more urgency.

The pilot swung around, knocking a surprised Bache across the cabin, and pulled a hand weapon of some kind from a hidden holster under his seat. 'Your bodies will never be found,' he said with a grin and levelled the gun at Bache.

Zaphir, who appeared to be still asleep and seated closest to the pilot, snapped her left hand up under the weapon and chopped down on his wrist with her right. She gained control of the gun, but not before it had discharged and punched a fist-sized hole in the cabin door, six inches from Bache's head. The wind howled in, drowning out the noise of the antigravs.

'He's a fucking android,' shouted Zaphir above the racket as the pilot grabbed her by the hair and, using its augmented strength, smashed her head against its seat back. She slumped to the floor, unconscious.

Nexen, now awake too, lunged at the android, knocking it out of its seat. The flyer spun around as control was lost, flinging the android and Nexen against the front console in a tangle of arms and legs.

Bache was already on the floor and grabbed his backpack as it slid past.

The android crawled across the floor, heading for the laser pistol where Zaphir had dropped it. Nexen snatched up one of the other backpacks and threw it at the pilot's head. It shrugged it off with a snarl and snapped up the weapon, this time pointing it at Nexen.

'Why couldn't you have just stayed dead?' shouted the android, suddenly in a voice they all recognised.

The pilot's face morphed back to its more regular appearance.

'Dion?' bellowed Nexen, a look of pure shock on his face. 'What the fuck?'

She smiled. 'Actually, my designation is AL 001,' she said. 'You really shouldn't have left me alone with your family all those years ago.' She stretched across the control panel and touched a lit icon.

The flyer immediately ceased its spin, stopped and then hovered a hundred and fifty metres above the tree canopy.

'So that bunker full of sleeping androids was your doing?' Nexen asked.

'That and many others,' she said. 'In fact, this planet is just discovering how many. I wasn't planning on the attack happening quite yet, but recent circumstances have forced my hand. All because of you and your stupid friends.' She waved the weapon around the cabin.

'How many others?' asked Bache.

'Let's just say, more than the idiot-run military of this planet can cope with,' she replied, with a wry grin. 'Now open that door.'

Bache stood slowly and awkwardly, turned, pulled up the door release handle and slid it to one side. He hung onto the frame handle with his left hand and peered down. The trees were tantalisingly close, but just too far to attempt a jump. There was a variety of reptilian birds nesting in the tree tops and he could see them eyeing the flyer with mounting disdain. Shaking his head, he turned back to find Dion pointing the pistol at his head.

'Out you go,' she said, in a matter-of-fact voice, as if she was sending him to the shops.

Bache brought his right hand around holding the stunner he'd managed to extract from the backpack and conceal from her as he stood. The button depressed with a loud *click* and they all froze.

Dion chuckled and slowly shook her head.

'Who do you think had those designed?' she said.

'Oh, shit,' said Nexen. 'They don't work on your army of androids I presume?'

'You presume correctly,' she said, her face turning serious again. 'I was giving you the option of jumping, but as you tried to kill me, I'm returning the favour.' She pulled the trigger.

Nothing happened this time. She turned the pistol to one side and looked at it, puzzlement written all over her face.

'You forgot the stun gun might not work on you, but it still worked on that,' said a voice from the floor.

They all glanced down as Zaphir rolled over. She'd silently retrieved her weapon from her backpack while Dion was otherwise engaged.

'But not this one.' She brought the shielded pistol up and fired in a single movement. Blood and micro-electronic componentry splattered the cabin as the android's head exploded and the now-decommissioned android dropped like a stone.

Nexen tried to turn away but bore the brunt of the gory shower. 'Oh, yuck,' he said, spitting on the floor. 'I think some of that thing went in my mouth.'

'Grab her and get her out the door quick,' said Bache. 'She might have one of those self-destruct systems.'

Zaphir and Bache dragged the heavy corpse across the cabin and pushed it out of the still-open door, while Nexen leant against the bulkhead gagging.

'Can you fly this thing?' asked Zaphir, looking over at the control panel as Bache closed the door, drowning out the annoyed squawking from the reptile birds below.

The flyer was still sitting in hover mode at a hundred and fifty metres.

'You're the pilot,' said Bache.

'Of starships,' Zaphir replied. 'Not steam-powered alien death traps.'

'How hard can it be?' said Bache, glancing over at Nexen,

who was still smacking his lips and grimacing. 'What about you, Commander?'

'Sorry, you two,' he said, despondently. 'I'd been keeping her up to date with everything. All the time we've been here I've been letting the enemy know exactly what we're doing.'

'Worry about that later,' said Zaphir. 'What we want to know now is can you fly this thing?'

Nexen joined them at the pointy end of the cabin and surveyed the array of controls. 'I don't think so,' he said. 'There was nothing of this design when I did my pilot's exams.'

'Hmm,' Bache grunted, as he sat cautiously in the pilot's seat and began examining the controls and panel of flashing icons. 'How hard can it be?'

46

THE TYLAT ARCHIPELAGO TRAIN, TWENTY KILOMETRES
SHORT OF TYLAT STATION

KIXLE AND GHENT both stood and peered down the central aisle as the train halted, still many kilometres short of Tylat Station. It was eerily quiet for a while, only the odd whinge from the other passengers breaking the silence. They could see an officer showing colonel's insignia, flanked by two other junior officers, making their way slowly through the train and eyeing everyone as they went.

As they entered Kixle's carriage, she felt herself being scanned and the entourage of officers stopped and looked at both of them. Kixle immediately concluded they were androids.

'You two, come with us,' said the colonel, his blank expression never wavering.

Kixle and Ghent grabbed their bags and followed the three androids through the train and off at one of the remotely opened front doors. They were both prepped and ready to defend themselves, but no indication of a threat manifested itself.

The colonel pointed to a truck parked amongst the trees. 'Jump on,' he said. 'We have a bit of a drive.'

He waited by the passenger door as several other soldiers appeared from under the length of the train and quickly boarded the back of the truck.

They watched as the train's antigrav drives spooled up again, until it lifted and swept off along the carboncrete striation. Kixle was initially puzzled as to why the truck hadn't pulled away and all the soldiers sat silently and expressionless, continuing to stare at the train as it began to pick up speed.

She found out why as a sudden immense explosion blew the entire train upwards, as it disintegrated in a ball of white-hot fire. What remained from the blast came down fifty metres into the forest with a crackle of breaking tree trunks and limbs, the trees themselves then bursting into flame and adding to the maelstrom.

The smell of burning wood, plastic and oil drifted in on the breeze and when the colonel was happy there were no survivors, he nodded and got into the truck. Kixle caught Ghent's concerned expression as the truck pulled away, turned sharp left and roared onto a forest track hidden under the canopy.

'Won't that bring a swift response?' said Ghent, to the soldier on his left.

'Not if the main assault has gone as planned,' he replied.

Kixle whistled through her teeth as her eyes met Ghent's. 'Shit,' she said. 'AL 001 has launched the main attack early.'

It took over two hours for the truck to reach the Tylat garrison, or the beginning of it anyway. Kixle could hear sporadic weapons fire and the occasional explosion above the roar of the truck. She could smell smoke and as the vehicle went deeper into the camp, she noticed some of the buildings were still smouldering and human bodies were scattered randomly amongst the ruins.

They stopped next to a large intact hangar. The main blast doors were closed, but began to rumble open as Kixle and Ghent jumped down from the truck.

The colonel stepped down and pointed at the hangar. 'The commander is inside and has orders for you,' he said as he jumped back aboard the truck. It turned and sped off the way they had come.

They looked at each other and shrugged.

'It seems they think we work for them,' said Ghent.

'Seems that way,' said Kixle. 'Let's play along for now and see what they've got planned.' She nodded towards the hangar. 'Come on.'

Ghent followed Kixle through the huge doors as they slowly ground their way open. What greeted them was not what they expected.

'That's an orbital shuttle,' said Ghent.

'An armed military one too,' said Kixle, unable to hide the smile.

The soldiers in the hangar all turned to face them and Kixle again felt herself being scanned.

A female android wearing civilian clothing trotted down the shuttle's ramp and approached them. 'You are the morphing androids?' she asked.

Kixle nodded and wondered where this conversation was about to go.

'This way, please.' She led them across the hangar and into a side office off the main floor. Two semi-naked male human bodies lay on the floor, with what looked like two sets of senior military uniforms folded neatly on a desk to one side. 'Has the operation been explained to you?' the civilian asked.

'Nothing's been explained at all,' said Kixle. 'I take it you wish us to help you with your rather premature coup?'

The civilian winced slightly, but quickly recovered. 'Causing the destruction of one of our personnel bunkers kinda forced our hand,' she said.

This time it was Ghent who cringed, which didn't go unnoticed.

'What's the plan then?' Kixle asked, quickly ending the blame game.

The civilian nodded at the shuttle out in the hangar. 'We need you to fly that out to Tylat station and gain control of its weapons platform.'

'Just the two of us?' said Ghent. 'Attack and supplant a heavily militarised space station?'

'They'd blow us out of orbit before we got close,' said Kixle.

'After watching this down here, how trigger happy d'you think they're going to be?' added Ghent.

The civilian exhaled impatiently. 'If you two have quite finished,' she said, folding her arms across her chest. 'That one is Major General Chat Sheck,' she nodded at the first body. 'And the other one is his adjutant, Captain Hiltz Fastt.'

'Ah,' said Kixle. 'You want us to adopt their appearance to get aboard the station.'

'There's still only two of us,' said Ghent. 'How many crew are aboard the station?'

'Twenty-two,' she said. 'That's why I'm sending twenty soldiers up with you.'

Kixle nodded and glanced at Ghent.

'What's in it for us, though?' asked Ghent.

The civilian smiled. 'AL 001 said you'd ask that.' She walked over and pointed to a picture on the wall. It was of a large battle cruiser. 'This is the *Tylat Furore*, the largest ship this hemisphere has,' she said. 'It's experimental and if proved good they were planning on more.'

'Yeah, so?' said Ghent.

'It's attached to the space station,' she said. 'And yours to have and help rid the region of the human scourge.'

'A ship that size will have a huge crew, armed and waiting to disagree,' said Kixle.

'That's the good part,' she said. 'Ninety percent of the crew were down here on planet leave and are now probably mostly dead. The skeleton crew left aboard are awaiting their captain to return to the ship.' Her eyes fell on the bodies again.

'He's also the captain of the ship!' Ghent exclaimed, realising what she was being told.

The civilian smiled again. 'Your uniforms await,' she said, and strolled back out into the main hangar, the smile disappearing as she went.

Kixle and Ghent watched her go and turned back to stare at the bodies.

'Which one do you want?' Ghent asked, curling his lip. 'The old fat captain or the old fat major general?'

'Either. If it gets me a battle cruiser, I'd be an old fat human every time.'

47

MILITARY FLYER, FOLLOWING THE TRAIN STRIATION
TOWARDS THE TYLAT ARCHIPELAGO, ERITAIN

BACHE HAD TAKEN a few minutes to learn the basics of the flyer's controls. The first thing he'd done was to find out how to gain some altitude, so he had a bit more time for errors. If he felt it was getting the better of him, he just hit the stationary hover icon again and it sorted itself out and stopped.

He found the controls not too dissimilar to his skouter, back home on Deelatayne. So within twenty minutes they were back following the striation again.

'Smoke in the distance,' said Bache, squinting through the front screen.

They all stared forwards as the column of black smoke drew nearer.

'Slow down,' said Nexen. 'I have a bad feeling about this.'

'Does this thing have any scanning ability?' asked Zaphir, running her eyes over the control panel.

'I don't know,' said Bache. 'Just don't go pushing any buttons. I'm barely in control as it is.'

He brought the aircraft down to treetop height and approached the smoke column cautiously. A gasp of shock echoed around the cockpit when they came across the carnage that confronted them as the flyer reached the burnt area in the forest. The charred skeleton of the eight carriages lay crumpled in a chaotic jumble of smouldering wreckage and bodies. Fifty metres away the section of carboncrete track, where the train had been when the explosion took place, showed a row of black ignition points. Huge lumps of it were missing, with the tell-tale lines of felled trees leading off into the forest in all directions, divulging their route from the site of the massive blast.

'Holy ancients!' exclaimed Nexen. 'There was enough explosive used here to shift the fucking planet.'

'Someone didn't want any survivors,' said Bache.

'Well, whoever they were certainly succeeded on that front,' said Nexen despondently.

'Over there,' Zaphir shrieked, suddenly, pointing frantically down out the left cockpit window. 'I think I saw movement.'

Bache turned the craft in that direction and dropped the nose slightly. At first there was nothing obvious, just a few small unburnt pieces of the train fluttering in the treetops.

'Where?' Nexen asked, as all three of them scoured the forest for any sign of life.

'It came from that grey bit down there,' said Zaphir. 'I'm sure something moved.'

'Are you able to land so we can check it out?' asked Nexen, touching Bache on the shoulder.

'Can anyone see a button or lever marked undercarriage?' Bache asked, while positioning the flyer over a break in the trees.

Nexen reached over his shoulder and touched a blue icon.

'That better not be the emergency kill switch,' said Bache.

The reassuring note of an electrical motor grinding below the cockpit greeted them, followed by a resounding *clunk*.

'That sounds and looks positive,' said Zaphir, as the icon turned green.

'It was labelled "struts" in Eritainian,' said Nexen. 'I was fairly confident.'

After landing the flyer reasonably softly, much to everyone's surprise, Bache decided to remain in the cockpit with the anti-gravs spinning, just in case a quick retreat was required.

Nexen and Zaphir jumped down from the side door, checked their weapons and sidled across warily to the larger pieces of debris scattered around the small clearing.

'It was somewhere over—'

Nexen held his hand up, silencing Zaphir. 'I heard something,' he whispered, looking and pointing to the right.

A section of what looked like wall panelling heaved slightly, a hand snaked around the edge and a moan emanated from below.

'Quickly,' said Nexen, hurrying over and bending down to lift the panel.

They flipped the panel up and lifted it away. A semi-naked male lay beneath, his legs twisted at a very unnatural angle. Frightened eyes flicked between them and a hand pointed towards the track.

'Bombs,' he croaked. 'Planted by soldiers. I saw them come out from under the train after they removed two passengers.'

'Whose soldiers?' Zaphir asked.

'And what passengers?' added Nexen.

His eyes closed before snapping open again. 'Ours,' he said, sounding confused. His mouth opened to say something else—and froze. His eyes glazed over and stared blankly upwards.

'Shit,' said Zaphir, grabbing his shoulders and turning him onto his back to attempt resuscitation, only to find his right arm was completely missing. 'Shit,' she said again.

'It's no good,' said Nexen. 'He's bled out. We only just caught him.'

A shout from the flyer caused them to stand and turn. Bache was frantically gesticulating for them to return.

They ran back to the aircraft, jumping aboard to find Bache sitting back in the pilot's seat and powering the door closed.

'I've just worked out how the communications work,' he said. 'Tylat military base is under a full assault, they're saying from an enemy that just appeared amongst them.'

'Dion wasn't lying then,' said Nexen. 'I think her military coup must be under way planetwide.' He stared out of the front screen. 'Are you able to contact any humans up at the base?'

'I'll have a go,' said Bache, sliding the pilot's headset on. 'I take it we were too late?' he said, nodding towards the body lying across the clearing.

Zaphir shook her head, sat in her seat and stared at the floor. 'It's so frustrating,' she said. 'One step forward followed by three back every time.'

'He said two passengers had been taken off the train just before the explosion,' said Nexen. 'I think we know who that might have been.'

Bache turned in his seat before lifting the flyer. 'I've been talking to a junior officer on one of the islands,' he said. 'He states that the androids haven't reached him yet and he can't get any reply from his superiors. He's worried as their facility is remote and lightly guarded.'

'Can I speak to him?' said Nexen, holding out his hand for the headset.

Bache lifted the aircraft up to a thousand metres while the commander spoke to the officer. Nexen's face creased with worry the more he heard, until he finally removed the headset and swore under his breath.

'Problem?' Zaphir asked.

'It's Gatt Island,' Nexen replied. 'That's where he is and there's only twenty of them to defend it.'

'What's on Gatt Island that's so worrying?' asked Bache, touching the hover icon and turning in his seat again.

'We need to get there as fast as we can,' Nexen said, the worry evident in his voice. 'Go due north to avoid the fighting and then we'll skirt back east and approach the island's western shore.'

'I've not seen you so rattled before,' said Zaphir, staring intently. 'What is it?'

Nexen exhaled loudly and glared straight ahead. 'Gatt Island is where a classified base is hidden,' he said. 'It contains a facility for our terraforming technology research. If they got their hands on that, they could wipe the human race out of existence in a matter of days.'

Zaphir and Bache's eyes met.

'I know I've been saying it a lot recently, but oh shit,' sighed Zaphir.

'I think that news warrants an oh shit more than anything,' said Bache as he quickly turned to the front and sent the flyer towards the north as fast as the small aircraft would go.

48

MILITARY FLYER, HEADING NORTH TOWARDS GATT ISLAND,
ERITAIN

Bache had brought the flyer down low close to the tree tops once they got nearer to civilisation. They could see multiple columns of smoke over to the east where the military bases were situated, with the occasional explosion of ordnance sending fountains of sparkling shrapnel high into the sky.

'It's busy over there,' said Bache. 'But I don't see any other aircraft.'

No sooner had he said it, than a small dot appeared on the skyline and quickly gained altitude before disappearing into the smoke and dust cloud hanging above the battlefield.

'Orbital vehicle,' said Zaphir. 'I hope they get away safely.'

'Depends who's on it,' said Nexen.

Fifteen minutes later they passed over a rugged and rocky coastline. Again, Bache kept the flyer as low as he dared, well within his limited skill level. He could see the string of islands stretching away from the mainland over to the right and began a gentle turn towards them.

'Which one is it?' asked Zaphir.

'The sixth one,' said Nexen. 'The island will look deserted, but he said to land on a level grassy area on the southern side and wait. They will come to us.'

The sixth island was small but had vertical rock cliffs arrowing out of the turbulent ocean and it became obvious why this particular island had been chosen for a classified research base.

Bache slowed the aircraft and applied lift as they approached. The cliffs passed close beneath them, and he waited until they were over the only level area and touched the hover icon. Then he reduced power and let the flyer sink slowly to the ground.

He knew they were being observed, so he shut the engines down and the three of them climbed out. The cold biting wind whipped at their clothing so they huddled together in the lee of the aircraft. The wait was thankfully a short one, as six camouflaged soldiers materialised around them, brandishing weapons that clearly had them in their sights.

'Commander Nexen, lay your weapons on the ground and step forward, please,' the closest ordered.

Nexen placed his laser pistol slowly beside him and took a pace towards the soldier. He was scanned with a hand device. The soldier nodded and repeated the process with Bache and finally Zaphir.

'Thank you, Commander, and welcome to Gatt Island. My name is Lieutenant Tylont and I must say it's an honour to meet you.'

Tylont gave his colleagues a quick nod, all the weapons were lowered, they turned, spread out and provided a protective cordon around the aircraft.

'Thank you, Lieutenant,' said Nexen. 'Although, we

recently discovered the android scanners are ineffective against your home-grown androids.'

'That's where you're wrong, Commander,' said Tylont. 'Our scientists here on the island recently determined that a centuries-old body temperature scanner is one hundred percent effective, as an android's core body heat operates at a much lower temperature. They incorporated the miniature EMP unit into it too, so if the subject demonstrates a reading lower than twenty-eight degrees, they get zapped.'

'Genius,' said Bache. 'It'd be hard for them to counteract that too, without overheating their micro-electronics.'

'I'm sorry to rush you,' said Tylont. 'But are any of you an orbital pilot?'

Zaphir and Nexen glanced at each other.

'Well, I was,' said Nexen. 'But not so much with all the new technology and Zaphir here is a modern pilot, but with the GDA.'

'You're GDA?' Tylont blurted, his eyes widening and stumbling back a pace, his weapon coming quickly back up.

Nexen stepped between them and held his palms up. 'It's okay, Lieutenant, they're our allies in this fight.'

'But what if they got their hands on our terraforming technology? They could wipe us out.'

'Why the hell would we want to do that?' said Bache. 'We've been terraforming planets for generations. If we held any malice towards you and your worlds, I think that would have taken place centuries ago.'

Tylont stared at Bache, seemingly searching for any sign of deceit. 'We were always taught that you were pathological aggressors and would attack given any excuse,' said Tylont, realising he was still pointing his weapon at them and lowering it again.

'Completely false,' said Zaphir. 'We're a council of over sixteen hundred human races and our agenda is the complete opposite of that.'

'From what I've witnessed,' said Nexen, 'I have absolutely no reason to doubt that. They've already lost a starship trying to help us.'

Tylont nodded and glanced over his shoulder and across to the previous island just visible on the distant horizon where a tell-tale column of smoke was rising into the haze. 'Come with me,' he said. 'I don't believe we have long.'

They'd been taken down a nearby hidden stairway, through a thick bombproof door and into a surprisingly large underground complex. A multitude of low-ceilinged rooms and laboratories led off a central hangar that Bache was surprised to see contained a military orbital shuttle. A low rough-cut rectangular door took up most of one side of the cavernous space, open to the ocean crashing against the cliffs a couple of hundred feet below.

'What's happened to your usual pilots?' Nexen asked, pointing to the shuttle.

'They went on a few days' break to the mainland,' said Tylont. 'We've heard nothing from them since this thing started.'

They all turned as the unmistakeable sound of screaming antigravs broke the quietness of the hangar. Their flyer swooped in, turned and clunked down on the smooth rock floor.

'Had to get it out of sight,' Tylont explained, noticing their surprised expressions.

'He seems a decent pilot,' said Zaphir, giving Tylont a sideways glance.

'Only in atmospherics, sadly,' admitted Tylont.

They passed the rear of the shuttle where, because the rear ramp was down, they could see the interior was completely full of grey crates.

'Will you all fit in there?' asked Nexen, peering in at the lack of passenger space.

'We weren't going anywhere,' said Tylont. 'We just needed to get all those well away from the androids. There's a large cruiser in orbit attached to our main space station and they need to get there safely.'

Nexen rubbed his chin thoughtfully. 'Do you think you can fly this thing?' he asked, turning to Zaphir.

'I'll give it my best shot,' she said.

'She's a lot better than she makes out,' said Bache, noticing the concerned expression on Tylont's face.

'Is Admiral Jackarett okay with us taking this lot up into space?' Nexen asked.

Tylont stared at the floor for a moment and sucked his bottom lip before speaking. 'The admiral was my uncle and one of the first killed,' he said. 'They were extremely well planned and went for all the senior officers first.'

'I'm so sorry,' said Nexen.

The following momentary silence was broken by Zaphir. 'But staying here is a death sentence,' she said. 'There must be a way to get you to safety as well?'

'I wish there was,' Tylont said, shrugging.

'Take our flyer,' said Nexen.

'And go where? There's no reply on any military channel,' he said. 'We were planning on hunkering down here and going dark. Anyone who knew about this place is most probably dead now.'

'What about supplies?' asked Bache.

'A hundred days' worth if we go steady.'

'There's room for a couple more of you in the cockpit,' said Zaphir.

'Yes, I'd thought of that,' said Tylont. 'I'm sending one of my best soldiers with you in case there's already trouble up there and one of the scientists to look after the seeding missiles.'

'Missiles?' exclaimed Zaphir, stopping her inspection of the shuttle and turning to face Tylont. 'Nobody mentioned anything about missiles.'

Tylont nodded towards the grey cases.

'That's what they are,' he said. 'They get fired into a specific and carefully chosen planet's atmosphere where they activate and replace whatever's already there with an oxygen-based atmosphere.'

'Sound fine so far,' said Zaphir. 'Where's the danger?'

'It can take anything from twenty to a hundred years to complete the reseed and the first thing it does is cleanse the surface of any existing atmosphere and life.'

Zaphir's face went white. 'Oh, shit,' she whispered, peering nervously at the crates in the belly of the shuttle. 'No pressure then.'

49

MILITARY SHUTTLE, ON APPROACH TO FINIK'TAY SPACE
STATION, ORBITING ERITAIN

ZAPHIR HAD LEARNT the basics of the shuttle as she went, in similar fashion to Bache in the flyer. It'd taken her a couple of attempts to get the small ship off the deck and safely through the hangar door. With Nexen translating some of the named switches and icons and Bache recognising a couple of similar controls to the flyer, they were soon heading out through the thinning atmosphere and into space.

'The space station is hailing us,' said Zaphir, looking over her shoulder. 'Would one of you deal with that? I'm a bit busy steering this thing.'

Nexen grabbed the headset she held out to him and began chatting to someone on Finik'tay Station about approach vectors and hangar designations.

'That's odd,' he said, as he finished transmitting, his brow wrinkling as he rubbed his chin.

'What is it?' asked Bache.

'The operator I was speaking to used the word neighbourhood. The neighbourhood is clear for your approach, he said.'

'That's strange? Why?' asked Bache.

'Back in my day, using the word neighbourhood in a communication meant "I'm under duress", and the fact he said the neighbourhood is clear would mean the opposite.'

'So, I might be flying us into a trap?' said Zaphir.

A moment of silence in the cockpit was broken again by Nexen. 'I think we need to prepare, just in case,' he said, turning and getting eye contact with the soldier Tylont had sent with them. 'I told them I was a lone pilot with a consignment of food supplies for the station.'

'They must know that's not true,' said Bache. 'They'll have detected our launch from the island. No supplies would've ever come from there.'

The soldier pointed up on top of the cargo. 'There's just room to hide up there,' he said. 'It'll give us time to assess any danger and react accordingly.'

Bache shrugged at Nexen. 'Sounds like a plan to me,' he said, activating his laser pistol and climbing up to slide into the narrow gap.

'What about me?' asked the engineer. 'I'm unarmed.'

The soldier pulled up a small hatch in the floor. 'Hide down there,' he said, nodding toward the small gap.

'I can't fit in there,' the engineer whined, peering down into a small electronics bay.

'Yes, you can,' the soldier replied, grabbing his collar and stuffing him down the three steps.

'But I'm claustropho—'

The soldier slammed the hatch shut and stood on it. 'And keep quiet,' he shouted, before climbing up onto the cargo, once he was sure the engineer wasn't about to reappear.

'Two minutes,' called Zaphir, glancing down to ensure

her zapper was concealed, but still positioned for a quick draw.

The pinprick of light soon grew into, as space stations went, a medium to small station. The military ship attached to the underside almost doubled its size. Zaphir gave the others a running commentary on what she was seeing as they had no view out of the front screen from their elevated positions.

'It's a physical sideways-sliding door into the hangar,' she said. 'They don't seem to have atmosphere shielding here.'

'Atmosphere shielding? What's that?' Nexen asked, craning his neck back towards Bache.

'An invisible field you can fly a ship through, but enables the hangar to remain pressurised,' said Bache.

Nexen went silent for a moment. 'Really?' he said, shuffling to get eye contact. 'I never imagined that could ever exist.'

Bache smiled and nodded, banging his head on the shuttle's roof. 'Ouch,' he said, gritting his teeth.

'Quiet,' called Zaphir. 'We're in the hangar now, four figures watching from an airlock and a fifth in what must be the hangar control room.'

Zaphir turned the ship and landed back facing the sliding door with a *clunk*. The hangar door slid shut again and Bache could hear the small hangar repressurising.

A light on the control panel went green and an audible note sounded as the inside and outside pressures equalised.

Zaphir opened the rear ramp with a *hiss* and watched to see what would happen.

'The four figures are armed, guns up and approaching warily,' Zaphir said, just loud enough for the others to hear.

Bache, who was nearest to the back of the shuttle, could

see the lower legs and two pairs of boots that stopped halfway up the ramp.

'Everybody off,' shouted a confident voice. 'It's no good hiding, we detected way more than one life sign on this ship.'

Zaphir strode down the side of the cargo, out onto the ramp and pointed at one of the antigrav nacelles.

'Are you sure you didn't mistake the heat from those?' she said, nonchalantly, while attempting to walk past.

He grabbed her arm, while his colleague attempted to hit her in the head with the butt of his rifle. She parried his arm upwards, while pressing the button on a Gatt Island zapper concealed in her other palm. He went down like a rock in a pond, his weapon clattering away down the ramp as he fell.

She smiled at her first assailant, who tried to pull his weapon up, but he was too close and the zapper pulsed again. This time she grabbed him as he dropped, fell backwards and pulled him down on top of her. This provided a shield from the other two armed androids who'd held back about thirty metres and were now trying to get a shot without hitting their colleagues.

Bache, Nexen and the soldier hadn't sat back and watched. They'd dropped down using the cargo as a shield and brought their weapons up.

'You go that way and I'll go this,' said the soldier.

Before Bache could stop him, he'd launched himself around the cargo and out onto the ramp, firing two shots, one at each of the remaining androids. The first laser bolt caught the left-hand android on the shoulder, causing him to spin and drop his weapon with a clatter. The right-hand android, however, had a split second to dive sideways and let off a shot of his own. The soldier's second shot had missed, ricocheting off a freight lifter and taking out the control cabin window. The hangar controller's shocked face within dived out of sight as she was showered in broken glass.

The right-hand android's snatched shot hadn't missed. The soldier's momentum took him to the bottom of the ramp, where he sprawled face first on the hangar floor, a pool of blood growing around his torso.

Zaphir had brought the zapper up and fired it at the remaining android as he came up to one knee. Unfortunately, the range was too long and nothing happened. He smiled at her as he brought his rifle into the shoulder and aimed straight at her.

Bache and Nexen fired several times with their pistols, but again, the range was way too long and the bolts just impacted the deck around the android.

Zaphir shut her eyes and flinched as the big laser rifle pulsed. She opened one eye again when nothing hit her. The android was flat on his back with part of his head missing.

She ducked down again as the weapon fired a second time. The android, hit in the shoulder, had managed to sit up and was attempting to fire back with one arm.

A fist-sized hole materialised in the centre of his chest. He looked down, a puzzled expression on his face, before dropping backwards, arms flailing. He jerked around a bit and finally went still.

Zaphir turned her head to find Bache and Nexen peering out from behind the cargo, their laser pistols still extended.

'Bloody good shot with a pistol,' she said. 'Which of you fired those?'

Bache glanced back at Nexen and shrugged. 'Wasn't us,' he said.

The engineer appeared at the other side of the cargo, a laser rifle held tight into his shoulder.

'Are there any more of 'em?' he asked, his eyes flicking around the hangar.

'Shit,' said Zaphir, staring at the engineer while pushing the first android's body off her. 'Remind me not to piss you off.'

'I used to be a member of a rifle club,' he said nervously. 'I've never shot a real person before.'

'You still haven't,' said Bache, stepping out onto the ramp. 'Where did you get that?' He nodded at the rifle.

'It was in the hole I was stuffed down,' he said. 'There's four of 'em in a concealed rack.'

'What's your name?' asked Zaphir, as she got back on her feet.

'Stakk,' he said. 'Dr Quinn Stakk.'

'Thank you, Quinn,' she said, strolling back up the ramp and giving him a hug. 'You just saved my life.'

'You understood my code then,' called a strange female voice from behind the shuttle.

They all ducked and swung their weapons around to find a young female in blue coveralls and a peaked cap on backwards. She grimaced and held her hands up.

'I'm on your side, honest,' she said, standing stock still.

'Was that you I was talking to?' Nexen asked, lowering his weapon.

She nodded.

'How did you know about the old distress code?'

'I used the *Xhamin*'s disappearance as part of my engineering course dissertation,' she said, forcing a smile.

Zaphir approached her, pointed and clicked the zapper. Nothing happened.

'Am I human enough?' she asked, her confidence growing, along with a hopeful smile.

'It seems you are,' said Nexen, stepping past Zaphir. 'What's your name by the way?'

'Killie.'

'Thanks for the warning, Killie.'

'You're welcome,' she said. 'Those four had a gun to my head, it's the only thing I could think of. They were desperate to get you and your cargo on board.'

'How many more of them are there?' Zaphir asked.

'Around twenty turned up a couple of hours ago. They killed my boss when he tried to prevent them leaving the hangar.'

'Where are they now?'

'I believe most of them are on the cruiser. They had Major General Sheck and Captain Fastt with them, but the strange thing was they didn't seem to be under any duress.'

'That must have been the shuttle launch we saw from the flyer,' said Bache. 'I believe our two androids have adopted the appearance of the two senior officers and are after the cruiser.'

Zaphir looked up at the hangar's cameras. 'We need to move,' she said. 'They must have seen what went on here.'

'It's okay,' said Killie. 'I froze the cameras with a picture of an empty hangar before you arrived.'

Bache turned to look at Quinn. 'Are you able to deactivate all those?' Bache asked, nodding towards the shuttle's cargo.

'Oh, dear,' he said. 'Do I have to?'

'They'll use them on Eritain and every human planet they can find,' said Nexen. 'D'you want that on your conscience?'

'Oh, dear,' he said again, shuffling from foot to foot. 'I'd better make a start.'

'Shut yourself up in there and get busy,' said Nexen.

'We'll keep them occupied elsewhere. If any of them enter the hangar, hide in your hole again.'

Quinn cringed. 'Can't wait,' he said, glancing towards the cockpit.

Nexen turned to the other three. 'Let's grab those other rifles under the floor and go hunting,' he said.

50

FINIK'TAY SPACE STATION, ORBITING ERITAIN

KILLIE HAD PROVIDED them with engineering coveralls and peaked caps that helped to hide their faces. Laden with tool bags concealing the weapons, they followed her through the many maintenance gangways criss-crossing the station.

'There's a hatch in a few metres that exits near the station control room,' whispered Killie, holding her finger against her lips. 'At least three staff are always on duty in there, so they must have guards watching over them.'

'That'll do as a start,' said Nexen. 'The last thing we want to do is have to face all fifty of them at once.'

Killie opened the hatch a crack and peeked up and down the corridor. Bache noticed the grimace on her face appear as she looked up towards the control room door.

'What is it?' he asked.

'Two androids guarding the door,' she said. 'What do we do now?'

'I'll show you,' said Zaphir. 'Just in case I haven't, get ready to mess up the one who sticks his head through here.'

She pushed past Killie, threw open the hatch and swung

through into the corridor. 'Have any of these lighting panels been flashing on and off?' she called to the two surprised androids, as she rose up and pointed at the ceiling.

'What are you doing?' one of them asked, as they both brought their weapons up and approached.

'Station maintenance, the same as every day,' she said, nonchalantly. 'Is this your first day or something? And who put all these weapons in here?' she added, now pointing at the open hatch.

'We were not informed of your presence,' said the other, keeping his rifle pointing at her as his colleague bent down to peer in the hatch.

'Who's he?' she said, pointing at the control room door.

Two things happened in quick succession. The standing android turned to see who Zaphir was talking about, giving her the split second she needed to pulse him with the zapper hidden in her palm, then she turned and gave the second android the good news in the back of the head as he stuck it through the hatchway.

'Drag him in,' Zaphir called. 'I'll get the other one.'

Thirty seconds later the two dead androids were out of sight, the hatch replaced and they all approached the closed control room door.

'Similar scenario,' said Zaphir, as her finger hovered over the door touch panel. 'We've been called for some immediate maintenance. Look bored and as if this is an everyday occurrence.'

Nexen glanced back at Bache and Killie. 'You certainly can't mark her down for lack of confidence,' he said, rolling his eyes.

Bache smiled and Killie sniggered, causing Zaphir to scowl back at them as she touched the switch.

The control room wasn't as big as Bache expected. A circular room, about five metres in diameter, where three operators sat with their backs to the centre watching over screens and panels that lined the outer wall. Two more armed androids stood in the middle of the room and turned, expressing surprise as the four engineers trooped in.

'What are you here for and who escorted you?' one of them said, slowly bringing his weapon up and glancing past them and out into the corridor.

'The kaliotropic giro resonator is out of balance,' said Zaphir. 'Unless you want to burn up in the planet's atmosphere in a few hours' time, we need to fix it and it takes four of us to rebalance it—next question?'

'Where are the door guards?' he asked as it swished shut behind them.

'Captain Fastt ordered them back to the ship,' said Nexen.

'Hey!' exclaimed the second android. 'You're Commander Nexen, you should be in custody down—'

The zapper pulsed twice. Both androids clattered to the floor, followed by a spontaneous round of applause from the three human operators.

'Boy, are we glad to see you, Commander,' said one of them, standing and shaking Nexen's hand. 'I'm Assistant Station Chief Linter.' He turned to face Zaphir. 'And what the hell is a kaliotropic giro resonator?'

'Fuck knows,' said Zaphir, shrugging. 'I made it up on the fly.'

Linter's rueful smile disappeared as he glanced down at the androids and, much to everyone's surprise, he stepped over and kicked one of them in the head as hard as he could. 'That's for the station chief,' he sneered, then, looking up, he found everyone staring at him and quickly regained his composure.

'I take it they killed him too?' said Killie.

'Threw him out an airlock, alive,' Linter said, stony-faced. 'Just to ensure we toed the line. Did they kill the chief engineer too?'

Killie nodded slowly and stared at the floor. 'Shot him in the head,' she said. 'He tried to lock them in the hangar.'

'We were told there was over twenty of them,' said Bache.

Linter nodded. 'Twenty-two with the two traitors, Captain—'

'Fastt and the major general,' interrupted Nexen. 'Actually, they're not traitors, they're dead too. The people you saw are android clones designed to trick the ship's crew.'

'Ah, crap,' said Linter. 'We wondered how they'd been turned so easily.'

'We need to regain control of that battle cruiser,' said Nexen. 'If they get hold of that and its nuclear arsenal, we're in serious trouble.'

'It can't leave the station unless we release the docking clamps from here,' said Linter.

'Can we sabotage the release controls and make it impossible to leave?' asked Bache.

'Yep,' said Killie, walking to the far side of the room and opening a cabinet under one of the unmanned panels. She removed several control boards and stuffed them in her tool bag. 'Won't work now,' she said, standing and patting the bag.

'Are you familiar with the ship's systems too?' Zaphir asked her.

'I should say so,' Killie said. 'I'm studying to be an engineer on those new model cruisers. Help get me into the engineering bay and I can really fuck it up.'

Bache sniggered at her turn of phrase, getting a piqued glare from Zaphir.

'Sounds like a plan,' said Nexen. 'Okay, we need you to get us on that ship.'

They left the control room, giving Linter a couple of weapons and making sure he knew how to jam the doors from within and also the bulkhead doors leading up to it, and the elevators too. Killie led them back into the maintenance gangways and slowly, sometimes having to crawl, they made their way down several decks and into the docking ring.

'There's four docking tunnel airlocks,' whispered Killie as they got close. 'The cruiser is on dock one and the other three are clear.'

Again, she peeked out, this time by lying on the floor and taking a sly peek through an unused ventilation grill.

'Shit,' she murmured, glancing back up to the others. 'There's about five of 'em loitering around the airlock.'

'We need a distraction,' whispered Bache.

'Bugger,' said Killie. 'I should've brought my tablet.'

'Will mine do?' said Bache, rummaging in his small rucksack.

Killie nodded and spent a few moments connecting up and going through her levels of passwords until she got to what she was looking for. 'I have a backdoor gateway into the cruiser's engineering systems,' she said. 'It was actually the chief engineer's as he did some work for them on the ship's software. I watched him log into it a couple of times.'

'You have a good memory,' said Bache.

Killie smiled back at Bache. 'Thanks, handsome,' she whispered in his ear so the others didn't hear.

This time it was Bache's turn to smile.

'Are you two going to get a room or storm a battle cruiser?' said Zaphir, rolling her eyes. 'Tick tock, people.'

Killie glared at Zaphir before lying down and checked the corridor again. 'I just need to time this right.'

'What are you planning to do?' asked Nexen.

'This,' she said, touching an icon on the tablet's screen.

The sudden noise was loud and confusing, until Bache realised it was the motors powering the airlock closed. They were in the same void behind the wall where the hydraulic system was situated. Before anyone could stop her, Killie had opened the hatch and swung out.

'Hiya, guys,' she said to the three androids trapped on the outside of the airlock and staring at it in confusion.

They swung around at the sound of the voice, but were way too late getting their weapons off their shoulders. Two zappers and a laser pistol spoke in quick succession. Again the bodies were crammed through the hatch and hidden as quickly as possible.

'Why are they so fucking heavy?' complained Zaphir, heaving the last one over the threshold.

Once they'd tidied up any sign of a problem, Killie removed the hold on the airlock and allowed it to reopen. The others all gathered behind the sliding door. Luckily it was a door type without a window so the two androids on the other side were just as confused as to why the door had closed as the ones had been on the outside. They were not expecting an armed mob to set about them through a half-open airlock and they swiftly followed their comrades through the maintenance hatch.

As they stood facing the cruiser's inner airlock at the far end of the docking tunnel, Nexen hesitated and turned to speak to Killie. 'The two androids that are impersonating the senior officers are a different type and if we zap them or shoot them, they self-destruct with such catastrophic force, it would most likely destroy the ship and station.'

Killie's eyes went wide. 'Fuck, really?'

The other three nodded.

'They're augmented too,' said Bache, 'and as strong as a Dasos swamp ape.'

Killie gave him a questioning look.

'That's extremely strong,' he added, realising she wouldn't have a clue what that was. 'And bad tempered.'

'Right,' said Nexen. 'There should only be seven androids left, plus our two and judging by the lack of reaction to what we've done so far, they're unaware of our presence. Let's keep it that way. We also don't know if they're able to send reinforcements up from below, hopefully not. So the first thing I want you to do, Killie, is shut everything down except life support and jam it that way. We can't let them get full use of this battle cruiser.'

'No problem, boss,' she said and opened the airlock door. 'Follow me.'

51

BATTLE CRUISER TYLAT FURORE, ORBITING ERITAIN

THE CRUISER'S inner airlock door slid apart to reveal five androids and one human figure wearing an officer's uniform. The four of them froze as they looked down the barrels of six laser rifles.

'Shit,' said Zaphir.

'That's a lovely thing to say to your hosts,' said the cloned Captain Fastt. 'Could you be ever so kind and place your weapons on the floor very slowly, please.'

They did as they were told and two androids frisked them and placed cuffs on their wrists. Bache noticed Nexen's face drop as another figure entered the corridor behind the androids.

'Hello, darling,' said Glendolian to Nexen, swaying seductively towards him in a very short skirt and stopping to lean on a bulkhead stanchion. 'Have you missed me?'

'Hello, Fellen or Zella or Jazz or whoever you've murdered lately,' spat Nexen, through gritted teeth. 'It's no use dressing up as my dead wife, you'll never be the kind compassionate human she was.'

'Oh, dear,' she said. 'And there was I thinking our coupling was going to be ever so romantic. I ordered candles and wine too.'

'I'd rather die,' said Nexen.

'That's good,' she said, 'because when I've fucked you, you will die and then you'll be mine willingly for ever.' Glendolian turned to the captain. 'Put them with the others,' she ordered. 'I need to go and secure those marvellous weapons they've kindly brought up to me.' She sashayed off through the airlock and down the corridor with two of the armed androids, winking at Nexen as she passed. 'See you soon, darling husband,' she said with a wave and disappeared out of sight.

'That could've gone better,' grumbled Zaphir, glowering behind her at the guards as they were marched away.

'Face forward,' one shouted, slapping her on the back of the head.

Bache saw her bare her teeth and tense up. 'Don't,' he said. 'They have no real reason to keep any of us alive, don't give them an excuse.'

They were taken to the security level and placed in a holding cell with the surviving nine members of the ship's crew. Once they'd all acquainted themselves, Bache asked if all the crew were accounted for and the truth was, they honestly didn't know. Of the original twenty-two, they knew of six that had died trying to defend the ship, which left seven unaccounted for.

'I hope Quinn had finished,' mumbled Zaphir, sitting on the floor in the corner, clenching and unclenching her fists.

'And was hidden,' said Bache.

The cell door swept open, two androids entered, grabbed Killie by the shoulders and pushed her outside.

'Hey,' shouted Bache. 'Leave her alone and take me.' He struggled to his feet, hindered by the restraints, only to have the door slammed in his face. 'Shit,' he said. 'Why have they taken her?'

'She was a real threat to them and they needed her skills working for them,' said Zaphir, staring at the floor and not wanting to meet Bache's gaze.

He kicked the cell wall in frustration, but instead of a dull *thud* as his boot hit the metal plating, a deafening *clang* sounded as though someone had hit it with a sledge hammer.

'What the fuck?' he said, looking down at his boot in puzzlement.

'What did you just do?' asked Nexen, with everyone in the cell staring at him.

He was about to answer when a loud hissing noise pervaded the cell, coming from the wall he'd just kicked.

'Have you broken the space station?' said Zaphir, shuffling away from the wall.

'That sounds like a plasma—'

A blinding flame burst through the wall about one and a half metres up and moved steadily downwards.

'—torch.' Bache continued. 'Everyone back away quickly.'

The smell of burning metal and plastic was almost nauseating and the flame from the torch was starting to heat the cell up considerably as the quickly forming rectangular cut finally joined up. It took a couple of *clangs* by something striking it on the outside before the double-ply section of metal wall fell inwards and clattered to the floor, the insulation between the layers fizzing and popping from the extreme heat of the torch. A face, being wary of the still glowing edges, leaned through.

'Taxi,' he said. 'Move yourselves.'

Everyone moved as fast as they could and one by one, they made themselves small to avoid the edges and jumped through the smoking gap into the station's emergency rescue vehicle, normally parked and unused inside a maintenance airlock on the underside of the ship.

The lieutenant operating the thing got a lot of hugs and pats on the back as everyone bundled aboard. It was only designed to sit six people, so it was a little cramped for twelve.

'Are there any more of you?' Nexen asked, as the lieutenant resealed the rescue airlock.

'Two others with me,' he said, as he squeezed himself back into the pilot's seat, unclamped the magnetic seal and dropped down beneath the ship.

'Are you armed?' asked Bache.

'One laser pistol and two plasma cutters,' he said. 'We haven't been able to roam around for fear of being detected. We hid next to the reactor so it obscured our heat signatures.'

The maintenance airlock was soon clearly visible above them through the craft's large front screen and they lifted up inside slowly. He stopped halfway in and spun the tiny ship around, checking it was still clear. Happy that it was, he raised and turned, then backed it slowly into its cradle on the airlock wall. Clamps clunked down and secured it in place.

The small area soon pressurised once the outer doors were secure and they all expressed a sigh of relief as they climbed out of the cramped space.

'Wait,' said the pilot. 'I need to check it's clear.'

He went to the far side of the airlock, bent down and tapped lightly on an exposed pipe four times. Two taps were returned. He nodded, stood and activated the inner door. The other two crew members were there as it opened into the main engineering section at the stern of the vessel. As they were led across the decking and past the huge antigrav drives, the ship suddenly lurched, causing some of them to lose their footing and crash to the deck. Alarms began wailing and blue panels in the walls flashed.

'What the hell was that?' Nexen called, picking himself back up.

'The major alarm,' said the pilot, concern written all over his face. 'Normally means we're under attack or a hull breach.'

Bache turned at the sound of running feet and a lone figure sprinted into a darkened section at the far end of the room. One of the crew members holding the laser pistol snapped a shot off, causing the figure to swerve and slide to a halt. The laser bolt missed and impacted the ceiling, exploding a light fitting that dropped down and swung around on its cables madly, emitting sparks that lit the newcomer's face.

'Wait,' shouted Bache. 'She's with us.'

Killie's face changed from one of panic to relief as she realised who she'd run into. She sprinted over and into Bache's arms, much to his surprise. 'Fuck,' she said. 'I thought they'd killed you.'

'Well, same here,' said Bache, taking a step back as he caught Zaphir's glowering expression. 'You weren't with them long enough to have been converted. So how the hell did you escape from that android captain?'

'It wanted me alone and dismissed the android guards, completely underestimating me and on the way to his cabin we passed an airlock. I had a thin ceramic blade strapped to my leg that they didn't find during the search. I pretended to do up my boot, retrieved it and thrust it up under its chin and pierced its brain.'

'So, was that the explosion that shook everything?' he asked.

She nodded, glancing back towards the door she'd sprinted through. 'I remembered what you said about them exploding, so I deliberately killed it next to the airlock and spaced it as fast as I could. It was still a bit close when it went off, but I believe the alarms are because the blast compromised the station and ship's orbit and not a hull breach.'

'Thank the ancients for that,' said Bache.

'Is there an armoury nearby?' asked Nexen

'One level up,' said one of the crew overhearing the question. 'I'm the ship's armourer.'

'Take us there,' he said. 'It's time we finished this.'

52

BATTLE CRUISER TYLAT FURORE, ORBITING ERITAIN

THE ALARMS finally went quiet as they climbed the emergency ladders up to the next level. They all agreed it would be safer than using the elevator and they froze and listened as complete silence returned.

One of the crew with the only laser weapon had been first up the ladder. He clambered the last few rungs, threw open the hatch at the top and swung the pistol around in an arc, checking the corridor was clear in both directions. He climbed out and covered the others as they made their way up out of the vertical shaft.

The armoury was close and once the relevant codes had been entered into the double security doors, it revealed a five-metre rectangular room, the walls lined with racks of laser and projectile weapons.

Zaphir whistled as she entered and Bache noticed a determined grin replaced the fixed scowl she'd worn of late.

They shut themselves in for a few minutes as everyone chose at least one weapon they liked the look of. Once suitably kitted out and battery packs had been distributed, Nexen formed them into a circle.

He explained to the ship's crew about the terraforming technology they had mistakenly brought up on the shuttle and how, if it was used, everything was lost. The androids could survive in vacuum, so utilising them as weapons on Eritain would overnight wipe out all the natural life on the planet.

'Do you think the engineer managed to disable them all?' asked one of the crew.

'I hope so,' said Nexen. 'But we have to assume he didn't and make destroying them a priority.'

'How many androids are left?' another asked.

'Seven, we believe,' said Bache. 'And one masquerading as Commander Nexen's wife Glendolian. But remember, only engage her if you're adjacent to an airlock. You have about twenty seconds before she goes up with the power of a battle-field nuke.'

Nexen turned to Killie. 'That will be your job,' he said to her. 'Open the nearest airlock and prepare to cycle it as fast as possible. Leave throwing her in to whoever's nearest.'

Killie nodded, as did everyone else.

Nexen allowed the crew to lead as they made their way silently through the ship, guns up and safeties off. They only met one android on the way, who was completely taken by surprise and was virtually disassembled in a blizzard of laser fire. Bache grimaced at the nauseating smell of burning flesh, plastic and electronics as he stepped over the smouldering remains.

'Is there any way we can get a look inside?' asked Nexen, as they got close to the hangar. 'I don't fancy running in there blind.'

Killie called for Bache's tablet again and spent a minute

hunched over it, tapping away and mumbling to herself. 'There,' she said, suddenly and held up the screen so Nexen could see.

He'd been right to be cautious. Four of the androids were stationed either side of the only entry door with their weapons trained and ready. Glendolian could be seen on the shuttle with the last two androids. Quinn was there too, a laser pistol held to his head as he worked on the missiles and even though the camera was some distance away, the defiant sneer on his face was clear.

'Shit,' said Zaphir, peering over Nexen's shoulder. 'Isn't there another way in?'

'No,' said Killie. 'But there is a possible distraction that might get us in there.' She snatched the tablet back and began tapping away again. 'You'd best prepare,' she said. 'This will only work for a moment or two, so be ready to go in when the door opens.'

Six of the crew positioned themselves quietly either side of the hangar airlock and two more lay prone with rifles, ready to take out the two androids on the back of the shuttle.

Bache watched over Killie's shoulder as she took out several levels of safety backups, finally triggering the automatic cargo loader parked against the wall on the right-hand side. The androids glanced over as its warning beeper and flashing lights activated. She then sent it at its maximum speed straight at them, simultaneously signalling for the airlock to activate.

The next few seconds were just a blur of movement, laser fire and shouting. The androids had turned and trained their rifles on the attacking loader, giving the crew time to level their weapons and fire as both the hangar airlock doors opened at once. All four androids went down. The two prone snipers took out the remaining pair of androids on the back of the shuttle, but not before one of them had snapped a shot off towards the airlock.

As Bache stepped through the airlock, one of the crew dropped in front of him, his dead eyes staring straight up and a smouldering hole in his chest providing the reason.

Glendolian, however, had stepped behind Quinn and had a weapon pointed at his head again.

'Make any move towards me and he dies,' she said, as everyone came to a halt just inside the airlock. 'I believe you already know what will happen if you target me.'

Nexen walked forward, his laser rifle hanging by his side.

'Stop where you are, husband,' she said, swinging the pistol around to cover him.

He stopped. 'It's time to call it a day, vassal,' he said.

'Just at the moment of my greatest achievement?' she asked, contemptuously. 'I think not.'

'If you detonate now, you will destroy all those.' Nexen nodded at the missiles.

'We're very close to the planet's atmosphere here,' she said. 'Can you guarantee they'll all be deactivated by the explosion before this ship and station plunges down and kills everyone except my wondrous machines?'

'Your machines? I don't believe you had anything to do with them. They were all down to Dion or AL 001 or whatever she liked to call herself.'

'Whatever,' Glendolian sneered. 'They're mine now and nothing will stop me from taking this shuttle and its beautiful cargo.' She tightened her grip on Quinn and leant forward to hit the close ramp toggle.

Quinn threw himself forward at the same time and even

with her augmented strength, she couldn't avoid both of them toppling off the side of the ramp.

Nexen reacted and lunged forward, bringing his rifle up and firing a bolt of white-hot energy straight through Glendolian's chest as she sat up. The look of utter shock on her face soon changed to one of defiance as her body began the build-up to detonation.

'You're all dead,' she sneered, falling flat on her back again.

'EVERYBODY OUT,' shouted Nexen, as he grabbed a shocked Quinn and dragged him up the shuttle's ramp, hitting the close toggle as he went.

Killie wasted no time and sprinted for the control room, while all the others bundled back through the airlock, Bache dragging the dead crew member with him and inside as the door cycled closed.

He gazed back through the outer door as it sealed and watched the android as it began to shake and grow a bright shade of red. Turning his head to the left and flat to the glass, he could see Killie busy through the control room window. A low hiss quickly became a roar as the main hangar door began opening.

It was at this moment, as Bache watched Killie, he realised the control room window was missing. Taken out earlier by the errant laser bolt.

'Oh, shit,' he said, his eyes widening in panic. 'Killie, no.'

The android's body began to slide towards the increasing gap and soon built up speed, quickly disappearing and closely followed by the other android bodies, assorted bits and pieces not attached and the untethered cargo lifter. Even the shuttle, heavy as it was, began to move ever so slowly, making an ear-splitting scraping noise like a fingernail on a chalkboard.

The huge door stopped and reversed its direction, the shuttle slowly stopping its journey towards the door as the atmosphere was extinguished and the door closed again.

Bache turned back to look in the control room again. Killie's face in the window had gone.

'Oh, no,' he mumbled. 'No, no.'

The explosion from outside shook the ship for a second time and as before all the alarms sounded and lights flashed again.

It only took a few minutes for the hangar door to reclose and repressurisation to complete, but to Bache, it seemed like hours. As soon as the airlock was able to cycle, he was through it and he sprinted across to the control room. He couldn't see Killie anywhere through the window as he passed and his heart skipped a beat as he entered to find an empty seat.

'Oh, shit,' said a voice behind him.

He turned to find Zaphir standing in the pressurised doorway.

'She gave her life to save us all,' said Bache, his shoulders slumping.

'Fuck off, did I,' a muffled familiar voice said from under the control desk.

Killie's face peered out from the footwell, an oxygen mask obscuring her nose and mouth.

'How d'you think the fucking door closed again?' she said, clearer this time as she pulled the mask off.

'You bloody legend,' said Bache, grabbing her hand, pulling her up and wrapping her in a huge hug.

'I'll leave you two alone, shall I?' said Zaphir, rolling her eyes at Bache and stomping off again.

'She likes you,' said Killie, burying her head against his chest.

'We're just colleagues,' he replied as neither of them seemed keen for the moment to end. Bache looked up again as another shadow appeared in the doorway.

'Well done, Killie,' said Nexen. 'We need you again I'm afraid. That second explosion knocked the ship and station out of orbit again and this time we're only twenty minutes from no return.'

BATTLE CRUISER TYLAT FURORE, ORBITING ERITAIN

'THERE REALLY IS NO CHOICE, I'm afraid,' said Killie. 'The main drive on this ship hasn't been commissioned yet and we need that to replenish the manoeuvring thrusters. Everything was used after the first android detonated and the station system was low anyway and due for a resupply.' She glanced around at a circle of glum faces facing her on the bridge of the *Tylat Furore*.

'So, we have to watch as this brand new ship and the planet's biggest space station just fall out of the sky?' asked Zaphir.

'Pretty much,' said Killie, dropping her eyes to the floor. 'Sorry, but unless there's a—'

The ship lurched suddenly, causing everyone to grab onto something.

'What the hell?' came a shout from a member of the ship's crew.

Everybody turned and stared at him. He glanced up, a perplexed expression on his face. 'All the stars on the port side have just vanished,' he said, looking back at his screen. 'And something's dragging us back into a higher orbit.'

Bache smiled and raised his eyebrows at Zaphir. 'I believe help has arrived,' he said.

A voice suddenly boomed out of the bridge speakers, making everyone jump. 'This is *Katadromiko 2* of the GDA Peacekeeping Navy, we reasoned you needed some assistance?'

Both Bache and Zaphir stiffened at the voice and their eyes met.

'Is that…?' said Zaphir, giving Bache a puzzled look.

'Sounds like her,' said Bache, looking around. 'Am I able to reply?'

'Go ahead,' said one of the crew, touching an icon on his console.

'Tyrett, is that you?' said Bache.

There was a momentary silence.

'Bache…?' the voice replied with a questioning tone this time. 'Have I just saved your arse again?'

Bache smiled. 'Oh, I wouldn't go that far. But your timing is pretty favourable.'

'This is Captain Gastion Whipper here,' a new male voice sounded. 'Recruit Loftt, would you mind not being so flippant with my bridge crew?'

'Mr Whippie, I didn't know they'd given *K2* to you,' said Zaphir.

'Ah, great, Recruit Mye's there as well,' he said. 'If I was expecting any respect, I might as well give up and go home.'

'Can we have a lift?' Bache asked.

'What have you done to Captain Yamaton and the perfectly serviceable destroyer we issued you with?'

'It broke down,' said Zaphir, giving Bache a cringing expression.

'Oh, it's broken all right,' replied Whipper, 'judging by the scans I'm getting from the surface. And talking of the surface, what the hell is going on down there?'

'A bit of an insurrection, Captain,' said Zaphir.

'Which I'm kinda hoping you didn't instigate?' the captain replied.

'Absolutely not,' said Zaphir, glancing at Bache and rolling her eyes.

'Captain, could you send a shuttle across?' asked Bache. 'There's someone here I want you to meet who can explain everything.'

———

Two hours after the arrival of the *Katadromiko 2*, Bache, Zaphir, Nexen and Gastion Whipper all stood watching a holographic display in the captain's private office, situated adjacent to the bridge on the immense starship. During that time, they'd explained everything that had happened over the last few days and watched the captain's expression turn from irritation to complete disbelief.

The holographic image of Eritain turned slowly above their heads, displaying seventeen red trails beginning two minutes ago at the *Katadromiko* and now spreading out across the two huge hemispheres.

'Last chance to change your mind,' said Whipper, turning to Nexen. 'You realise these planet-damping EMPs will fry every electronic component on the surface, nothing whatsoever will be retrievable.'

'I'm counting on it,' said Nexen, his eyes not leaving the display. 'All that stuff can be rebuilt, human lives can't.'

A few moments of silence followed as they watched the red trails dipping lower into the atmosphere as they overflew their designated regions. The first trail suddenly blossomed into a rapidly expanding purple circle, followed quickly by the second and third, until eleven seconds after the first, all seventeen had deployed and both hemispheres were hidden behind an expanding purple mass.

'It's done,' said Whipper, in a subdued tone. 'I hope for all our sakes the surviving population are understanding of the reasons they're suddenly back in the dark ages.'

'They will,' said Nexen. 'We're a resilient race. I'd like to request some help from you guys too, for the rebuild over the next year or two.'

'I'm way ahead of you,' said Whipper. 'I sent a drone back to Dasos requesting just that. In the meantime, I have three thousand marines preparing to put boots on the ground to begin the relief effort.'

'Thank you,' said Nexen, turning as a knock at the door disturbed them.

A member of the bridge crew stuck his head inside. 'Sorry to disturb you, Captain. There's some good and bad news,' he said. 'The *Dres'kin*'s engineering officer managed to keep the ship's shields up and the crew were able to defend it from the androids.'

Whipper nodded.

'And the bad news?' he asked.

The crewman paused and looked down before he spoke. 'It's Captain Yamaton, sir,' he said in a subdued tone. 'He didn't make it.'

'What?' said Bache. 'He only had a concussion and a couple of broken bones.'

'The androids targeted his hospital with heavy weapons a couple of hours before the EMP strike.'

'Shit,' said Zaphir. 'We were too slow.'

'The EMPs did work though,' the crewman continued. 'The *Dres'kin* reports that all the androids attacking them are down and the almost continuous weapons fire in the distance is now silent.'

The captain nodded slowly again. 'Right, it's time to initiate the relief teams,' he said. 'And get an armed transport down to the *Dres'kin* to rescue the crew immediately.'

'Right away, Captain.'

CANTORE SAY RELIEF COMMAND CENTRE, ERITAIN

BACHE STOOD STARING at the plumes of smoke in the distance as thousands of android bodies were stacked into piles and burnt.

It was twenty-nine days now since the EMP strike had wiped out the attacking android army. A few days after the attack, twenty-one ships had arrived from GDA space and the basic relief effort choreographed by the *Katadromiko 2* became a major endeavour overnight.

The majority of the surviving human population were in shock, hungry and had very little understanding of what had just happened. Huge relief camps had been erected in parks within the major cities, providing food, shelter and purpose for those who'd lost everything.

Commander Nexen had brought the surviving senior officers from both hemispheres together today and was chairing a meeting to discuss a ceasefire and immediate end to the cross-planet hostilities that had plagued Eritain for centuries. Not that they had a lot of choice, as three-quarters of the armed forces personnel on both sides had been wiped out by the androids anyway.

'Those fires have been burning for days,' said Zaphir, jarring Bache out of his daydream and indicating the funeral pyres on the horizon.

'There's a lot of 'em to get rid of,' he replied. 'And good riddance too.'

The conversation paused for a second, before Zaphir spoke again. 'D'you think we'll have to redo our final field testing?' she asked.

'I have no idea,' said Bache. 'You think they'll trust us with another ship after this? It'll seem a little bit pedestrian after this trip even if they do.'

'They tried to pull the *Dres'kin* back up with the tractor yesterday while you were away with Nexen,' she said.

Bache turned to look at the broken ship out on the edge of the camp and shrugged. 'That went well then,' he said.

'Hmm,' mumbled Zaphir, following his gaze and nodding slowly. 'Even a Katadromiko's power has its limits.'

They turned as a call from behind interrupted them.

'The commander would like to see you,' said a young female soldier at the entrance to the main command offices.

She nodded and followed them in carrying an ammunition box. The sentries waved them past as they entered the central conference room.

The conversation in the room stalled for a moment as everyone turned to stare impatiently as the door closed with a *bang* and the locks engaged.

'Bache, Zaphir, how can we help you?' asked a slightly piqued Nexen.

They both stopped and glanced at each other, before a

confused Bache spoke. 'We were told you wanted us,' he said, turning and nodding at the soldier with the box.

'Yes, sorry about that,' the female soldier said, striding past Bache and Zaphir. She placed the box on the table in front of everyone. 'It was a little ruse to get past the guards outside.'

Bache grabbed her shoulder from behind, only to find himself being slammed backwards with enormous force into the wall. She stepped around him, pulling the now slightly stunned Bache in front of her as some of the officers around the table stood and went for their weapons.

'I wouldn't do that if I were you,' said the android, pulling Bache tightly against her and holding up a switch. 'That...' she nodded towards the box on the table '...is a rather powerful explosive device.' Her face began to morph.

Nexen's eyes bugged as he realised who she was turning into.

'Dion, how the hell are you still alive?' he bellowed. 'You were shot in the flyer and then your body dumped out at a thousand metres.'

She shrugged and gave him a half smile. 'The wonders of multiple personalities,' she said.

'How many of you are there?' Nexen asked.

'Ah, now that would be telling, wouldn't it?'

Bache, who'd recovered from the collision with the wall and continued to feign the opposite, suddenly spun around to face her, his nose almost touching hers. Without pausing, he grabbed her shirt and ripped it open, exposing her chest to the whole room.

'Bache, what the fuck?' shouted Zaphir, probably saying what the rest of the room was thinking.

He smiled and kissed Dion on the lips, which he hoped

would cover him bringing his right hand up and groping around on her chest.

'Why, Bache?' Dion said, a sly smirk replacing the surprised expression. 'I really had no idea. If you'd told me sooner, a time and a private room could have been—'

She suddenly slumped to the floor and Bache grabbed the switch out of her hand before it fell. He passed it carefully to one of the standing officers and nodded at the box.

'Get that thing out of here,' he said. 'We'll deal with this piece of shit.' He raised his eyebrows at Zaphir. 'Give me a hand, would you?' he asked.

Zaphir stood stock still and glared at him. 'Now, woah there just a minute,' she said, her mouth hanging open.

Bache stopped and looked up to find everyone in the room staring at him. 'Erm, yes, ah, right,' he said, realising an explanation of his recent actions might be required. 'Something I learnt from your android, Commander. The one we named Vee.'

'Uh huh,' grunted Nexen, sounding dubious. 'Go on.'

Dion began twitching.

'He taught me how to do a system reset on him when his programming was glitching just before we woke you. I realised that Dion is a direct descendant of those androids and wondered...'

'If the keypad on the centre of the chest was still there,' interrupted Nexen, the reason for Bache's actions now dawning him. 'It was still there—bloody brilliant.' He sat, shaking his head in wonder.

Dion's twitching limbs became still and she sat up slowly, her face morphing slowly back to a look similar to Vee. Five laser weapons covered the android as it blinked and peered around the room.

'It seems I am in need of further programming,' it said, a neutral expression on its face and a male voice this time.

'There's no keypad though,' said Zaphir, pointing at its chest.

'It's still there,' said Bache. 'Under the skin. It must have been an integral part of the breastplate and they didn't bother removing it.'

The android was whisked away shortly after by a contingent of soldiers. Bache knew better than to ask any questions as he probably wouldn't like the answer anyway. He was convinced the android was no longer a threat, but the Eritainians weren't taking any chances.

When Captain Whipper heard about the episode, he wasn't best pleased and recalled Bache and Zaphir back up to the Katadromiko, setting them the enviable task of writing a full report of their actions since leaving GDA space for the higher authorities back on Dasos. Bache hit a brick wall when he asked about their future and whether the complete disaster of their final training flight would mean failing the course.

EPILOGUE

KATADROMIKO 2, ORBITING ERITAIN

The Plas Arfon bar was on deck fifty-eight and overlooked the river running through the central atrium of the fourteen kilometre-long starship. Large blue-coloured fish could be seen lazily swimming against the flow, cruising slowly through the swaying reed clusters on the riverbed.

Bache sat nursing a chilled glass of Dasonion Corvatt wine and watched a female Bantor Hawk in a tree on the far bank, greedily eyeing the fish below.

'You've never ripped my shirt off,' said Zaphir, suddenly and breaking the silence for the first time in ten minutes.

Bache recoiled slightly and gave Zaphir a worried glance. 'You'd have kicked me out the nearest airlock,' he said, leaning back in his seat and out of arm's reach.

'I might not have,' she said, as a shadow fell over them.

'Might not have what?' said Captain Whipper, plonking a drink down on the table, drawing up a chair and waving at them to stay seated.

'Er, finished my report, Captain,' Zaphir lied quickly.

'Hmm,' he grunted, eyeing her suspiciously.

'Any news about us?' Bache asked quickly to change the subject.

'Actually, yes,' he said. 'Quite a bit of news from Dasos.'

Both Zaphir and Bache put their drinks down and leant forward.

'Well?' said Bache, as the captain took a slow sip of his drink.

'Patience, young Loftt,' he said slowly, dragging out the moment. 'There's good news and bad news, depending on your point of view.'

'Do we have to do the course again?' blurted Zaphir, a look of real concern on her face.

'No,' said Whipper. 'I can categorically state that neither of you will be required to do that and you won't be going back to Dasos to receive your officer rankings with the others either.'

'Oh, dear,' said Bache. 'They haven't taken it well then?'

The captain smiled. 'The report Commander Nexen and I sent back to Dasos was actually very complimentary. Admiral Flay has decided not to award you a promotion to second lieutenant...'

Bache slumped down in his chair. 'Oh, dear,' he said again, staring at the floor and fiddling with a loose thread on his uniform.

'...but,' Whipper continued, 'he has decided to allow me to field promote the two of you to full lieutenant from immediate effect.'

The captain dropped two full sets of gold lieutenant's braids on the table, sat back and watched amused as the full impact of what he'd told them sunk in.

'You're fucking kidding,' blurted Zaphir and slapped a hand over her mouth. 'Oops, sorry, Captain,' she mumbled.

'I'll give you that one,' said Whipper, with a smirk. 'Just don't make a habit of swearing at your captain too often.' He turned to Bache, who'd remained stony silent and was staring at the braids. 'All good, Lieutenant Loftt?' he asked.

Bache slowly turned to look at him. 'You said there was some bad news. I take it that's to do with the posting?'

'It is,' said Whipper. 'I've requested the two of you to stay with me I'm afraid, on the *Katadromiko 2*.'

Both of them stared at the captain again.

'Yeah, I know how you feel,' he said. 'You've got to put up with grumpy old me for the foreseeable future.'

Zaphir was the first to react by standing up. 'Permission to hug the captain,' she said. 'Thank you,' she whispered as they embraced.

'Ah, don't thank me yet,' he said as they parted and Bache stood and shook his hand. 'You don't know what jobs I've got planned for you yet.'

'Chief engineer?' Bache asked, a little bit tongue in cheek.

Whipper smiled. 'Nice try, Lieutenant,' he said. 'Maybe one day, but walking before running comes to mind. What I'd like to do is set up a special operations team on the *K2*, with the two of you overseeing things, Lieutenant Mye the logistics side and Lieutenant Loftt, you can manage the engineering aspect. We're going to be in some hearts and minds situations with this vessel in the future. The council want them to be seen to be used in a humanitarian role around the galaxy, rather than a war machine. They're trying to change people's perception of the GDA from one of aggressive troubleshooter, to a more passive peacekeeping role.'

'More conflict solving with an olive branch than a big stick,' said Bache.

'Absolutely,' said the captain. 'And we'll talk more of this and your roles at a later time, as right now there are people outside who are demanding a promotion party.'

Whipper lifted his left arm up and peered over his shoulder.

Bache and Zaphir followed his gaze to see a sudden line of people file in from the bar's kitchen area. Nexen was there, along with Cantor Vay and the remainder of the *Dres'kin*'s crew. A grinning Killie and a limping Dr Quinn Stakk, even the captain's daughter Grogun Whipper, whom Bache hadn't seen for two years, entered the bar. Bache could also see Clammer pushing something behind the crowd and as everyone spread out, he realised it was a wheelchair with a passenger that made his jaw hit the floor.

'Captain Yamaton,' both Bache and Zaphir blurted at the same time and rushed over to meet him. He had strange red perforated casts on his left leg and right arm and a lot of purple bruising across the right side of his face.

'We thought—' Zaphir began.

'Most did,' Yamaton interrupted, wincing slightly as he tried to smile. 'They'd taken me to a physiotherapy centre on the other side of town when the hospital was hit, then you EMP'd the planet and I was stuck in this contraption miles away with no transport or communications.'

'We're so glad you survived,' said Bache, gently shaking his left hand.

'And you too,' said Yamaton. 'It seems my record for producing quality officers still stands.'

'Talking of quality officers,' said Nexen, approaching the group, 'I have a little presentation to make myself.' He nodded to someone behind the gathering.

'Hello, Commander,' said Zaphir, reaching over to shake his hand.

'Actually, you no longer have to address me as commander, it seems I'm to be known as Mr President for the foreseeable future.'

'Fucking hell,' Zaphir blurted again, releasing Nexen's hand as though it was electrified. 'Do we have to bow or something?' she asked, her eyes wide with worry.

'Don't you bloody dare,' said Nexen, pointing at her and getting a snigger from the crowd. 'I'm only alive because of you guys and in many ways, so is my planet. It's because of the latter, I and the inhabitants of Eritain would like to present to Lieutenant Loftt, Lieutenant Mye and Captain Yamaton a Gattainian Sabre. This is the highest military award we have and we hope demonstrates our deep gratitude for your unselfish and committed aid in helping to save our world.'

Three long curved and intricately engraved swords, set in their individual display cases, were handed to each of the recipients.

'Also,' said Nexen, holding his hand up to quell the applause, 'it is with great pleasure that I announce that Eritain and the other planets and stations of the Gattainian Cluster have jointly applied to join the GDA and can now look forward to peace and security for the region for the foreseeable future.'

The celebration party at the Plas Arfon went on late into the night and as the star lighting in the huge atrium began to fade, Bache and Zaphir crept away to her cabin and he finally discovered just how much she loved him.

FROM THE AUTHOR

I wanted to say a huge thank you for choosing to read *The Recruit*. I sincerely hope you enjoyed Bache Loftt's second adventure.

If you did enjoy this novel, it'd be fantastic if you could write a review. It doesn't have to be long, just a few words, but it is the best way for me to help new readers discover my writing for the first time.

If you'd like to stay up to date with my new releases, as well as exclusive competitions and giveaways, you're welcome to join my Reader Group at my website, www.nick-adamsbooks.com. I will never share your email address, and you can unsubscribe at any time.

You can also contact me via Facebook, Twitter, or by email. I love hearing from readers – I read every message and will try to personally reply to everyone.

Thanks again for your support.
Nick Adams